Unearthed

Emma Makarova

ISBN: 9798565488227

PublishNation
www.publishnation.co.uk

For Daisy

The best sister a girl could wish for:
a true friend and honest critic

Any faerie story told on a Friday should be prefixed by saying, "a blessing attend their departing and travelling! This day is Friday and they will not hear us." This prevents faerie ill-will coming upon the narrator for anything he may chance to say.

Superstitions of the Highlands & Islands, 1860

A person may cause evil to others not only by his actions but by his inaction, and in either case he is justly accountable to them for the injury.

John Stuart Mill, *On Liberty*, 1859

Sollas, Isle of North Uist, Scotland, July 1849

Mammy pulled me up the hill towards the black flag. Her hand was wet and cold and squeezing mine too tightly. Our feet squelched and slipped in the peat bog, and the sodden heather and grass soaked through our shoes to our feet. My heart hammered in my chest like the waves at Cod Point, but Mammy wouldn't stop, and when I tripped and stumbled over a rock she dragged me on. "Thugainn, Morag!" she said in a voice that was so sharp, I swallowed my tears and stumbled on behind her. Mammy's pockets were bulging full of stones that clinked and bounced as she ran. The sack in her left hand bumped against her leg. Her hem was stained and splattered dark with mud and wetness was rising like the tide up the back of her dress. The wind whipped the rain into our faces as we ran. I felt like I was swimming. I had a mouthful of water and everything was blurry. I am the rain and the rain is me.

We reached the flagpole, made from the boat's mast that had washed up on Sollas beach. It leaned in the wind as though it were still aboard the ship racing over the waves. Mammy dropped my hand, and the sack, and clung to the pole trying to catch her breath. Her breathing sounded like Mr MacIver's jagged saw and her hair was plastered flat against her head so that her face was skull-like with two dark circles under her eyes. She yanked the line of rope and hoisted up the black flag. It hung there like a dead thing.

Mammy suddenly froze and stared down at the Lochmaddy road below us. The rain was blowing across the bog in great rolling drifts so that the road appeared and vanished, appeared and vanished in the mist. Mammy gave a single terrifying shriek that ripped a hole in the mist and for a heartbeat the rain paused, cowering. In that moment I saw what she had seen. They were coming. Raise the flag, yes raise it up, for they were coming. Coming for us.

Six months earlier

Chapter One

Sollas, January 1849

Darkness was creeping over the village as I stepped out of the schoolroom for the last time. As soon as I closed the latch behind me, the wind started tugging at my bonnet and the salt spit breeze spattered my face. Out at sea a black storm front was banking and I clutched my slate and bible to my chest, ducked my head, and ran for home through the winter twilight. At the Church of Scotland the words of the psalm that Miss MacAllister had just read to us came back to me, "they are like the chaff that the wind driveth away." My eyes filled with tears, but the wind slapped my cheek so I ran on, past the empty brown fields that were waiting for planting. There was no shelter between here and our croft. Now the wind came screaming up over the sandbanks, whipping my bare legs as it went shrieking away over the empty moor. I could just make out our croft, huddled low with the others, the smoke rising sideways from the thatch. Some of the crofts had a faint candle glow in their tiny window. Ours was dark. My dress was speckled with rain as I flung open the door.

"They've closed the school."

"Heavens, Morag, shut that door quickly," Mammy said. I could hardly see her in the gloom. She was crouching by the hearth in the middle of the room blowing desperately on a smouldering peat turf beneath the griddle. Her dark hair tumbled down her shoulders and her face glowed orange in the fire.

She glanced up at me. "This wind is blowing the fire out and I'll be late with Da's supper." As she said it there was a fierce gust that sent the smoke swirling back through the thatch and set the chain that hung the griddle from the beam creaking back and forth.

"Auch." She sat back on her heels, coughing from the smoke. She wiped her eyes and smudged soot on her brow. "I only want to cook some barley scones for goodness sakes." Mammy could

5

mend a net and plant a rig as fast as a man, but she did not have the knack for cooking.

"You'd better light the candle," she said, still coughing.

I laid my things on the table, took off my bonnet, and lit the candle stub. But the door opened and an icy blast swirled into the room snuffing it out. It was Da, his jacket wet, and a pail in his hand which he handed to me with an inch of foaming milk still warm from the cow.

"I've shut up the cattle. Let's hope the byre roof holds," he said.

"I'm having an awful job with the fire," Mammy said, still on her knees, flapping her arms against her sides. "The supper isn't ready at all."

Da took off his jacket and hung it on the peg on the door. He knelt on the thick flags of the hearth. "A good hearty breath is what we need here." He blew on the fire steadily until the flames leapt up and caught first one dried peat, then another. Then he heaved himself into the chair beside it to cook the scones, the toasted barley smell making my stomach rumble. My stomach rumbled and ached all the time the entire year before, on account of The Hunger.

"I don't know what we'll have those scones with," Mammy said, standing up and brushing earth from the hard floor from her skirt. "Some herring I suppose." She lifted the lid of the barrel in the corner and peered in. The salty dried fish smell sneaked past her and hung about the room.

As she passed me the cup for the milk, I said again, "The school has been closed. Miss MacAllister is going back to Edinburgh."

The words caused an ocean swell in my chest and Mammy turned to look at me, her face made sharp by the light of the candle and the fire. "Well, how are you supposed to learn your lessons?"

Da did not look up, but pushed a turf carefully into the flame with his boot.

Mammy looked at him. "Did you know about this, Artair?"

Da shifted in his chair. "Only this morning from Mr Morrison. There are a lot less bairns than there were last year, Ceit. And

6

Morag will be fourteen this year. She won't have need of lessons for much longer."

My heart pitched like a boat on the waves to hear him say this.

Mammy sat down at the table and picked up the knife. She gripped the bone handle and began cutting up the herring into thin strips, shaking her head. "Tsch! There's still plenty of bairns in Sollas who need teaching. Is this from the new factor?"

"Mr Morrison said it was the Society in Edinburgh who made the decision to close the school," Da said.

"The Society, my elbow. We know who's behind it." She muttered something under her breath, and the wind howled about the croft making the candle gutter and dip.

"Miss MacAllister gave me these because she said I was gifted in the English," I blurted out, picking up the slate and bible.

My teacher had bid me stay behind when the others had gone. "You're a good girl, Morag," she had said putting her hand for a moment on my head. "And gifted in the English and your letters too." She had lifted her gaze to the high school room window. "It's such a shame, such a shame." And her blue eyes had watered in the winter light.

Mammy wiped her hands on her apron then took the bible, tilting it towards the candle on the table so that the gold cross embossed on the cover caught the light. She looked at the foreign words and frowned.

"And what is wrong with the one we have in Gaelic?"

"It's to learn my letters, Mammy."

"English letters." She pursed her lips and pushed the bible back towards me.

After we had eaten, Da put the kettle over the fire for some tea and Mammy and he settled in their chairs beside it. I sat on the bench by the table. My heart was sinking like a stone at the thought that I would never sit at my school desk again, nor stretch my hand up as high as I could, hoping, just hoping, to be chosen to give the answer. The wind was still shrieking around our croft trying to find its way in. Last year the MacIver's thatch was ripped half-off in a storm and I peered up at our roof beam that was groaning in the gale. I took up my slate and started drawing to take my mind off the roof. I began to draw a princess, which was my favourite thing to draw, and the chalk squeaked against the slate. I'd only ever seen a picture of a princess once in a newspaper clipping that Miss MacAllister showed us. It was Princess Victoria sitting on a special chair with a lovely dress, having a crown placed on her head to make her into a queen. I imagined the princess in my drawing had a fine green velvet dress and I drew her riding a horse, but the legs of the horse went wrong and I turned them into a bush instead so that the princess was peeping over it.

"Look," I said, lifting the slate and tilting it in the light of the fire to show them. "A princess. I'd like to be a princess and live in a fine castle with lovely clothes."

Da chuckled.

Mammy said, "Well you are a princess. You are related to Somerled, the great Laird of the Isles. Don't forget that."

"Will you tell us a story, Mammy?" I asked, putting the slate away. "A story about the piskies? About when Margaret MacNeish caught them dipping their fingers in her butter before she went away to America."

Mammy sat back and closed her eyes with a faint smile on her face.

"Pale gold butter, Margaret MacNeish had the knack for it alright, the creamiest thing you ever could imagine eating, melting on a hot scone." She licked her lips and opened her eyes. "No, I think I'll tell you a different story as we are talking about princesses."

She waited a moment as Da placed another peat turf on the fire and I went and sat on my bed in the corner.

"Now," she said, "tell me, what is our clan name?"

"*Clann Ùisdein*," I said. "Clan Donald of Sleat"

She nodded.

"Yes and the founder of the clan is *Uisdein*, Hugh, and Hugh's granddaddy was of course the mighty Somerled, the Laird of the Isles." She glanced at me to make sure that I was listening. "But before him, Somerled's great grand-daddy was Conn of the Hundred Battles. Conn was a High King of Ireland who came across the sea to our islands."

The turf settled in the fire and the flames started to lick it. Da and I knew to wait quietly to let Mammy's mind wander back through the stories of all the families who had gone before us.

"This is after the people built the stone circle at Pobull Fhinn, but before the Norsemen came," she began. "Conn sailed over from Ireland with a fleet of long boats, and as he pulled up on the shore of Traigh Iar beach he saw a beautiful woman standing on the sand. She had dark brown eyes and a pelt of long dark hair that fell all the way down her back. Her name was Sheonag MacCodrum. Conn and his men built blackhouses overlooking the sea and after a while Sheonag became with child by Conn and gave birth to a wee girl that they called Morag, just like you. But all was not well, you see, Conn, being from Ireland, did not know about the *Cu Sith*."

Mammy paused and I hugged my knees in fearful anticipation.

"One dark November night, a few weeks after Morag was born, the village was woken by the most dreadful howl. Fearing it was a wolf, Conn and his men leapt from their beds, picked up their swords, and ran out into the dark. Sheonag called to them to come back. But it was too late, they had gone. Poor Conn. If only he had known. It was no wolf, but the *Cu Sith*, the ghost hound who did the bidding of the fairies. The fairies have a terrible thirst for milk and the Cu Sith had come to steal the nursing mother for her milk, and take her back to the underworld.

There was a second blood-chilling howl, much closer this time. Sheonag clutched baby Morag to her. She kissed the baby on its soft head, laid it on the bed, and then ran out into the dark, down towards the beach. A third howl and there it was, the enormous Cu Sith, standing on the top of the dune watching her, ghostly green and its eyes glowing in the dark. Away Sheonag ran, down the sand. The Cu Sith sprang after her, its great tongue lolling over its sharp teeth, spittle flying from its jaws.

Down to the sea Sheonag went, kicking up the wet sand, her bare feet sliding on the wet kelp. She could hear the snarl of the Cu Sith behind her. As she reached the surf she glanced behind to see it almost upon her. Her feet were in the water now, and as soon as she felt the waves around her knees, she transformed. For of course she was a MacCodrum, so she was a selkie, and she

9

dived beneath the water having transformed into a smooth brown seal."

"And what about Morag?" I asked fearfully.

Mammy smiled. "Auch, she was raised by her father and the villagers and she grew up into a fine young lass. But when her father, Conn, returned to Ireland, she would not go. For as you know selkies can only return to land for a wee while every seven years and she wanted to see her Mammy. Every seven years Morag went down to the sea and waited for her to come. And so she stayed on our island and married and had children of her own, and her children had children, and so on, and she lived in a blackhouse overlooking the sea for the rest of her days."

"Just like us," I said.

"Aye," Mammy said, glancing at Da. "Just like us."

Da stretched and stood up. He looked up at the roof beam that had fallen silent. "Morag, you can fetch some more peat, before we turn in, seeing as the wind's dropped."

I opened my mouth to protest, but the closed it again. I used to be afraid of monsters. But Da said that now that I was thirteen there would be no more stories if I made a fuss. I opened the door and stepped into the night. Our neighbours had already snuffed out their candles, their windows were dark, and the sudden blackness was like having a sack pulled over my head. The wind had gone and everything was strangely still, save for the distant roar of the waves and the sound of my own shallow breathing. I closed the door behind me and my hands felt along the rough stone wall, my feet slipping in the mud towards where the peat turves were stacked against the side of the croft. Da had covered them in an oilskin and my fingers found the waxy cloth, beaded with cold rain, which had half blown off in the wind. When I fumbled to pull it towards me, something on the other side of the stack moved. It was an inky shadow against the deeper black. My heart shot into my throat and began beating there. Whatever it was gave a low animal moan and pulled hard at the oilskin so that it was ripped out of my hands. My feet slipped nearly sending me over in the mud and my arms made wild circles to save me. When it rushed past, I caught a hot animal stench, felt the brush of hair on my hand, and the oilskin, and animal, was gone.

Chapter Two

London, January 1849

Our carriage rattled towards Notting Hill, and I watched how our breath became trapped in foggy blooms against the cold glass as it tried to escape. A damp vapour, like the ghosts of passengers-past, rose from the seats. Stale, dank, sour. Even my hands had turned clammy inside their gloves. Was it from the miserable cab atmosphere, or the dread of being shut in?

I glanced at Aunt Caroline beside me, upright and silent. Her hands were folded neatly in her lap. Beneath her new bonnet her mouth was a thin line of anxiety. Every now and then her lips worked silently as she practised her vowels. I looked at the dim reflection of my own new bonnet in the carriage window. The satin brim was so wide that my view was reduced to a pink frame. A horse with blinkers.

While rubbing the misted window, I looked out as best I could. Our rented barouche, its wheels clogged by the filthy streets, had become stuck behind an omnibus as we made our way through Kensington. There was the clang of its bell and its driver yelling at someone to get out of the way. It had been over a year since I had been this way through London and I hardly recognised it. Where the World's End public house had once stood was now a pile of rubble, and an entire row of houses had vanished like missing front teeth. It was to make room for the railway, according to the news sheets that Mr Betts had wrapped the fish in. *Another one thousand miles of track to be laid across Britain.* On Fridays Aunt Caroline attended her embroidery circle. I could slip down to the kitchen and unwrap the fish, read the news, then wrap it back up, being careful to rinse the haddock smell from my hands. Sometimes, I was unlucky and it would be wrapped in advertisements for Parrs Life Constipation Pills. He favoured *The London Post,* Mr Betts, which would not have been my choice. Still it was better than nothing.

I rubbed the window again and saw two workmen dressed in greasy overalls connecting wires to telegraph poles beside the road. Not to the poles directly, of course, but to the ceramic insulators. Grandpapa and I had attended a lecture on telegraphy two years ago at the Polytechnic. There was an audacious plan to lay a great transatlantic cable from Ireland to Canada. Instead of twelve days by fast ship, a message would be pulsed across 2,500 nautical miles in a matter of minutes. The audience had expressed doubt that it could be done, but sitting at the back of the hall, taking care to keep my face down, I had reckoned it was possible. Many things had seemed possible two years ago.

Our carriage had reached Bayswater where the city gave way to cottages and fields. We passed an old lady prodding her dirty cattle along the road with a stick.

Aunt Caroline suddenly poked me in the arm. "Remember, Maria, let me do the talking today. No philosophising or scientific views - that last gentleman was quite put off by all that. And goodness knows chances are slim what with the cholera this year. Besides, the doctor forbids that sort of talk. It will only excite you."

I said nothing but shifted in my seat and felt the steel fastening of the corset pressing into my back.

"It's not too tight, is it?" my aunt asked, smoothing my skirt with a small gloved hand. I caught a waft of her lavender scent and looked out to where they were building crescents of new villas on the old racecourse.

Since the doctor had declared I was well enough, I had been taken along to E. Moses and Sons to be stuffed and trussed into a dress of stiff blue taffeta to take part in the season. The assistant had not remarked directly on my hair, but she had called a boy to bring a selection of bonnets that came down low on the cheek and closed in on the face. "These can also be worn indoors," I heard her whisper to my aunt. Then came an endless string of social functions in the chosen bonnet. So much sugar, so much cream, I could feel the flesh thickening again on my bones. My hair was re-growing.

We came into Notting Hill and a crane hung motionless like a hangman's scaffold over a row of dilapidated cottages. One had its roof smashed in, the beams were like a ribcage exposed to the sky. I wondered what type of gentleman lived right out here. Not that I cared, for I saw these trips as a parlour trick that I was forced to participate in.

When I was a child of nine or ten, Grandpapa had taken me to St James Theatre to see a magician perform. He had a card trick called the Vanishing Lady, in which he made the Queen of Spades disappear from his hand. Then, under the pop and sizzle of gas light and with the swirl of purple silk he made it reappear, by magic, in the pocket of a gentleman chosen from the audience to help him. The trick had drawn gasps and applause, but Grandpapa explained afterwards that it was based on the simple principle of distraction. The dim gas lighting and the swirl of the coloured silk distracted us whilst the card was placed through sleight of hand in the gentleman's pocket. Aunt Caroline had her own trick she would play in Notting Hill. The Unwed Lady. Using the principles of distraction she would attempt to place me in the pocket of some gentleman. It gave me satisfaction that she had yet to successfully perform it, but I knew that time was running out.

"We will review your health in three months," Doctor Fortnum had said at our last appointment in December. "Just to ensure there has been no relapse and that no further treatment is required." He had stroked his oiled moustache with his long thin fingers as he said it and I was forced to look away. It was nearly February already.

When our carriage swept through tall gates, I noticed the wide gravel driveway to the house was lined with lime trees that had been savagely pruned; their stunted branches grey against the January sky. The mansion had a new portico entrance whose columns glowed white like bone. We pulled to a stop. When travelling with Grandpapa I had always jumped down from the carriage without the coachman's help, but as I made my way to open the door, my aunt gripped my arm. Her grasp was like the claw of a falcon gripping its prey and she did not release it until the door was opened for us by the coachman.

Then she smiled and reached up to tuck a curl of hair into my bonnet.

"You know, I think your colour is returning at last, Maria. The doctor will be so pleased. He returns from Paris next week, I believe. He's been visiting the asylum at Salpêtrière."

Then she took the coachman's hand and descended the carriage steps in her dainty slippers. That word. It was like the flash of a knife hidden inside a velvet coat. I followed her meekly into the house, my large feet crunching the gravel.

Grandpapa always said the quality of a gentleman could be determined from his handshake and I was certain that if I ever happened to shake Godfrey MacDonald's hand it would be a damp, limp thing. I vowed to myself that I would never touch it. He had a face that looked as though it had never been outdoors and very pale hands. On the right one he wore a large gold signet ring which he rubbed every now and then as he sat opposite us. Straight backed and solemn-faced, he seemed, at first glance, much older than his twenty-four years. His vowels were perfectly clipped through generations of breeding which Aunt Caroline, despite her practice, would never perfect. And yet on closer inspection I saw that his hair was done in a schoolboy fashion, combed flat with a lot of hair-oil. He had splashed on too much cologne so that it wafted across the table in a youthful cloud, and his dinner jacket was too large for him, as though he had borrowed it from his father. In fact, sitting here alone in the dining room beneath the crystal chandelier, it was as though his parents were out for the day and he was playing house.

"I didn't see your name on the guest list for the Winter Ball, Your Lordship," my aunt said, cutting a tiny piece of jellied pigeon.

His Lordship paused with his fork of jellied pigeon in mid-air. He tilted it from side to side as though observing how the wobbling golden jelly caught the light.

"I've hardly been up to town since my parents passed away," he replied.

His parents were not out for the day then, but deceased. That was something we had in common. I bit my lip and hiding my face in my bonnet I examined my fork. It was stamped with a coat of arms. A gloved fist brandishing a cross like a weapon.

"And you are now heir to your family's estate," Aunt Caroline remarked. "You only have the one brother, I believe?"

Had I not been sitting directly opposite Godfrey MacDonald I would have missed seeing him flinch. Then there was a slight curl of his lip.

"That's right. Alexander."

He took a gulp of his wine.

My aunt dabbed her mouth with her napkin and smiled. "It's the Countess of Wexford who made our introduction to you. She and I are friends."

She had only met the countess once at a charity event, but she collected these connections like miniature china dolls that she showed off to everyone.

"I ran into her son, Bill, at the Polytechnic last time I was there," Lord MacDonald said.

I looked up.

"Do you mean the Polytechnic on Regent Street?" I asked him.

He gave me a smile as wan as winter sunlight.

"Yes. I attended a demonstration of the camera. I'm rather a fan and have just bought one. Have you been there?"

I put down my fork and glanced at my aunt.

"Why, yes, I've been there several times, I greatly enjoy-

"Shops." Aunt Caroline placed her hand on mine. "That is what we go to Regent Street for. It offers some excellent shopping, especially now all that construction is finished. We often enjoy an afternoon there, shopping, don't we, Maria?"

Lord MacDonald looked at us holding hands across the table. Aunt Caroline smiled and squeezed my hand, but underneath her nails dug into my flesh. I felt my eyes prick with tears at the pain which the baron no doubt took for joy at the thought of an afternoon of shopping. I could sense that her trick, The Unwed Lady, which she usually saved for after dessert, was to begin.

She glanced up at the chandelier.

"Your house must feel empty with both your parents now sadly deceased. All of these wonderful things, but nobody to share them with. Maria lost her parents too, when she was very young." She sighed. "And yet despite tragedy one must look to the future. Your Lordship must look forward to happier days, to marriage, for example."

At this, she lifted my hand and turned in her chair towards me. Lord MacDonald followed her gaze. He regarded me as though being forced to come back and admire a curiosity in a museum that he had already decided was un-interesting. I knew what he saw. A nineteen-year-old girl wearing a pink trimmed bonnet and a defiant look on her face. He looked away, but Aunt Caroline was prepared for this and now she began her trick.

"Did you ever happen to hear of naval officer Edwin Smith?"

Godfrey MacDonald knitted his brow.

"He served as a captain in the Navy during the French wars. I wonder if you have heard of him as he was decorated for bravery. Anyway, no matter. He was Maria's paternal grandfather and after Maria's parents died he was appointed as her guardian. He lived as a recluse in Norfolk where she was raised." She shot me a warning look. I had been known to tell people all about my upbringing at this point. "He invested all his money in the railways."

"Before the financial crash, I trust, Mrs Blunt?"

"Oh yes, your Lordship, he sold his shares well before then. At the height of the boom in fact."

Here it came. Her distraction - a dazzle of vast, unexpected wealth.

She leaned across the table so that her string of pearls clinked against the plate. "He made a fortune." She mouthed the sum at him, her powdered mouth puckering around the fat, juicy figure. She sat back and gave a sad smile.

"He passed away last year and left his entire fortune to Maria. Her inheritance weighs so heavily upon us since his passing. We hardly know what to do with it."

Grief and bitterness washed over me. My inheritance had become a millstone around my neck and was going to drown me. Godfrey MacDonald looked at me with new interest and I glared back at him to leave him in no doubt. I saw that his eyes were a very pale blue, the same as my aunt's.

We were ushered into the drawing room. No books. Only paintings of MacDonald ancestors and a collection of finely upholstered silk chairs. My aunt took a digestive brandy and I watched her fall asleep. Her face so usually carefully composed, quickly slackened. The rain beat against the windowpane and I listened to the long, slow tick of the Grandfather clock. Lord MacDonald sat in the chair opposite. He was staring into the fire and drumming his fingers upon the armrest. His face was pensive, and very white, like milk in a tall glass. He made no attempt at conversation, not that I cared. Soon we would get back into our rented barouche and I would refuse to ever see him again. Although, it would have been interesting to talk to him about his camera and the Polytechnic. I remembered my descent in the diving bell.

"They have every type of invention and scientific curiosity," Grandpapa had said on our first visit when I was eight-years-old. "But there is something you must try first." He whisked me through a hall of new inventions where the air was filled with the whoosh and clank of automatic machines. At the end of the main hall an enormous tank of water had been sunk thirty feet into the floor. A great cast iron diving bell hung over it. It was suspended from a crane to lower it down and I peered into the depths. "We've never sent a child down before, especially not a girl," the operator said, looking at me with doubt. Grandfather slipped him a coin. I was shut in and the brass door was screwed shut behind me. Then came the suck of the pump, the terrible grating of the chain as it turned in its windlass, the dimming of light through the thick plate glass, and then the awful pressure in my ears, until pop! There was a sudden rush of murky green water around the seal and the freezing water began to-

"Would you like to see the library?"

I startled. Lord MacDonald was leaning forward, his voice a whisper.

"Pardon?"

"I thought you might like to see the library."

He glanced at Aunt Caroline, asleep in her chair, and I glanced at her too. Her chest was rising and falling slowly, a fleck of saliva bubbled at the corner of her mouth. Lord MacDonald placed his hands on his thin knees and stood up. I did too, but at the doorway, I hesitated. How long would she stay asleep? How much time did I have? That marvellous word. Library. It beckoned me and I hurried out to cross the polished marble hall where Lord MacDonald opened a door.

"Oh, my goodness."

I stood in amazement looking about me. The room was chilly with the lamps and the fire unlit, but on every wall, from floor to ceiling, were shelves and shelves of books. I stood for a moment in disbelief then I went around them running my finger along the spines and breathing in the familiar smell of sweet, musty paper. There must have been five times more books than Grandfather had ever had. Here were books on gardening and architecture, science and travel, the latest by Dickens. A whole shelf of Austen waiting for me like old friends.

"What an incredible collection."

My eyes rested on a large leather-bound volume with *Kosmos* written in gold on the spine and I ran my fingers over the embossed letters.

"You have a Von Humboldt," I exclaimed. "How on earth did you manage to get a copy? They ran out of print almost immediately." I turned to Lord MacDonald who was watching me from the doorway with his arms folded.

He smiled and shrugged. "My mother was an avid book collector."

I walked about the library touching the books in wonder, stopping here and there to exclaim over some volume or other. I pulled a copy of Charles Lyell's *Principles of Geology* from the shelf. I remembered how a willow leaf had once served as a bookmark in my copy. I had only read as far as the chapter on the Pliocene.

"My parents were both progressives," Lord MacDonald said following me into the room. "They felt they had to keep themselves informed with current thought and they took it upon themselves to read everything." He stopped in front of a small glass-fronted cabinet. "My mother called this her 'cabinet of radicals'."

I went over to the small glass-fronted cabinet and opened the door. It contained a collection of liberal pamphlets. Mills, Smith, Wollstonecraft, and one by the philanthropist, Robert Owen, *A New View of Society*. I had read many of them before. I looked around me at the books lining every wall and then to where Lord MacDonald was now standing, by a table in the centre of the room. I quickly considered my position. Since Grandpapa's death the inevitability of marriage had been bearing down upon me like a huge, unavoidable ship and I, an exhausted swimmer, had been trying to out-swim it. What if I now chose to be hauled aboard onto a ship of my own choosing? With this pedigree of library, this broad range of thought, it could turn out to be a lifeboat of sorts.

I went and stood beside Lord MacDonald and followed his gaze to the table. Spread out before him was a map made of thick, yellow parchment. It was curled at the edges from being repeatedly rolled. Drawn upon it, in blue ink, was a maze of islands and islets, like scattered jigsaw pieces. I peered to read the calligraphy in the spare winter light.

"North Uist," I said. My arm brushed his as I bent over the map and I heard my voice tremble a little.

He must have taken this for girlish nerves at reading out loud, for he said, "Yes, that's right, your pronunciation is spot-on," in a teacherly sort of way.

In truth, I did feel nervousness, not at reading of course, but at having to show a sudden, softer, change of heart. I thought he must be nervous at being alone with me too, for he cleared his throat before speaking again.

"This is the MacDonald estate in Scotland which I inherited last October when my parents died."

His voice was rather stiff and I assumed it was the emotion of losing his parents only a few months ago. He didn't look at me, but leaned closer over the map so that I caught a waft of his strong cologne. He put a long white finger on North Uist and his finger trembled a little.

"I've had this map since I was a boy. I even took it with me when I was sent down to Eton. I used to hide it under my mattress and look at it at night when the other boys were asleep. I can name all the beaches."

I looked sideways at him, his ears were reddening. I imagined him as a young boy and felt a stab of sympathy to think of him in a cold dormitory, reciting the names of beaches in the middle of the night. Hadn't I been a lonely child myself and also known a chilly bedroom far from home?

The blush was spreading from his ears to his cheeks, and to spare him more scrutiny, I turned back to the map.

"Sollas," I read aloud, looking at where his white finger rested upon the north of the island. The map had been divided into narrow columns. "What are these markings?"

"There's a plan of improvements for the whole estate. Sheep farming, that sort of thing. The whole place needs modernising."

I nodded in approval, thinking of Owen's pamphlet in the cabinet, *A New View of Society*. Owen had modernised his mill in Lanarkshire and improved the conditions for his workers. Across from North Uist was a larger island marked as Skye where, on the south side, was the symbol of a castle. I placed my finger on it.

"This here is a castle?"

"Armadale Castle, that's the clan seat." He held up his hand bearing the large gold signet ring to show me. "I'm the clan chief now."

The ring bore the same mark as the knives and forks. The gloved fist wielding the cross.

"I was given this ring by my father at Hogmanay, or Scottish New Year's Eve. My parents always held an enormous ball at the castle to celebrate." His voice became animated. "There's a tradition that a guest is chosen to go out and knock on the door at midnight. He's the first-footer, you see, the first person to come in over the threshold in the New Year. He's welcomed in with some black bun and a dram of whisky to bring good luck. When I was sixteen my father chose me to be the first-footer. The whole company of guests was waiting to welcome me into the castle and when I tore open the bun this signet ring was hidden inside." He grinned and waggled his ring finger. "That's when I knew that someday I would be the clan chief and the estate would be mine."

His eyes were shining and one might almost think him handsome, from a certain angle, with his fine, pale features and dark hair. He looked down at the map. "The whole lot's mine, the estate, the castle. You should see the view from the top windows."

From the hallway, I heard my aunt calling my name. My stomach tightened. I must not be found in here, in the library, at any cost.

I glanced once more around me, at all the books, then I looked at Godfrey MacDonald, my mind made up. "I would very much like to see the view from the castle." I offered my hand.

He nodded, then took my hand in his and shook it. His grip was hard and very cold.

Chapter Three

Sollas, March 1849

It was early March and I was out on the moor clearing the grass that had grown over the peat-banks since last summer. The day was cold and I pulled at the tough sedge-grass with freezing hands. The damp had seeped through my apron to my knees and I sat back to blow on my numb, dirty, pink fingers. All around the chilly wind was whipping waves across the dark surface of the lochans that studded the moor. Looking down towards Sollas, the moor gave way to land that was ploughed up into narrow rigs ready for planting. And on the other side of the crofts was the wide machair where the cattle grazed which ran straight onto the long white beach. Filling the horizon beyond was the restless, pewter sea and the empty grey sky. Mammy said there was nothing between us and America and I thought of my friend, Eilidh, who had gone away over that horizon with her family last year on account of The Hunger.

A hooded crow gave a sudden mournful caw and I turned to watch it fly over the moor towards Eaval hill. The hill rose out of the flat land like a fin breaking the water. On the other side of the hill, at Langais, the land was all bogs and lochs, and no crop would grow there in the marsh. It was a wild place where the fairy circle stood and where we children were not allowed to venture alone. I gave my fingers a final blow and began clearing the peat-bank once more. Underneath the spiky sedge-grass was the slab of rich peat we used in our fires. It was like the fruitcake Miss MacAllister had once shared with us at Hogmanay and the memory of those sweet, dark crumbs made my mouth water. I would have usually been in school at this time if it hadn't been closed. I thought longingly of the little stove that had warmed the schoolroom during winter months causing our misted breath to catch on the high schoolroom windows. It had been my job to come in early each morning to clean out the stove and light it before lessons began. These were often the best times of the day if Miss MacAllister happened to come in early too, for though she spoke the Gaelic she liked to hear me practise my English, especially if I recited a psalm, being religious like she was. I thought of the stove now standing cold and unlit in the empty schoolroom with the peat stack mouldering by the door.

I shivered, remembering what had happened that night by our own peat stack a week ago. The dank, ripe smell of the creature had stayed in my nostrils for days. Da had not believed me when I came crashing through the door to tell them. It was only the wind, Da said, that had blown the oilskin away, and my imagination had done the rest. He had frowned at Mammy and said that there were to be no more tales like that after dark, but Mammy had watched me carefully as I told them of what I had seen. She made no comment on whether it was true or not which was unusual in itself. Later though, as I brushed my tangled hair before getting into bed she spoke sharply, "make sure that every hair from that comb goes in the fire." That had set my heart racing again as that was only done to ward off evil. Now I could not leave our croft without glancing at our peat stack. Sometimes I would promise myself not to look at it, but my eyes would creep there on their own imagining what sort of creature had hidden there in the dark. I was grateful that the days were finally lengthening beyond the night of winter.

I heard a shout. Standing up and wiping my hands on my apron, I saw Cormac MacIver running and leaping over the tussocky ground towards me. He was fourteen already, the oldest in the class, since Eilidh had gone away. A sandy haired boy with a freckled face who I noticed had suddenly grown taller, his legs now sticking out of the bottom of his trousers.

"Red Hugh and Seamus MacRae had a fight," he said breathlessly. "And Mr Morrison has called a meeting in the schoolroom."

We ran along the side of the ploughed fields, clumps of earth and straw sticking to our shoes, and up the road to the schoolroom. What a strange sight it was from the doorway. Grown men of the village were all squeezed behind our small desks, others leaned against the walls for lack of chairs. Mr. Morrison the minister sat at Miss MacAllister's desk and Red Hugh and Seamus MacRae stood before him.

23

Red Hugh spoke. "It's always been the way here to rotate the rigs between families so that everyone gets their turn in the best soil." He was a big man with a red beard and hair and having the eyes of the room on him made the colour rise up in his face, too, and his lip tremble. "And it's my turn for a decent rig this year," he added, scowling at MacRae.

"That's not fair," Seamus MacRae said, folding his arms. "Last year the whole village had the rot and you couldn't grow anything, in good soil or poor. I say we keep the rig we had last year." MacRae looked like he'd come off the worse for the fight. The collar of his shirt was ripped and he had a red welt on his cheek.

"It was your decision to plant tatties man, you could have planted turnips or oats. If you planted tatties, then it's your own fault."

"Come on," MacRae's voice rose. "You know that oats won't take in the soil here. You'd not get the yield to feed y'self. It's only tatties that will feed a family all year round, if not for the damned rot."

There was agreement on this from around the room.

"At least you've got a rig that's half decent," someone called. There was muttering and grumbling around the room.

"The rig I been given this year is so poor it will hardly grow a weed," someone else said.

Mr. Morrison stood up. He was the minister of our Free Church a short man with a pink face and a booming voice used for delivering his sermons outdoors, as we had no building to meet in.

"What I propose is this. In view of The Hunger last year we will begin anew this season. The fields are divided into forty-two working rigs and we will divide them into lots. Each family will draw a lot."

Red Hugh began to protest, the planting had started already, and others joined in.

"No," Mr. Morrison said, lifting his hand. "It is quite the fairest way, given the circumstances. Everyone in agreement, say Aye."

Everyone looked around the crowded room. Even a daftie could see that there were more families than forty-two. To give everyone a lot, all the exhausted rigs would have to be ploughed and planted too. There was not enough land to feed us all.

Da was leaning against the wall. He was chewing his cheek. "Mr. Morrison." He stepped forward. Everyone turned to look at him and I pushed through and went to stand beside him. "I have another suggestion. I'll go and speak to the new factor and ask for a wee bit more land. I've been thinking about it and we don't need much, an extension of twelve rigs to the west should do it. If we plant turnips there the first year, with some cloverage in the second, we'll greatly increase the yield."

The men looked at each other and nodded, but Red Hugh scoffed. "The new factor, Colonel Crawford? And how will you speak to him, seeing as he doesn't speak the Gaelic?"

Da looked down at me and put his hand on my shoulder. "I'll take Morag, she speaks the English well, her teacher said."

My heart beat fast with pride, but I was careful to look down at the floor. There's no pride in being too smart, Mammy always said.

* * *

That afternoon I dressed in my Sunday best with my bonnet and shawl. Some folks stood and watched us leave, a few wished us well, and a couple shook their heads. Cormac was the only one to accompany us out of the village, his hands stuffed in his pockets to keep warm. He was a good head and shoulders taller than me now, I realised as he hopped and jumped over the ruts in the road beside me.

"The colonel's house has fifteen glass windows and a wooden staircase that goes right up to a second floor," Cormac said. "It's as big as the Inn at Lochmaddy."

It was well known that the old factor had been put out of his job once the old Laird had died. And that this new factor, a colonel, was from London. He had not been seen in the village yet.

Cormac walked with us as far as Grenitote beach and then he turned back, leaving Da and me to walk on alone. I missed Cormac's chatter now for Da walked silently beside me frowning at his boots and chewing his cheek. I looked out to the sea to where a great silver-grey cloud was hanging low against the pale spring sky, so low it was touching the water. Down on the beach foaming white breakers crashed onto the sand and left a trail of wet shiny kelp along the shore. The kelp had once been our gold, before I was born, Mammy often reminded me. That was during the French Wars, when half the men were away fighting Napoleon for his Lairdship. Cut off from their supplies in France, factories paid dearly for the soda ash that could be got from the kelp to make their soap and glass. The estate, Mammy told me, urged the islanders to abandon crofting and turn to kelping. They even brought more workers from the mainland, and from as far away as Ireland to work so that the population of Sollas and the other villages swelled to several hundred. Cutting, drying, pounding the kelp, all day, every day. Even with extra workers it was hard work and dirty too, but nothing was as filthy as the burning. They built big pits up on the beaches and all day long the smoke made your eyes water and the smell burned your chest. Burning and burning the kelp until only the sticky black tar was left that could be sent to the factories. But it clothed and fed us at least, Mammy always said, and gave us money for some lace, tobacco, new boots and beer. And then the French war ended. It was said that we had won, but it felt like the opposite Mammy said, for suddenly the potash was no longer needed. The kelp wasn't gold anymore, it was only plain old seaweed again. Only good now for putting on the crops, and when the crops got the rot, for eating.

As we came around a bend in the road, Colonel Crawford's house came into view and we stopped in awe. The house was perched on raised ground and sat with its back to the sea. Solid and square under a dark slate roof, the light bounced off the double row of glass windows. All around the house the land had been ploughed up into rig upon rig of rich dark soil, as far as the eye could see.

"Do all these rigs belong to the colonel?" I marvelled. I had never seen so many before.

Da knelt and picked up a handful of soil and it ran easily through his fingers. "Aye." He stood up. "Look there's Alasdair MacInnes."

The thin figure of Mr MacInnes could be seen bent digging in the furthest rigs. Da had known him since they were boys and now he worked on the estate. We started towards the house and Mr MacInnes straightened up and headed towards us. When he reached us he crossed his arms and blocked our path up the driveway. He was a thin man with a sour look on his face.

"What are you doing here?" he asked without so much as a *how do you do.*

"Good day to you, Alasdair," Da replied, "I'm after having a word with the colonel."

"He won't want to see you."

Da smiled. "If you don't mind Alasdair, I'll speak to Colonel Crawford directly."

"Whatever it is you want to say to him, you can say to me. I represent his authority." Mr MacInnes stood up tall.

Da looked over to the rigs where MacInnes had been working, then back at him standing in his dirty old clothes. He had a smear of earth on his cheek. "Pardon me, but you look more like his labourer."

MacInnes leaned closer to Da. "Watch yourself, MacDhomhnaill," he growled, "you're in no position to be talking to me like that."

Even I could smell his rotten breath.

Da stepped away from MacInnes, the colour was up in his face. "I would ask you to kindly show us to the colonel."

At that moment the front door of the house opened and a gentleman dressed in a fine suit appeared on the top step.

"MacInnes," he called.

The gentleman walked out of the house towards us and MacInnes slunk over to his side. He was tall, this gentleman, and his yellow hair was brushed neatly over the top of his head like raked sand. He wore high black leather riding boots, so shiny that the light gleamed like two silver pennies on the toes. He smiled at us as he approached and my heart lifted.

Da took off his cap and folded it in his hands. He looked at me, giving me a nod.

"Good day, Colonel Crawford. I was hoping I might have a moment to speak to you. My name is Artair MacDhomhnaill from Sollas."

I translated Da's words into English, my voice shaking a little, but Colonel Crawford only gave me the briefest of glances.

"What is it you want to say?" He smiled pleasantly enough at Da, but his English words had the ring of pebbles thrown upon on a frozen loch.

Da did not speak English, but he looked uneasily from the colonel to the smirking MacInnes and back again.

"Well, sir," Da hurried, "It's about the division of the fields into run-rigs over at Sollas. I have been giving it some consideration, sir, and well, I have a plan of improvements. I, we, would like your permission to extend them onto the pasture land, only by twelve rigs, but this will improve the yield considerably and enable families to-"

The colonel quickly raised a hand, and my translation trailed away. His hand was very clean, as though it had been scrubbed, and each nail was like a pale pink shell.

"MacDonald, is it?" Colonel Crawford said. "There will be no extension of the rigs into the pasture or elsewhere. As I understand it, none of you have paid rent for two years. You are living on his Lordship's estate for free."

I translated carefully, concentrating on getting the words right. Da frowned and shook his head and I stared down at the light bouncing off the colonel's boots.

"But, sir, we've had the rot these last two years and The Hunger. And with the kelping gone, and no work, none have us have earned a penny. We have a real chance this year, sir, if we can just have a wee bit of land or be able to use the land we already have differently, then-"

"It will not happen," the colonel said. "That land has already been allocated for other purposes." His voice was as sharp as frost and his smile had gone. "I suggest you concentrate on getting your affairs in order, MacDonald. Now, good-day to you. I have a shoot to get to."

He turned on his heel and headed quickly back to the house.

"But, sir," Da called after him, "if you could talk to his Lairdship, perhaps we could have a chance to present our case to him."

But the colonel didn't look back.

MacInnes gave us a dirty grin, the sort Murdo Macaulay gave when he had snatched your bonnet and wouldn't give it back. "Colonel Crawford doesn't speak the Gaelic," he sneered. "And his Lairdship will certainly not want to speak to you. What are you gonna do, go all the way down to London?"

"MacInnes," Colonel Crawford shouted from the steps. "Fetch my horse."

We watched MacInnes slope off, then we put our heads down into the wind and headed home.

Chapter Four

London, April 1849

It was only six o'clock, but I had been awake ever since Godfrey had half-dressed a few hours earlier and returned to his own bedroom. He had woken me up by tripping over a chair, and once he'd gone I got up to wash myself with the flannel and soap that the maid had laid out on the washstand the night before. I had thought I'd seen her smirking as she laid them out and I felt myself blushing to know why as I washed between my legs. Still, a wedding night was no worse than other things I had endured, and at least it had been over quickly enough, I thought, as the cold water trickled down my thighs. I lay in the fuggy darkness thinking of the books I wanted from the library. Thackeray, Scott, Austen, Von Humboldt. I repeated them to myself over and over like a liturgy.

As soon as sunlight appeared through the crack in the curtains, I swung my legs out of bed into my slippers, wrapped my blue damask shawl over my nightdress and pulled my bed cap down over my cropped hair. Godfrey had made no mention of the fact that I had kept my bed cap on. I tucked a few stray strands up into the lace-trimmed cap then opened the bedroom door and listened. Already the household was stirring, the smell of baking bread curling up the stairs from the kitchens. From out on the gravel driveway there was a crunch of a cart's wheels and the clink of milk-cans. I padded along the hall, pausing to listen at Godfrey's door, but there was no sound from within. Sunshine was streaming through the rose-light window on the landing, illuminating a huge painting. It was of Armadale Castle on Skye where we were heading today. The castle sat upon a lawn that rolled right down to a beach on the Sound of Sleat. Godfrey had told me of the time he had taken a wager to swim from that beach out to the rocky point and back again. All the village lads had cheered him on.

We were catching the eleven o'clock train this morning and our luggage was to be collected at ten o'clock sharp. With that in mind, I hurried along the landing to the staircase.

"Put the chairs back in the dining room and His Lordship wants to rid of those boxes and this painting."

I froze and flattened myself against the wood panelling at the top of the stairs. Peering below I could see the liver spots on the butler's polished bald head. He was speaking to a footman.

"And set the table for breakfast. His Lord and Ladyship will be eating at eight o'clock this morning."

I cowered at the top of the staircase. I am the mistress of the house now, I told myself, but on this first morning in my new home my title, Baroness MacDonald of Sleat, was like a grown up's dress on a child. More than that, instinct told me to conceal my ambitions wherever books were concerned. My sessions with the doctor had taught me that much. I wondered if Doctor Fortnum had seen the announcement in the *Times* that I was now married. I saw him smiling beneath his oiled moustache - *another patient, cured!* I shuddered.

There was a whistle at the back door and I watched the butler hurry away. The footman disappeared into the dining room, but I waited a moment longer before continuing downstairs. Across the marble hall I hurried past a stack of boxes and a painting to the library door. My heart beat fast with happy anticipation. Thackeray, Scott, Austen, von Humboldt. It had been a year since I had been allowed to read anything other than The Bible. I turned the handle, but it was locked. I tried it again, rattled the handle hard.

"Your Ladyship? May I help you?"

I wheeled around, my shawl slipping off my shoulders. It was the butler.

"Ah yes, please." I pulled the shawl around me, drawing myself tall, we were nearly the same height. "I wish to go into the library, but the door appears to be locked."

The butler frowned. "It is locked under instruction of His Lordship."

"May I have the key then?"

He sniffed and made small, sorry bob of his polished head. "Regretfully, Your Ladyship, I am instructed not to give you the key."

I opened my mouth to tell him that he was mistaken, but his gaze slid to the marble floor and remained there fixed on the tiles. I understood plainly. Aunt Caroline had got there first. The footman appeared in a doorway and stood looking at me curiously. I couldn't help it, but my hand flew to touch my night cap. With as much dignity as I could muster I lifted my chin and walked away. I glanced at the stack of boxes. The top box was open and filled with all the pamphlets from the library. *On Liberty* by John Stuart Mill lay on the top. As I went up the stairs, I heard the footman's whisper echo in the hall below. "Is her Ladyship religious, what with wearing a head covering all the time?"

Then the butler's sotto reply. "It was an illness, apparently."

An illness. I wondered when my aunt had told Godfrey? It would have been once the engagement was agreed or even when I had been safely wed. Had she told him about Dr Fortnum and his methods too?

I lingered at the top of the stairs until I saw the butler and footman had gone then I hurried back down and rummaged in the box of pamphlets. Why was Godfrey getting rid of these? I glanced at the painting leaning against the wall. It was of a young man with curly blond hair posing beneath the MacDonald coat of arms in a velvet coat. It was titled, *Alexander*. This must be Godfrey's brother, I realised. Godfrey had only spoken of him once and I could see it pained him. "It's better that you don't have to meet him," he had said. "He's estranged from the family and he's become a bitter sort of fellow, prone to outbursts and violence."

I looked at the painting again. They looked quite different, the two brothers. Where Godfrey was thin and pale, Alexander was broad and had a square chin. He looked as though he enjoyed outdoor sports or boxing. He stood in an easy, confident pose with his hand clenched on the top of a ceremonial sword. I heard footsteps coming from the dining room and quickly made for the stairs.

Back in my room I went over to the carved oak travelling trunk that stood beneath the window. I had planned to pack all the books I wanted from the library in it, but now it would only be filled with corsets and bonnets instead. I pulled the only book I owned out of the trunk. *The Female Instructor: A Young Woman's Guide to Happiness.* My aunt had given it to me on the last night I had spent with her. She had come into my room and sat on my bed beside me and had tried to stroke my cheek. I jerked my face away, it was far too late for such gestures. "I know you think I'm a monster, but I only wanted to help you, Maria." Her lip trembled a little and she seemed smaller suddenly, and older. She looked down at the book and I saw that the skin was becoming creped on her delicate hands. "I'm sorry that I was not – well- that I was not-" she stopped. What was she going to say, that she was not my mother? She sat up straight and sniffed. "Well, I have done my best, as my sister would have wanted, and now you are getting married. And see, I have bought you a book." She thrust it at me. "To help you in the female sphere."

The female sphere. That tightly hemmed circle. Well, I would not open the book after what she had done. I tossed it back into the trunk. Instead I looked at the pamphlet that I had taken from the box downstairs. It was *The Rights of Woman* by Mary Wollstonecraft. I felt a little barb in my heart, for Grandpapa had had me read from this when I was a child. I opened it and my eyes fell on the words:

"I have a profound conviction that the neglected education of my fellow-creatures is the grand source of misery I deplore."

"Yes, very good," Grandpapa had said as I had tripped over Miss Wollstonecraft's words. I did not understand half of them, but I liked the sound of them in my mouth; *con-vic-shun, ed-u-cay-shun*. We had been sitting together at the reading desk in the library that looked out onto the garden. Grandpapa's smell of cigars and Pears soap came back to me all of a sudden. I felt the familiar shape of grief, an empty hollow in my chest. Yet reading Mary Wollstonecraft's words again stirred the old flicker of defiance in me. Like breath blown on a glowing ember. I thought of the painting of Armadale Castle hanging out in the hallway. As the family home, the castle would surely have a library too.

With that I put Mary Wollstonecraft's pamphlet in the bottom of the trunk and I set about dressing for the journey.

* * *

I watched Godfrey dozing opposite me in the carriage to the station. His dark lashes were closed and his face was so pale it looked made of alabaster. The sudden recollection of how his naked buttocks had glowed white in the dark sprung to mind. He had turned away to undress last night, fumbling with his buttons and braces. My husband, I repeated to myself as I looked at him now. My husband. It was like jabbing a lip that was numbed with cold to see if there was feeling yet. The word had no significance though, no resonance, it was just a word. I tried to think of married couples I knew, but they were few, for Grandpapa had not socialised. There was Mrs Hobbs, the housekeeper in Norfolk, and her husband who worked at the mill. I saw him squeeze her bottom once when he thought no one was looking. "Nigel," she had exclaimed, blushing. I could not imagine Godfrey doing that to me.

We had reached Drummond Street and the pavements were busy with people streaming towards the station. A brass band played as we pulled in under the great Euston arch and the station yard had a carnival air and was crowded with people dressed in their Sunday best all come to see the spectacle. Our coachman pushed through into the Great Hall and we came out onto the platform. Beneath the wrought-iron roof stood a locomotive of burnished brass and green. A crowd of gentlemen was gathered around the engine talking to the driver. It was 0-6-0 engine by the looks of it. I stopped to take a better look.

"No leading wheels then?" I asked, squatting down to examine the wheels. The group of gentlemen spectators looked surprised.

"That's right ma'am, just the six drivers on three axles," the driver said wiping his blackened hands on a rag.

In front of me, Godfrey had stopped. He wheeled round. "Maria!"

I stood up.

"And what is the capacity of the tank?"

Godfrey came back towards me and gave the gentlemen an apologetic glance. He gripped my elbow and pulled me towards him so sharply that I stumbled. The driver put out an automatic hand to steady me.

"Do not touch my wife."

Wife. It had an ugly sharp sort of sound. He marched me up the platform towards the first-class ladies' carriage. The pressure of his fingers causing pain in my elbow. He dropped my arm and gave me a stern look.

"You cannot go grubbing around locomotives and talking to their drivers. It won't do."

I rubbed my elbow.

"I only stopped for a moment to look at the engine. You really hurt my elbow, Godfrey, dragging me up the platform like that."

"I didn't mean to hurt you my dear." He gave my shoulder an awkward little pat. "But you really must learn. I'll see you when we change at Birmingham."

Then he went off down the platform.

You really must learn. I thought of the book, *The Female Instructor* in my trunk. Doctor Fortnum had used those words too. Though what he had meant was "un-learn" of course. A porter opened the door to the first-class ladies' compartment and helped me to step aboard. There was a hushed atmosphere within. A woman in black was reading The Bible and two ladies in silk dresses had their embroidery out upon their knees. I shuddered at the thought of my own embroidery, and of Elizabeth Dingle who had once tried to teach me.

"I'm travelling to York," an elderly woman informed me as I took a seat beside her next to the window. She was a duchess, apparently, and she offered me a sweet, but I shook my head and looked out of the window. Shops and stalls had been set up along the platform to serve passengers. Next to the pie-seller was a stall with a newly painted sign that said WH Smith's. Its tables were stacked with piles of books and copies of *The Times*. A good omen, I thought.

Further down the platform, amidst the busy to and fro of coalmen and porters, I caught sight of Godfrey. He was talking to another gentleman who had his back to me. This fellow was as tall as Godfrey, but broader and wore a dark green velvet coat.

Despite his fine clothes he appeared dishevelled though. The back of his coat was crushed as though he had slept in it. Whatever he was saying, Godfrey looked grim and was shaking his head. Then the man drew closer and took Godfrey by the lapel. Godfrey was saying something now and I saw him pull out his gold pocket watch. Then he pointed up the platform towards my carriage. I drew back quickly and when I looked out again, the man had gone.

There was a long, sharp whistle then came a sudden jolt accompanied by a fearful clanking, the scrape of metal, and a rush of steam past the window. The duchess beside me emitted a small cry of alarm and plucked at my sleeve with a papery hand, pressing her handkerchief to her mouth. I felt a rise of excitement finally build inside me. The hiss of the pistons was like my own breath (yesss!) at the thought of leaving my aunt and Dr Fortnum behind. The brass band struck up in double time, and as we pulled away from the station, the crowd of spectators waved and cheered, and some boys jumped onto the tracks and ran along besides, waving their caps. For a moment, I imagined that they were all there to bid me farewell, *Good luck Maria, Good luck and God Speed with your new life,* and I waved back.

Slowly, slowly we inched away, gradually pulling out of the station, until the engine built up steam and then we flew, flew out of the city at four and twenty miles per hour and London gave way to countryside. It was not the jolt, rock and bump of a horse and carriage, but the relentless pull of a wonderful machine. Great clouds of steam, like dragon's breath, rolled past the window, accompanied by an occasional shower of embers and sparks, the smell of cinders and smoke creeping in. Through a hedge, there was a glimpse of a canal boat and its dray, moving so slowly they looked frozen still. A crow flapped away from a fence post in alarm, its wings beating in slow motion. All the time I urged the locomotive faster in my mind, onwards towards the future.

Chapter Five

Sollas, April 1849

Three weeks after our visit to the colonel I woke up in the middle of the night and heard Da get up and open the door. Though I could hardly see him I knew he was standing barelegged in his shirt at the open doorway. I could feel the chilly night air creeping past him and into our croft. The hairs on my neck prickled and my ears strained in the dark too. Then he shut the door and got back into bed and I lay staring up at the dark thatch, my heart ticking like a kettle heating over the fire. A short while later he got up, opened the door, and stood there listening again. I sat up in bed and through the open doorway I could see the glint of the moonlight in the puddles out in the road. I saw Da step outside and stand there in the road, stock still, the light from the moon shining on his pale shirt. Then the moon was snuffed out by clouds and he vanished. I got out of bed, the floor cold on my bare feet, and went to the door.

"Da," I called, my voice like the rasp of a file. "Da?"

"Shhh, Morag," his voice said from over near the peats.

My mouth went dry as I strained to see him, then the moon broke through the clouds and I saw him again, the shape of him, at least, beside our peat stack. "What are you doing?" I whispered.

"Listening to the wind."

I listened too. The wind was coming in off the sea and whistling between the houses making me shiver. "What for?"

"The wind has turned and I'm listening for a sand-wind." Then he came back inside. "It's hard to tell, but it's coming from the North West all right. I'll go at first light and check."

I got back into my bed and rubbed my icy feet together to warm them, pulling my sheet over my head and feeling my breath against it. I lay for a long while with the memory of that feral smell and that brief brush of hair, wondering what else beside the sand-wind was out there. I remembered how this time

37

last March we were woken early by a strange keening sound. It was Old Ma MacNeil, on her knees, out in the rigs, crying bitterly. Cormac's mam was first to reach her, but the old lady wouldn't budge, she kept crying and wailing. By now near enough the whole village were gathered, some stood still like statues, some shook their heads, others simply turned back into their houses. My Da stood in our doorway, pulling on his jacket. Mammy laid her hand on his arm and told him there was no reason to go and see for himself, he knew what was out there right enough and why not have some tea first? But he shook her off and strode out anyway, being my Da. His dark outline could be seen against the dawn sky, out in the rigs, tearing up the sick tattie plants, their leaves black and blighted, heaping them for burning. That burning smell was worse even than the acrid smell of kelp burning, because it meant that The Hunger had come, creeping through the rigs, rotting the tatties, and causing an achy, hungry belly that the pappy, watery taste of meal never filled.

When the first light fell through the window, I woke and saw Da pull on his boots and tuck his shirt into his trousers. Mammy was still asleep, her dark hair spread over the pillow of their bed like kelp on a beach. As he lifted the latch quietly I fetched my shawl and followed him. Everything in the village was cast in the grey shadow of dawn, the first light just stealing over the sea. I walked silently beside Da, glancing at the peat stack as we passed it, my eyes swivelling left and right. We went out to the run-rigs, some already sown with tatties, barley, turnips, and black oats. Soon they would all be vying for space in the narrow strips, but now the first tiny plants had just begun to push through the earth and were shivering in the cold breeze. Da knelt down, running his hand across them and through the soil of each rig. Then the next and the next, checking for the tell-tale grittiness that might have been sand-drift blown in on the wind. He stood up, satisfied. The light had reached us now, so that colours were appearing, the tiny leaves of the plants turning from black to bright green.

I squeezed his hand. "No sand then, Da?"

"No sand," he said, standing up. "And the plants look nice and healthy." He glanced along the rig and frowned. "But what's that?"

At the far end of the rigs, the plants had been trampled down, as though something had run through them in a narrow path two feet wide across all the furrows.

He went across to look, bending down to examine it, and I bent to look as well. There was no boot print or hoofmark, but the plants were completely ruined, their shallow roots torn, the earth around them kicked up as though something had been running fast.

"Could it be deer?" I asked.

Da hopped over each rig following the trail. "I don't think so."

"Or a rabbit?"

"It was something much bigger than a rabbit to ruin the plants like this and there are no droppings or prints."

We reached the end of the rigs where the ploughed land gave way to sedge grass and wild moor again. I looked out at the dark lochans and thought, what creature leaves no prints? The trail had stopped so we turned and followed it back towards the houses and the sea, and I hurried along with a pricking feeling in my hands and feet.

"Something bigger, more like a dog, I'd say," Da said scratching his chin.

My stomach turned a somersault.

No one had a dog in Sollas, except Seamus MacRae. He had bought a dog for his daughter at the fair. It was a mangy brown cur with runny eyes, but the girl loved it and had tied her only blue hair ribbon around its neck.

"It's probably that dog belonging to Seamus," I said. "Don't you think, Da, Seamus' dog?"

But Da did not reply. We had come to where the sandbanks had been built to protect the crops from the sand and we stood looking down on the beach where the fishing boats were pulled up on the shore huddled together like roosting hens.

"Granddaddy's sandbanks will keep the sand from coming in," I said, keen to be away from thinking about dogs and what might have made those tracks.

"Well it wasn't just Granddaddy who built them, you know." Da smiled. "Everyone helped after the sand wiped out the turnip crop, all the people from Dunskellar and Middlequarter too. Even

Laird MacDonald helped, he sent men over from Skye and he paid for all the tools."

I remembered the story Granddaddy had told of the old Laird MacDonald. Of when he and the men had returned from fighting the French wars for the Laird. The celebrations at the Taigh Chearsabhagh Inn at Lochmaddy had lasted three nights and they had drunk the place dry. The Laird had been carried aloft on the shoulders of his men and carried out into the street followed by the fiddlers. That was when there was money for drinking, Granddaddy had said, and before they had realised their victory had wiped out the kelping.

"Well maybe the Laird will help again, with the rigs I mean," I said.

"The old Laird is dead," Da said, kicking a tussock of grass with his foot. "It's his son that is Laird now."

"Halo there!"

We startled and turned to see Mr Morrison, the minister. He came and stood beside us on the sandbanks, looking at the boats below.

"I think we'll meet on the beach this morning as it is fine," Mr Morrison said, looking towards the sea. "Nothing like the roar of the sea to raise our spirits."

Da squinted up at a seagull flying overhead and said nothing. Since The Hunger Mammy had wrapped our bible in a cheesecloth and put it at the bottom of her wedding chest.

The minister put his hand on Da's shoulder. "As it says in the Book of Hebrews, *faith is the substance of things hoped for*." That's what I'll be preaching this morning, Artair." He patted Da's shoulder and smiled at me too. "Faith and hope, that's what we need, to put our faith in the unseen."

I glanced back at the rigs, shivering to think of what the unseen might be.

"I better be going," the minister said, clapping his hands together. "I'm away to see Seamus. His daughter is in need of an encouraging word since that wee dog of hers died."

Chapter Six

Glasgow, April 1849

The dining room of the Buckshead Hotel in Glasgow was done out in burgundy and gold fleur de lys wallpaper with a matching crimson carpet and drapes. Rather than conjure luxurious splendour it gave the room a claustrophobic effect which the dim wall lamps served to heighten. The hotel must have been a staging post for travellers, for as I came down for breakfast I recognised some of the people who had stayed at our previous hotel. There was the elderly gentleman with the natty red cravat who had sat opposite us for dinner in York, and there was the young lady that looked like Elizabeth Dingle. I felt a stab of dislike as sharp as the prick of an embroidery needle as I went past. She had the same strawberry blonde hair. My own hair was carefully hidden beneath a blue bonnet with lace trim.

Godfrey was seated at our centre table already. I would have chosen a table by the window, overlooking the street, but it seemed that guests were arranged by social order like a pack of cards. Those with titles were given the brightest, centre tables, the other guests were arranged around the sides and dingier corners of the room. Godfrey had his back to me, reading the paper and I hovered behind him for a moment trying to catch a glimpse of the news. Something about trouble in Ireland again, but the waiter came hurrying over to seat me.

Godfrey lowered his paper a fraction as I sat down, the bright light of the chandelier caught the gleam of his hair oil.

"Did you sleep tolerably?" He asked.

I thought of the rattle of the loose window casement, the smell of salty effluent seeping up from the docks, but a husband did not wish to hear about these minor complaints, the *Female Instructor* had advised. I had glanced at the chapter entitled, *Useful Hints to Married Women* and it recommended that, "cheerfulness and good humour should be particularly sought by married women." So, I placed my napkin in my lap and smiled.

"I slept well thank you, did you?"

"I did, quite tolerably, thank you."

Now that our exchange was complete he went back to his paper. I scanned the back of it hungrily, but there were only advertisements for starching powder and farm machinery. The front page was obscured by his hand. I frowned and racked my brain for some topic of conversation. "Never be afraid of a gentleman's intellect," Grandfather had said to me. He had been ill by then, the breath rasping in his chest. I looked across at Godfrey reading the paper. The problem wasn't intellect, but his chilly politeness. It was difficult to think of anything significant enough to pierce its facade.

"Godfrey," I said suddenly, "why was the library in London locked?"

"Hmm?"

"The library. In Notting Hill. It was locked."

A waiter arrived and lifted the lid of a silver dinner tray and a cloud of fishy steam rose from it. I wrinkled my nose as he placed a plate of kippers in front of me and cleared Godfrey's plate. Godfrey spread his paper over the table and went back to it.

"Well?

"Well, what?"

"About the library."

He frowned down at his paper. "The whole house was being locked up, Maria, ahead of our departure. Not only the library, the drawing room, the cellars, the whole lot."

"Yes, but I wanted to--"

A porter appeared at our table.

"A telegraphic message, Your Lordship."

The announcement of a novelty such as a telegram had drawn a look of interest from the tables next to us. Godfrey did not notice as he tore it open. As he read it, his lip gave an involuntarily curl and his jaw clenched. I watched him read it several times then rip it up and throw it onto the table. He slumped back in his chair, staring in front of him.

"What's happened?" I asked.

He said nothing, but pushed back his chair, and stood up.

"Godfrey? Wait. What time are we departing this morning?"

He looked down at me blankly.

"What time shall we leave to catch the steamer to Skye?"

He shook his head and blinked at me. "Oh, we shan't be travelling today after all."

"Not travelling? But I thought you wanted to be on Skye as soon as possible?"

He frowned at me and lowered his voice. "Look, I have a lot of responsibilities now and the estate trustees have requested to see me urgently here in Glasgow."

My heart sank at the thought of a day spent in the hotel bedroom staring at the florid wallpaper.

Without any further comment he had set off from the table.

I froze. He had left his newspaper behind. I was careful not to look at it, but instead took a mouthful of fish and chewed slowly, watching Godfrey leave the dining room, willing him to go. But at the door he stopped and walked quickly back. He picked up the newspaper and folded it in half.

"Forgot this. I'll see you for dinner tonight."

He did not meet my eye.

He had been told of the doctor's orders. "No reading of novels, newspapers or any material that may aggravate Maria's condition."

I stared down at the miserable kippers. A wave of hot shame followed by a burst of frustration went through me. To think that even here I was not beyond the doctor's reach. It was vital to tell Godfrey the truth of what happened last summer, but how? We were hardly ever alone. Godfrey played cards almost every evening and there was no conversation during his nightly visits to my room.

The young lady who looked like Elizabeth Dingle was getting up from her table. As she passed me she smiled, but I looked away to the blank space left by the newspaper. My eyes fell on the ripped pieces of telegram that Godfrey had left scattered across the tablecloth. I reached across and collected them and returned to my room.

At the writing desk I put the pieces of telegram together. It had been sent from Paisley station to Glasgow this morning, the signals were recorded by Mr P.Watts, telegraph clerk. The message had been sent for the sum of thirteen shillings, that was as much as Mrs Hobbs had earned in a week. Something urgent then to use the telegraph. I imagined the rapid clicks up the line, the twitch of the needle, as Mr P. Watts deciphered the message and copied it out in his curly handwriting.

After what you have done?! You'll pay for it.

I frowned. It was a strange message to have paid thirteen shillings for. Sent using a new Wheatstone single needle telegraph by the look of the punctuation marks. And then I saw that the message had been sent by a Mr Alexander MacDonald. That was Godfrey's brother. *After what you have done?!* The accusation jumped from the paper. *You'll pay for it.* I thought of the portrait of Alexander I had seen in Notting Hill, of the tall man with broad shoulders. A bitter fellow, prone to outbursts, Godfrey had said of his brother. And violence, I remembered, thinking of Alexander's fist clenched upon a sword. Where was Paisley? Hopefully nowhere near here. I collected up the pieces of telegram and went and dropped them into the grate. A chill went through me as I watched them slowly curl and blacken. They were like the fragments of charred paper that had swirled across the lawn in Norfolk.

From down on the Clyde came the sudden, mournful wail of a steamer ship and I went to the window. Across the wide street there were large villas and other hotels and I watched carriages drawing up outside our hotel to take guests down to the ferry. There was the girl who looked like Elizabeth getting into a cab. Down on the windowsill, there was a deep crack that ran along its length and the husk of a dead fly had fallen into it. I turned away. I would not think about Elizabeth and what she did, or I too would end up at the bottom of a dark crevasse.

I went over to my trunk and pulled out Mary Wollstonecraft's pamphlet and my eyes fell on the words:

The woman who strengthens her mind through proper education will become the friend and not the humble dependent of her husband.

When we reached Skye, I decided, I would tell Godfrey exactly what had happened last summer, the whole truth, and perhaps he would tell me what had happened with his brother. With that, I put the pamphlet back in my trunk and picking up my bonnet and gloves I went downstairs.

Chapter Seven

Sollas

The salty wind tugged at my hair and the wet sand made a *schlllupp* sound as it sucked at my feet. Beside me crouched Cormac, digging with his bucket for cockles. I looked up, the sky was so blue and vast that I felt dizzy from it. We had the great expanse of beach to ourselves, and the sea, at low tide, was just a thin fold of white on the horizon. It all seemed so empty, the sky, the beach, and I suddenly felt the loss of school like a punch in my chest. It had been two months since it had closed and I missed doing my arithmetic on my slate, hearing the squeak of the chalk as I added and subtracted. Miss MacAllister had promised to bring in a book called an Atlas that showed all the countries in Europe, but now I would never see it. Instead, I was down on the empty beach collecting cockles for a soup.

In The Hunger, we ate so many cockles that the salty, fishy taste was always on my breath and wet sand was always under my nails from digging them up with the bucket. Sometimes the whole village would be out cockling at low tide, a whole crowd of old and young, scrabbling in the wet sand for something to eat. It took an awful lot of cockles to fill one belly, stewed up in nothing but water and a handful of wild sorrel leaves. No one spoke or sang, but just turned over the sand in silence looking for the cockles, one eye on your neighbour's bucket to see how many they had. Da said that The Hunger brings on a madness in folks that leads them to become craicte in the head. Like Colin MacCuish who cut up his boots so that his bairns could chew on the leather. When he got on the boat he had bare feet like his bairns. Mammy says you must be pretty craicte to think that going away on the boat will make things better.

I gave up looking for cockles and followed the bird tracks on the wet sand instead, hopping and jumping wherever they went.

Following the tracks made me start singing my favourite song about a baby that is stolen away by the piskies.

"I've found the wee brown otter's track, the otter's track, the otter's track, I've found the wee brown otter''s track, but ne''er a trace of baby, O!"

Cormac was still turning over the sand with his bucket, smiling and scowling at the same time. I knew he liked that song from when he was a wee boy, but he thought it was babyish now. I danced ahead of him, singing it and his face got redder and redder.

"Give over with your faerie songs." He threw a piece of seaweed at me. "And get back to cockling."

"Missed," I shouted and raced ahead of him, swinging my empty bucket wildly. I glanced over my shoulder, but he was still bent digging. I stopped running and at that moment, he leapt up and charged towards me, catching my shawl and planting a long, wet piece of seaweed on my head over my face.

"Got ya." He laughed.

We fell onto the sand and laughed and laughed, me with my seaweed hair over my eyes. It was a funny sound, our laughter, like something we hadn't heard in a long time. A seagull was strutting about on the sand nearby and it squawked loudly as though it was trying to join in.

"Cormac," I said, standing up and brushing the sand off my dress, "you believe in faeries, don't you?"

He stood up too, looking at me uncertainly. "My Ma says we are only to believe in the Lord Jesus now." His cheeks reddened. "But my aunty tied a bannock to the front door when she had her baby, so the faeries wouldn't steal him and when she went to the door afterwards the bannock was gone."

"Yes, yes," I said, "but what about other things?" I tried to keep my voice light. "Like, I don't know, the Cu Sith."

He looked at me darkly. "My aunty says not to say its name. If you say its name you summon it. It's bad luck, like the devil."

I thought of the story Mammy had told me about Shonag MacCodrum. She had looked into the fire and had boldly said the name of the Cu Sith that night of the storm.

He looked at me. "Why are you asking?"

"My Mammy told me a story, that's all." I swung my bucket and walked away.

"Well, was it on a Friday?" he asked anxiously, catching up with me. "If It's on a Friday, It's double bad luck."

I stopped and looked at him. "Why is it double bad-luck?"

"Because that's when my aunty says the sith are abroad."

We heard the clip of a horse on the coast road that ran beside the beach and saw Reverend MacLean from the Church of Scotland riding past. He sat as straight as a piece of chalk on his bay mare. The reverend's stone church was for the gentry and he didn't come to the village much, unless he was compiling information for his statistical account. Then he wouldn't leave us alone, asking questions about returns and yields of barley and turnips, about diseases and deaths. Mammy had told the reverend several times her views on his church, but I don't think he put it in his report.

"Good-day, Reverend," Cormac called out.

The reverend swung round in his saddle and pulled his horse to a stop.

"Are you children from Sollas?" he called in Gaelic.

"Yes, sir." We stood up, brushing the rest of the sand off ourselves and scrambled up to the road.

The reverend looked down at us, his white hair stuck out from underneath his black hat and his thin nose was nipped pink in the cold wind.

"You can run an errand for me then," he said. "Go straight home and tell people that there is a meeting up in the stone church this afternoon. Everyone must attend."

We stood looking up at him. Sometimes Miss MacAllister would give us a scone for helping her with an errand.

"Chop, chop," he said and we got going.

As soon as I told Mammy, she told me to run and fetch Da straightaway who was down on the back beach collecting kelp. The tide was on the turn, the waves began to race up the beach, and I saw the figure of Da down by water, heaping kelp into his barrow to put on the rigs. He stood up slowly when he heard about the meeting. He didn't say anything, he just rested his hand on the wooden barrow and looked out at the sea.

Near enough the whole of Sollas turned out to the meeting, close to one hundred families. We stood up at the front, Mammy with her black Sunday bonnet and grey dress. No one spoke or asked after each other, we just gazed around at the stone columns and polished wooden benches, whilst Reverend MacLean stood at the front wringing his hands and gazing up at the roof. The church door swung open suddenly and a cold blast of spring air rushed in. Colonel Crawford came sharply down the aisle, the tap, tap, tap of his shiny black riding boots echoing in the silence. He was followed by Artair MacInnes slinking along behind him. He wore high riding boots like the colonel's, except they were brown and tatty looking. Reaching the front of the congregation, Colonel Crawford nodded sharply to the reverend and climbed up to the pulpit. We gazed expectantly up at him. MacInnes hung at the bottom of the pulpit steps and no-one gave him a second glance.

"Charles Shaw, the sheriff, has been delayed," Colonel Crawford said, his brassy voice echoing off the walls. "I will open the meeting in just a moment."

The reverend interpreted from English to Gaelic for the congregation. Everyone began looking at each other. No one spoke, but their eyes said, "Why is the sheriff coming here to Sollas?" The factor's job was to represent all of Laird MacDonald's business on the island, but the sheriff dealt with the law and keeping the peace.

Mammy bent down to speak to me. "Morag, out you go now and play and take the wee ones with you – and you, yes, you too Cormac."

I looked at her, but she had her no-nonsense face on and I filed out of the church taking Cormac's wee sister and brother, Mairie and Angus, by the hands. Other parents saw we were going and sent their children too, and we stood outside, the cold wind whipping our bare legs. The sleek horses belonging to the colonel and the reverend were tied up nearby and Cormac went to fuss them and pick them handfuls of grass.

Mairie tugged my hand. "I'm hungry." I looked back at the church door, thinking of the look on Mammy's face, as solemn as a stone carving.

"Yes, I'm hungry too," Angus said.

I looked down at them. "Come on, we'll go home and I'll go to the byre and fetch some milk."

I pushed open the byre door and the sweet, warm tang of the cattle greeted me. Light filtered from the high spaces between the wall and the roof giving a dim musty light. There were three cows that were ours amongst the others, and they nudged me, a mother and her two daughters, hoping that I had come to take them out to graze. They barged me with their shaggy golden sides and their big pink tongues licked their noses.

"Give over," I said, in the voice that Mammy used with them, pushing them back. I reached for the pail and stool, then froze as something caught my eye. There in the corner of the byre, in the straw, something dark was huddled. Panic fluttered in my chest like a trapped bird, my face growing cold then hot, then cold again. There was definitely something there. I picked up a cattle switch that lay by the door.

"Halo?" I called, "Who's there?"

But there was no reply, no movement from the shape in the corner as I stepped towards it. Closer now, I saw that it was our oilskin used for covering the peat stacks. It had been heaped in a bundle and all around it the straw had been trampled in a flat circle like a sort of den. I swished through the straw with the cattle switch and it hit something so I kicked back the straw with my foot. It hit something hard. Crouching down I saw what it was. A long bone, like from a human leg, slashed with teeth marks, the end snapped off. I turned and pushed my way past the cows, out of the byre, down the road to our croft, my hand shakily rattling the latch, slamming the door behind me. The two children were sitting on my bed and they looked up at me their eyes like saucers. I leaned against the door my breath rasping in my chest.

"Did you fetch us some milk?" Angus asked.

My breath was slowing, but the wind rattled the window suddenly and started my heart thumping again. I knelt to tend the fire with shaking hands, but my breath was hardly strong enough to make an ember glow.

"I'm hungry," Mairie said.

"How about a story," I said quickly. "A nice story instead?"

I sat down in Mammy's chair, my feet not quite reaching the floor and laid my trembling hands in my lap. I looked at the pair of them sitting on my bed, my mind racing for some pleasant thing to tell them.

"Did you know my Mammy saw a mermaid when she was a young lass?"

"No, she never," Angus said.

"She did. She swore on cold iron that she did."

They looked at me seriously then and I took a breath, trying to stop my heart from racing, trying to remember how Mammy told the story.

"It was a hot summer's day and my mammy and her sisters were cutting kelp for burning on Colla beach on Benbecula. It was so hot that my mammy had it in mind to wade out and cut the kelp where it floated in the shallows. So she wandered away from the rest of the group, past the nets laid out on the sand to dry, and tucking her skirts up she waded into the water. The sea was lovely and cool on her hot legs. She waded here and there, cutting the kelp with her knife and tossing it back onto the sand. When the water was nearly at her waist, there right there in front of her, was a small splash. She looked up expecting to see an otter, or even a seal, but there was just the flash of a silver fin and ripples in the smooth water. She stood still and waited, perhaps it was a shoal of rock cod come into the shallows for some reason. A little way out, bubbles appeared on the surface and she could make out what looked like a pale creamy body just below the water. Was it some strange white porpoise she wondered?"

"Porpoises are grey, not white," Angus said. "Our Da's seen one."

I nodded. "Well, my Mammy turned to call to her sister, Fionnalgh, to come and look and as she did the creature thrashed in the water, spraying Mammy with silver droplets. She caught a flash of arms and long hair, twisting under the water."

"A mermaid," Mairie said.

"Mammy stumbled back out of the water, and as she did, the creature partly surfaced. She had dark eyes and long yellow hair that streamed down her shoulders and her bare chest. Mammy saw then that the mermaid's tail was caught in the net of a fishing pot and that she was trying to pull herself free. Behind her some of the men from the burning pits and the other lassies were coming down the beach to see what was going on. They caught sight of the creature and began racing down the sand, grabbing the nets that lay about."

"Did they want to catch the mermaid?" Angus asked, "in their nets?"

"Yes," I said solemnly. "They did. The mermaid struggled and twisted in the water, her tail was stuck fast, and some of the lads waded in towards her. Some had rocks and stones in their hands ready to throw, but my Mammy turned to face them and she pulled out her kelping knife. "No," she said to them in her crossest voice. Then she turned and waded out to the mermaid and cut her free."

"So, she escaped then? The men didn't catch her?" Mairie asked.

"Yes, she escaped. She was last seen leaving a trail of silver bubbles as she swam off into Colla bay."

"And did your Mammy ever see her again?"

"No, but the mermaid left her something on the beach the next day." I stood up and went over to Mammy's carved wedding chest where she kept The Bible, wrapped up in the cheesecloth, along with her best things. Carefully I lifted the heavy lid, the chest smelled like the wooden pews in the stone church. It was in the breast pocket of Da's suit that Mammy kept it. I reached in with my two fingers and took out a scrap of red velvet cloth, then I showed the children what was wrapped inside.

A tiny pearl, as big as a baby's toenail, shaped like a teardrop. Its creamy lustre gleamed in the dim light. "A mermaid treasure."

"They're magic they are," said Angus. "You can throw it back in the sea and make a wish and the mermaid will help you."

We stood looking at the treasure lying in my palm.

"I'd wish for a bonnet with lace," Mairie whispered.

"I'd wish for a never-ending plate of tatties," Angus said.

I wrapped up the pearl and put it back in the chest. My wish didn't fit into words, only a feeling for everything to be go back to the way it was, for the school to be open again, for the creature in the byre to be gone. As I put the treasure back in its place, the croft door opened and Mammy and Da came in.

"Da," I said.

"Not now, Morag," Mammy said, lifting her hand. "Take Mairie and Angus back home." Her voice sounded hoarse, like after coughing. I glanced at Da, but his face was grey as ashes, and he sat down in his chair.

"But-"

"Morag!" Da's voice was sharp, and when it was like that, there was no arguing with him.

"Come on," I said to the children, hoping Da heard the huff in my voice, and I led them home, going the long way round to avoid going past the byre.

* * *

The next morning, we were woken up by an awful clanking sound. The light was already at the first plank in the table and Da grabbed his trousers, Mammy her shawl. We opened the door and looked out. There was Red Hugh right outside our door, pulling a handcart, pots and pans tied to it, his wife sitting bundled backwards on top. Other doors were opening, other people were looking out too. Old Ma MacNeill's white hair stood up in tufts and Cormac's Da's shirt was still unbuttoned.

"Where are you going, Hugh?" Da called.

The great figure of Hugh stopped and set down the cart and he turned towards us. "We're leaving," he said. He looked around at the open doorways on either side of the road. "Going to Glasgow."

Mammy pushed past Da and went out to the cart to where Hugh's wife sat.

"Moira, don't leave," she said. "What is there in Glasgow for you?"

Moira bit her lip and tightened her arms around a kettle on her knee.

Hugh spoke for her. "I have a cousin in Glasgow, he said there was work there and a decent place to live."

"But you have somewhere to live, Hugh," Mammy said. "You live here."

Hugh shook his head, his colour rising. "Call this living, what we've bin doing these past two years? Scraping a mouthful off the land and not even that?" He glanced at his wife.

"I'm with child," Moira whispered to Mammy, "and I can't lose this one."

52

Mammy looked to Hugh. "The Hunger is over," she said. "The plants are healthy this year, the cattle are fattening again, and your crowdie is the best in the village." She looked up at Moira and put her hand on her arm.

"I've already sold my cattle to Seamus," Hugh said, red-faced. "I've bought our ticket for the steamer to Glasgow." Then he looked at Mammy and at the rest of us too. "Did you not hear what Crawford said up in the church? Do you not realise what that means? I'm leavin' while I still ha' the chance."

He picked up his cart and moved slowly away, Moira watching us until they were out of sight. I remembered my friend, Eilidh, last year, bundled onto the cart as her family made for the ship to America. The chain of ox-eye daisies I'd made for her had bounced around her neck as she rattled away.

From her doorway opposite Old Ma MacNeill watched them go. "Maybe now I'll have some milk again," she remarked.

"What's that?" Mammy asked, still standing in the road, watching them go.

"That Moira, she put the eye on me," the old lady said, sniffing. "After I wouldn't lend her salt. My cow's been dry a week."

"Tsch!" Mammy said.

"Scoff if you will," Ma MacNeill replied scratching her white head, "but she was fey that one, like her mother."

"And my best cheese pail's gone," Marseil MacRae said coming out from her doorway, "I expect she took it too."

"You'll have just left it in the byre, Marseil," Mammy said to Cormac's Ma. "What would anyone need with a cheese pail in Glasgow?"

At the mention of the byre, I remembered the oilskin. "There's been a creature in the byre," I said to our neighbours and they turned their attention to me.

"It stole our oilskin and then it trampled the plants."

"Auch, Morag," Mammy said. She glanced at the two other women then frowned and shook her head at me.

"It's true," I protested, ignoring her signal. "And now it's made a den in the byre, with bones, cracked open for the marrow."

"That's enough now," Mammy said, "go inside."

"No," Ma MacNeill, said, coming over her threshold into the road clutching the edge of her shawl with her gnarled fingers. "Let the girl speak. What did you see, Morag?" She was the same height as me and she looked at me with her watery eyes. Mrs MacRae stepped forward too so the three women stood around me in a tight circle with me at their centre.

"I didn't see it," I told them earnestly, "but I felt it. It rushed past me in the dark, it was hairy and big, and it moved fast and it had a stench of a dead animal and then out in the rigs it left no prints."

Marseil put her hand to her mouth and clamped it there, as though words were trying to wriggle out the sides.

Old Ma MacNeill chewed her lip and looked at me with the breeze blowing her tufty white hair. "Marseil," she said, turning to Mrs MacRae, "go and fetch your best steel knife and meet us at the byre."

Chapter Eight

Glasgow

The hotel foyer was crowded with guests leaving for the steamer and with porters who carried their travelling trunks to the waiting carriages outside. I stood in their midst, stepping left and right out of the way. On the wall there was a map of the different steamer routes to Cumbrae Island and the isles of Arran and Bute. I was searching for something and when I found it I put my finger on it in surprise. Paisley. It was where the telegram had been sent from and it was only a few miles from Glasgow.

"Might I recommend the Argyll Arcade, Your Ladyship?" The head porter said. "It has a magnificent glass roof and there are several purveyors of high-quality dresses and silks."

I looked at him in dismay. Shopping? I caught a glimpse of Godfrey making his way towards the hotel drawing room with his beloved map under his arm. There at the door waited a group of older gentlemen, each dressed in grey. These must be the dratted trustees who had delayed our journey. I watched them enter the drawing room together then they closed the door behind them.

"Lady MacDonald?"

I felt a tap on my arm. A short, dark haired woman stood beside me her face as round as a currant bun. "You are Lady MacDonald, I believe?" the lady said, bobbing in a curtsey.

I looked at her blankly for a moment and the lady withdrew ready to apologise for her mistake.

"No. Yes, I mean yes, I am Lady MacDonald." The title still felt like as ill-fitting as a borrowed dress.

The woman bobbed again. "Oh, I'm so pleased. I thought I had made a mistake." Dimples appeared in her cheeks and she gave a bubbling laugh. "I am Mrs Frances Russell, my husband is Dr William Russell, he's a physician. We live in a villa across the street and dined here last night. Our friends pointed you out. I'm so pleased to make your acquaintance."

I noticed how Mrs Russell's voice rose and fell musically. "Are you Scottish, Mrs Russell?"

The woman gave a fresh laugh. "Why no," she exclaimed, "I'm American, from South Hadley, Massachusetts."

Massachusetts. Grandpapa had always spoken darkly of the place, it was the cradle of independence and he had not been sympathetic to American patriots and their mischief. Before I knew it, however, the American lady had proposed we have tea together and I found myself at a window table in the dining room. Mrs Frances Russell, please-call-me-Fanny, launched straight into her life story. The youngest of four daughters, her father, a Scottish émigré, and Presbyterian church minister, had decided that Fanny should accompany him on a visit to his former congregation in Glasgow. Whilst aboard the ship she had a strong feeling that she would meet her future husband in Scotland, a strong *Godly* feeling. Well, who should she meet at a prayer meeting that very first night? The man that she is now married to, Dr William Russell. Wasn't that plainly the Lord's will? He was twenty-five years her senior, but really, did that matter? They have been blessed with two children, so despite his age, there's nothing missing in *that* department. Her voice lowered as she shared a confidence, rose again in a tinkling laugh and despite myself, I heard myself laughing along with her like a scale played on a forgotten piano. The American was only a few years older than I, but she possessed a sort of no nonsense, bustling energy. There seemed nothing she could not fix. Did I suffer from headaches? She would bring me some of her lavender cure. Had I tried Forbes tincture for shinier hair? I held my breath when she said this, but she was only referring to her own shiny thick dark hair tied in a bun. She made no mention of mine hidden under its bonnet.

"And what about you?" Fanny asked. "Tell me all about you." She poured more tea and settled back in her chair with an eager look on her face.

I felt my insides shrink rapidly. Sharing confidences had not gone well for me in the past and well, what on earth was there to say about this year? I shrugged. "There's nothing much to tell, really."

I glanced up at Fanny and saw a look of disappointment on her face. "Well, where did you grow up?"

I would keep it brief and stick to essential facts. "Norfolk. From the age of six I was raised by my paternal grandfather. My father died from cholera when I was a baby and my mother from consumption when I was six."

Fanny's hand flew to her mouth. "Oh, I'm so sorry. You poor thing. To lose both your parents, how awful."

"It's alright. I was very young, I don't remember them really."

I had no memory of my father and hardly any of my mother, except that she was always in bed and that I had to be quiet. I remember thinking it was an adventure to travel on my own in the carriage that my grandfather had sent to collect me. I had arrived very late to Norfolk and there was no sign of him. The housekeeper, Mrs Hobbs, had shown me directly to bed and tucked me into chilly sheets that did not smell like home. She had pinched my cheek, her fingers smelling of onions, and warned me roughly that good girls stayed in their rooms.

"But was your grandfather up to the task? Fanny asked. "Mine was a curmudgeonly old soul and I don't think he could have raised a girl on his own."

"Oh yes, my grandfather was, well, extraordinary. He taught me everything he knew. He passed away last year." There it was again, the feeling of being winded at the realisation that he was really gone. I remembered my first night at his house in Norfolk. Mrs Hobbs had taken the lamp away with her and left me in a smothering silence. I had climbed out of bed and drawn back the curtain, but there was no moonlight, streetlight, nor any light from other houses. It was so silent and so dark I thought I had suddenly become deaf and blind. In panic, I felt my way to the door and fumbled along to the top of the stairs. Down below was a soft, golden beam of light coming from under a door and like a small, pale moth I trembled towards it, clinging to the bannisters. Pushing open the door, vision and sound were suddenly restored. The room was brightly lit with lamps and there was the sonorous tick of a clock, the sizzle of a log in the grate. Beside the fire sat an old man with his whiskered face turned down to a book.

57

"What is this place?" I asked, wonder thawing my voice as I looked at the coloured spines on the shelves around me. He had looked up in surprise. "Well, it's the library of course." His voice was growly, the same as a bear's would be if it could speak. Then he lifted me onto his knee and began to read aloud.

"And after your Grandfather passed?

"My mother's sister, Aunt Caroline, came to fetch me. She and her husband had lived in British India for most of my life. He was with the East India Trading Company, but he died of typhoid. She had just arrived back in London."

I had watched in fascination as my aunt had stepped out of the carriage. Having never been in the company of ladies before, she seemed an exotic creature. She was dressed in black and her hair was curled in ringlets. It was so neat compared to my own hair which was always tied up in a loose bun or plait to keep it out of the way. When Aunt Caroline took off her gloves I saw that each nail was clean and polished, unlike mine which were bitten and stained with ink. And her scent! I don't think I had ever been close enough to a lady to smell one before. Mrs Hobbs had an odour of beef stew and onions, but my aunt's skin smelled of lavender cologne as she pressed her dry lips to my cheek.

"Your aunt must have been delighted to find her niece all grown up," Fanny said, smiling at me.

I looked into my teacup and said nothing. "Feral" was one of the words she had used when she found me lying on the grass the day after she arrived. I was reading Charles Lyell"'s *Principles of Geology* with my long dark hair loose around my shoulders.

"And tell me," Fanny asked, "what hobbies do you enjoy?"

Steam model making, I thought. Hiking over the fens in a pair of rolled up trousers at dawn. Telegraphy, the study of it, the idea that we might connect almost instantly to a person who is standing on the other side of the ocean. Grandpapa and I had built our own telegraphic model in the garden. WULD YU LIK SME TEA I had spelled out with the letter board as the clicks came across the wires we had strung over the lawn.

But I said nothing of this to Fanny and sipped my tea instead.

"Sewing perhaps?" Fanny prompted. "I love needlework. I have just finished a kneeler for our church, a Celtic knot design."

I thought of the embroidery circle in Norfolk that my aunt had made me join. "You really must try, dear," my aunt had said, but I only went once. I had never been in the company of girls before and we had nothing in common. They seemed to me to be simpering dolls whose conversation centred on fashion and society gossip; round and round their chatter went in small vicious circles as they stabbed their needles through the cloth. I had sat next to a quiet girl, Elizabeth Dingle, with pale blond hair. My embroidery quickly became a matted mess and she had tried to help me with it. Aunt Caroline had bought me a sewing basket full of silk threads and a large pair of steel scissors, but I refused to ever go back.

I swallowed and shook my head at Fanny.

"No, I don't care for sewing."

"Well, what about reading then?" Fanny pressed, "everyone likes reading."

"Oh yes," I heard myself blurt out. "Grandfather and I had an enormous collection of books between us, books about everything, science and arts, as well as literature."

I felt a bitter wash of regret slosh over me at the mention of my books. I bit my lip and gripped the teacup so hard I thought I might snap the china handle.

"Didn't you wish to go to college, being so well-read?"

I looked up at the American with circumspection. I had told Elizabeth that I wanted to go to college. Aunt Caroline had invited her over after I refused to take part in any more social events. I had been showing Elizabeth the miniature steamboat that grandfather and I had made for the pond. She had seemed quite interested. "As soon as we return to London, I am going to continue my education," I had told her, as I knelt beside the pond, the water dripping from the boat onto my lap. "You're a blue-stocking." She had gasped and I had looked up to see the horror in her eyes. It had been a terrible error to tell her, I had realised too late.

I looked at Fanny sitting opposite me and gave a silly, dismissive laugh which I hoped concealed my true emotion.

"Well, perhaps when I was much younger, of course, but-"

Fanny interrupted me. "My sister, Amelia, attended the Women's Seminary in our town. She came top of her class in chemistry and they've asked her back to teach."

I put down my teacup and stared at her.

"What? Why are you looking at me like that?"

"To teach? Chemistry?"

"Yes, of course."

I thought of the lectures that Grandpapa had smuggled me into at the Polytechnic, dressed in one of his suits and top hat.

"It's just... I don't know... you talk about it as though it is quite an ordinary thing for a woman. In England we are not even allowed in public libraries. Our first women's college only opened last year. It was opened by Mrs Jesser Reid and-"

"Oh, I know Mrs Jesser Reid. She's a darling," Fanny waved her hand, dismissively. "She lived here in Glasgow for a while and she told us all about the plan for her new ladies' college down in London. Her late husband had a shipping business here. It's his money she's used to set it up."

I sat back in my chair and shook my head in disbelief. It was like having a secret that you thought nobody else knew and then discovering that everyone already knew it.

Fanny leaned forward and lowered her voice. "She's had a difficult time setting it up though. She just can't get any professors to come along and teach, they seem to think teaching ladies is not a good idea." She sat back. "Reading is such a pleasure though, and college or no, at least you still have your books." She sighed and looked around her. "Do you think It's too early for cake?"

No, I wanted to cry out, I do not still have my books. They are gone, all gone. That day came rushing back to me all at once. Elizabeth's mother had come straight round to call for my aunt. She must speak urgently to her, in private, she had some disturbing information that Elizabeth had shared with her. After she had gone I had been sent to my room. "I am at my wits end with you, Maria," my aunt had cried as she had locked the door. "You are a young lady." It had sounded like an insult. I went to the window and watched the shadows begin to lengthen in the garden below. There was the gardener coming onto the lawn and I watched as he began to set a fire. That's an odd place for a bonfire, I thought, for it will scorch the grass. I watched the steel and flint catch the tinder and begin to lick the twigs and sticks, then saw him build it higher and higher with branches. And there was my aunt coming out into the garden, even more unusual, for she did not like the damp English evening air. And then I saw in horror what followed her. There was a line of servants and each of them had an armful of books, books that belonged to my grandfather and me. Novels and encyclopaedia, journals and atlases. Despite my screams, my hammering at the glass, then my frantic pounding at the door, they threw each book onto the fire until each page was blackened and burned.

I felt a wave of nausea rising at the memory and I dug my fingernails hard into my hand until I could feel blood nearly pricking there.

"It probably is a bit early for cake," Fanny was saying, looking around the dining room at the waiters collecting the breakfast plates. She looked back at me.

"Are you alright? You look awfully pale."

I blinked, exhaled, struggled to keep my voice even. "I think I shall take some air."

I stood up and Fanny stood up too looking at me in concern. "How long are you staying in Glasgow?"

"Not long, until tomorrow perhaps."

"And have you seen much of the city so far?"

I looked down at the throbbing red crescents I had gouged in my hand with my nails. "I have seen nothing at all."

"Well come on then," Fanny said, standing up, "I shall show you."

Chapter Nine

Sollas

We made for the byre and by the time we reached it more folk had come out to see what was going on, the story of the creature snaking back through the crowd. I was at the head of the party with Old Ma MacNeill leaning on her stick and beside her, Marseil MacRae brandishing her steel chopping knife. Mammy shook her head and followed behind.

"I had a tingling this morning when I woke up," Marseil said, "on my left cheek, right here." She pointed a finger at her veined cheek. "That means a visitation."

Cormac's Ma spoke up loudly from the back. "As the Book of Leviticus instructs, *Seek not after spirits to be defiled by them.*" She crossed herself. "Someone should call the minister about this foolishness."

But others ignored her and muttered of the omens they had seen too. A cow laying on its left side, three crows sitting on a roof, a peat iron gone missing. From inside the byre came the sound of cattle snorting and kicking to be let out.

"Where's that knife, Marseil?" Ma MacNeill said.

Marseil produced the knife, its blade was the same colour as the dull, grey sky overhead. "Now, stick it in the door there," the old woman said, pointing with her bent finger.

Marseil gripped the handle and drove in the knife, wiggling it back and forth, the wooden door splintering around it until the blade was well sunk in. "That'll stop the creature getting out."

"Now, careful, open the door." The party pushed forward, but Ma MacNeill turned to them. "No, just me and Morag."

We peered around the door into the sharp, tangy gloom and the cattle, who had been shut up since last night, pushed at us to get out. Mrs MacNeill drove them back with her stick.

"It was over there," I whispered, pointing at the back corner to where the den had been. Now there was nothing except cobwebs and shadows. The straw looked no more trampled than it normally did and the oilskin was gone. I kicked my foot through the straw, but there was no sign of the bone either.

I felt my cheeks growing hot, my lip trembled. "It was here," I said, "it was."

But Old Ma MacNeill was turning the straw over with her stick.

"What's that, Morag," she said peering down, "what's that down there?"

I bent down and sifted through the straw. It was pieces of broken egg-shell, pale blue and so fragile that I could see my fingers through the fragments as I held them. I looked up at the rafter, but there was no nest that I could see.

"Hmm," Ma MacNeill said. She put them in her apron pocket and turned to go, pushing the cows aside with her stick.

The waiting crowd had grown larger in those few minutes and it jostled us as we emerged from the byre.

Mammy pushed her way through. "Well?"

When I cast my eyes to the floor she turned to the crowd.

"You see, there is nothing to be afraid of," she said. She pulled the knife from the byre door and handed it back to Marseil. The disappointed crowd began to turn away.

"Wait," Ma MacNeill said, gripping Mammy's arm. She leaned on her stick as she pulled the shells from her pocket. She stared up at Mammy. "That's the work of a changeling or some such, wouldn't you say, Ceit?"

Mammy looked at the shells lying in the old lady's wrinkled hand.

"It's a dark sign," the old lady muttered.

"Perhaps," Mammy said softly, "but there are darker happenings we should be concerning ourselves with, Mrs MacNeill." She looked sharply at me. "Come on, Morag, you can help me take these poor cattle out."

Mammy passed me a cattle switch and picking up one of her own she let the cows out. She drove them up the road past the rigs and out onto the machair beside the sea. I followed behind, my cheeks still blazing, but there was a knot in my stomach, waiting for Mammy's cross words at leading the village a merry dance. But Mammy didn't say anything and the more we walked, the more I thought. It had been there, the oilskin, the den, the bone. My eyes hadn't tricked me and now I glowered at Mammy's back up ahead and the knot in my stomach burst into hot indignation.

"It was there," I blurted out, running to catch up with her. "You saw a mermaid once, so you should believe me."

She turned and looked at me, then kept on walking. "I believe you," she said.

"What? You said that it was nonsense."

"I never said it was nonsense." She stopped and frowned at me. "I never said that. I only said not to go stirring people up."

I looked at her standing there with her brown hair wisping around her face. For the first time I noticed the lines around her mouth and on her forehead, shadows beneath her eyes.

"People get stirred up awful easily, Morag. Before you know it, they will all be stuffing their pockets, instead of their bellies, with what little oatmeal they have."

I knew she was talking about last year, in The Hunger, when Colin MacCuish sprinkled his family's meal ration all around his doorway. He thought it was the faeries who had cursed the tatty crop and he wanted to ward them off. Then he doused his whole family with the contents of the chamber-pot as protection, his wife, their children, and all their belongings, so that the reek of mastair wafted through the whole village.

Mammy reached her hand out to me. "Come here," she said and I gave her my hand.

It was like being pulled inside from the cold rain and we walked along for a moment, hand in hand.

"Cormac's wee brother, Angus, didn't believe me that you had really seen a mermaid on Benbecula," I told her.

She looked out at the sea. "I will never forget that day for as long as I live."

The cattle were moving slowly along on the machair and we followed them swinging our switches by our sides. The new spring grass was coming through, russet turning to green, and the cattle pulled at it greedily with their thick tongues.

"Look," she said, pointing with her switch to where a soft white plant trembled in the breeze, "the first bog cotton. And look, out there, the divers are back." She pointed out to sea, where a large flock of birds bobbed on the waves. The way she spoke brought my teacher, Miss MacAllister, to mind. Now Miss MacAllister would have a new class of children to whom she would show her Atlas of Europe instead.

"I miss school," I said pulling my hand away from Mammy's and whacking the grass with my switch. "I miss my lessons."

Mammy stopped and put her hand on her hip. "Well, I could teach you something. What do you want to know?"

I stood looking down at the beach to where redshanks and turnstones trotted bobbing their heads across the wet sand. "What is Glasgow like?" I asked.

"Glasgow? Well, It's a big town."

"Like Lochmaddy?" I asked.

"No, Glasgow is a lot bigger than that and it has a lot more people."

"And does it have a school?" I asked, thinking of Miss MacAllister.

She looked at me and frowned. "It has lots of schools. Churches, schools, houses, all squeezed together." She was looking down to the beach now. "Granddaddy went there on his way to the French wars." Her face clouded over, remembering something. "Dirty," she said. "The river was dirty with an unnatural sheen. And soldiers from his regiment caught all sorts of diseases, from, well from, all sorts of places." She pulled her shawl around her.

"I would still like to see it though," I said, "and to go to school."

She frowned at me. "What do you need school for? You've already learned more lessons than me."

"I wanted to see the Atlas of Europe."

"Tsch. Europe, my elbow. There's nothing good in Europe." She looked like she might spit. "Killed the kelping, did Europe. There was money here, and good money too, until they could get the potash cheaper from France again." She gazed out towards the sea. "All along these beaches local folk made their living, burning the kelp, It's what Sollas was built on. Some thanks for fighting their French war."

I turned away from her, and as I did, I saw that someone was coming along the road from the direction of the colonel's house.

They were stumbling along in a sort of half run, glancing over their shoulder. As they came closer, I saw that it was a girl, a few years older than me. When she saw us standing in the machair she slowed to a walk and I saw her face was drooping like a flower inside her bonnet and that she had been crying.

"Halo," Mammy called and the girl stopped, her eyes were puffy.

"What's your name?" Mammy asked.

The girl glanced behind her. "It's Hilda."

"I don't know your face," Mammy said. "Where are you from?"

The girl bit her lip. "I'm from over on Skye, from Armadale, but I work at the colonel's house now." Her eyes welled with tears. She folded her hands, and as she did so she winced. Mammy, being eagle eyed, looked down. "What's this now?" She frowned, taking Hilda's hand in her own. Across Hilda's palm was a raised pink welt and the palm was swollen around it.

"It's nothing," Hilda said, pulling her hand away. "Except my own fault."

"Who struck you?" Mammy asked.

Hilda began to cry. "It was nothing, but my own fault."

She was interrupted by the sound of a horse coming fast along the road from the direction that she had come from. It was Mr MacInnes riding hard towards us. He rode right up to us onto the machair and pulled up his horse so close that I felt the heat from its flank and caught the whiff of its hot hay breath.

"You get back to the house now," he said to Hilda.

Hilda shrank back and she trembled like a breeze through tall grass. Mammy snatched angrily at the reins and bridle of the horse.

"That's no way to speak to the girl," she said jerking the horse's head upwards, "and I'll thank you get your horse out of my face."

Mr MacInnes looked down at me and grinned showing his rotten teeth. "You're a fine lassie, maybe you want a job at the colonel's house too?"

Mammy dropped the reins and pushed the horse away, slapping it on its flank with her cattle switch, so that it twisted sharply, nearly un-seating Mr MacInnes. It trotted away smartly, tossing its head.

Mr MacInnes wheeled around, but Mammy brandished her switch at him. "Come any closer and I'll use this again."

The horse pranced a little on the spot, but he did not drive it closer. He turned his attention to Hilda instead. "You'll come back to the house now."

"No, she will not," Mammy said. "She'll come home with me for some butter for her hand."

But Hilda stepped forward towards the horse, her feet stumbling in the grass.

"There's no need to go with him," Mammy said, but the girl kept walking.

"Yes, that's right, your uncle wants to keep his job after all," MacInnes said. He freed his feet from the stirrups and jumped down, then pushed the girl up roughly onto the horse, his hands on her behind.

"I'll be seeing you soon." He spat over his shoulder as he remounted, then spurred his horse away down the road, the girl clinging to his back.

Chapter Ten

Glasgow

Outside the Buckshead hotel, Fanny hailed us a cab.

"Take us to City," Fanny instructed the driver as it pulled up beside us.

He looked at Fanny with circumspection and shook his head.

"Two ladies like you? That's more than my fare's worth, Ma'am." His accent was musical and he sucked the air through his yellowing teeth as though playing the harmonica.

"We'll tip you generously," Fanny said waving her purse at him and climbing into the carriage. She bade me sit beside her and settled onto the seat spreading her dress around her.

"We are not ladies that wish to waste our time on silly amusements, are we?"

"Oh no," I agreed as we pulled away and rattled past the Argyll Arcade with its glass roof. "The only thing the hotel porter could recommend was choosing a new dress."

"Ha." Fanny squeezed my arm. "You know, when I saw you standing in the hotel, I thought that you looked like a woman of a higher purpose, just like myself."

I thought of the extraordinary conversation I had had with Fanny over tea. To discover that her sister had been to college and was a teacher and that Fanny knew Mrs Jenner Reid. These things could not just be a coincidence, could they? Were they some sort of sign? We were passing a large redbrick building with a large sign that said MacDonald and Maclure Printing Press. A good omen. The streets were thronged with smartly dressed people and our carriage turned right beside a theatre where an organ grinder was playing a garish tune. Everything hummed with possibility and the world suddenly seemed large and inviting.

"My husband and I feel the Lord has laid a special calling on our hearts," Fanny said. "We want to share it with visitors, especially such an important visitor as yourself."

"And what is that calling?"

"You'll see."

Our carriage was crossing over the river and we were leaving the wide streets and villas behind. On this side of the river the street was narrower and crowded with houses, some looked nearly derelict, though there were signs of life. A line of grey sheets hung out to dry, a slurry of effluent ran through the gutter. Two women stood in the street with baskets on their arms and watched our carriage pass.

"Did you know, I met your brother-in-law, Alexander, last year," Fanny said suddenly. "At a fundraising ball."

"Really? I have never met him. He's a bit odd, the black sheep of the family apparently."

Fanny raised her eyebrows. "Well he seemed a charmer to me. Very dashing with his broad shoulders and blond hair. He had all the ladies queuing for a dance."

"I believe he lives in Paisley."

Fanny frowned. "Paisley? Why would he live there? No, he had come up from London for the ball."

What was Alexander doing in Paisley then just a few miles from the hotel? Fanny pursed her lips as though to say something more.

"What is it? Go on, tell me."

She lowered her voice.

"There was a huge family row apparently last October. They say it killed their mother."

I thought of Alexander's accusation: *After what you have done! You'll pay for it.* I felt a small beat of alarm and Fanny glanced out of the window.

"Oh look, we are entering City Parish." She called up through the roof trap, "take a left here, driver."

Our carriage turned so sharply that I had to brace myself against the window. It was as though dusk had suddenly fallen, the window frame was now filled with towering dark tenement buildings, built so closely together that just a crack of daylight was visible between each one.

"These are known as the Closes and Wynds," Fanny whispered.

It was the eerie silence that struck me. There was no hustle or bustle of daily life, no merchants or barrow boys, no dogs or horses. Yes, there were people, but they just stood crowded in doorways, or at the side of the road. Empty shells of people with faces cast grey in the strange light, who stared at us with vacant eyes as we passed them. And the smell. Even through the glass, I could smell it, huge rotting heaps of rubbish and human waste that was piled high in the middle of each tenement yard. Beside one of these heaps, children were playing barefooted, poking the piles with sticks. Seeing the carriage, they began to run alongside, waving their dirty sticks at the window and I drew back in horror, gagging behind my hand.

"Two or three families often share a single room and people are even packed into the earth cellars below," Fanny said, covering her nose with a handkerchief. "And yet still more and more people arrive from the Highlands each week, using the last of what little money they have to get here."

I looked at the dark buildings pressed so closely together on either side of the narrow street. "Why do they come here?"

Fanny sighed. "It was the potato famine to start with, but now they just keep coming. Poor souls. Hoping for a better life, I suppose."

"I'll turn about here or we'll become stuck," the driver called down to us.

I felt a wave of panic at the thought of being trapped in such a place, the dread of confinement rising in me like bile. As we negotiated the turn, a small girl of about six or seven with bare legs appeared in a doorway and watched us. In her arms she held a large, dirty-looking baby, dressed in a single rag.

Fanny called to the driver to stop and I watched in alarm as she opened the window. "Come here, girl." The girl moved hesitantly towards us. Her skin had a white pallor beneath the dirt, her hair was dishevelled around her small, pinched face. The baby was strangely quiet and had a runny nose.

I wished I had something to give her, a penny or something to eat.

Fanny kept her purse closed. "Where are you from?"

70

The girl looked at Fanny, cocking her head like a sparrow.

"What is your name?"

The girl said something in another tongue that was soft and melodious.

"You see," Fanny sighed, "not a word of English."

The girl struggled to lift the baby towards the window, saying something again in her own language. The baby suddenly wailed.

"No, no," Fanny said, closing the window quickly, instructing the driver to move on. "Take us up the north side of Parliamentary Road," she called.

I realised that I had been holding my breath as we re-joined the main street. We rattled away, back across the river, and I wondered what life lay ahead for that ragged girl standing in the muck holding that baby. Was she trapped forever in that stinking, rotten place?

"Here we are," Fanny said, banging on the carriage roof and I peered out to see tall black railings. Behind the railings was a handsome regency building and I felt my hands grow clammy inside my gloves. It looked just like the offices of Doctor Fortnum on Harley Street in London.

"What is this place?" My voice was dry in my throat.

"It's the poorhouse," Fanny said, "but we can't go in and visit today, there's an outbreak of cholera."

I stared at the poorhouse behind its respectable black railings. It might have been a town hall or a hotel, but I shuddered to think who might be within its walls and what might take place there.

"Even on the best of days the conditions inside are quite dreadful," Fanny said, as though reading my mind. "Only last month, my husband was called to attend a young woman in great difficulty in childbirth. The infirmary had no space for her and there was no privacy. The women and girls were two to a bed and the girl lay on a filthy pallet on the floor. William called for hot water and towels, but the women only stared at him. Most only spoke Gaelic, and those that had some English explained that they were only allowed to draw water from a pump once a day and that was all gone. As for towels, there were none of course – only a thin, dirty, strip of blanket, the whole place hopping with lice. They often have to burn their effects and shave the women's hair."

My hand jumped involuntarily to my bonnet and I remembered the cold blade of the scissors against my scalp. I turned my face away from the window.

Our carriage pulled up outside the Buckshead hotel. The street was empty now, the guests having departed and the new ones yet to arrive. On the corner, opposite the hotel, stood a man in a velvet coat and a top hat. He was tall and broad, but despite his fine clothes, he had a dishevelled sort of look, and I felt as though I had seen him before. He was still there as we took a seat by the window in the dining room. He appeared to be watching the hotel entrance. Looking at him I realised where I had seen him. It was the same gentleman that Godfrey had been talking to on the platform in London. He kept glancing at the hotel and then he took a pocket watch from the inside of his coat and consulted it. Its gold case winked in the sun. I peered closer, but the waiter brought the tea and cakes and when I looked out again, the man had disappeared.

"It's an awful situation here in Glasgow," Fanny said, pouring the tea. "The problem is that more and more people arrive in the city each month because of the wretched potato famine. That's why the Highland Relief Board was set up. My husband and I are both members. I'm talking about the Glasgow section, of course, which is much superior to the Edinburgh one." She frowned. "We often host dinners to raise money for famine relief. I served the most delicious lobster terrine last time. All the guests complimented me on it, I shall give you the recipe."

She dabbed her lips. "Are you eating that cake?" She eyed the untouched cream fancy on my plate.

I shook my head.

"You're very thin," she remarked as she took it from me. "Have you been unwell?"

I looked up to see her looking at me in concern and I blushed.

"It's the shadows under the eyes which give it away," she said, lowering her voice. "My third sister, Margaret, was the same after a long bout of influenza."

After my aunt burned my books, I had stopped eating and speaking. My throat had been raw for several days from screaming and the charred smell of paper was caught in my nostrils. It did not matter whether my aunt had pleaded with me,

72

or shook me, it was as though all the words inside me had vanished like smoke. I stood in front of the dresser mirror and stared at myself for long periods of time. My reflection stared back at me from the dim glass, my pale face framed by long dark hair. "You are a young lady," my aunt had implored. Perhaps I looked like them, but I could never be like one of those young ladies from the embroidery circle. I had grown up reading science journals, building model boats and visiting the polytechnic. I had survived the diving bell. I remembered how the water had come rushing in around me, my breath exploding in my lungs as the machine was cranked urgently back to the surface. It was a miracle, observers remarked. No ordinary girl could have held her breath for so long. I looked at myself in the mirror. Was I really just an ordinary girl? On the dresser was the basket with embroidery threads and the large steel sewing scissors that my aunt had given me. I picked up the scissors and chopped off a piece of my long dark hair. I watched it fall, then I cut another and another. Big chunks of soft dark hair fell around me like feathers. I brought the scissors closer and closer to my scalp until there was only an uneven dark fuzz left. My nose looked enormous on my face, my eyes huge inside their dark circles. Now I was not ordinary.

Fanny touched my hand. "If you need a physician, my husband is a wonderful doctor."

Aunt Caroline had taken me to see a physician on Harley Street. Doctor Fortnum was a well-dressed gentleman with a purple silk cravat and a manicured moustache. He sat behind a desk in a wingback chair that matched the green leather couch in the corner and he took notes as my aunt, trembling and tear-stricken, had explained everything to him. She blamed herself of course, she should have come to fetch me sooner, but how was she to know? My grandfather was my legal guardian and he had been a respectable man, a navy captain, decorated, twice. If only she had realised how I was being ruined. Her voice had ended in a sob and the doctor had offered her a handkerchief. She had made every effort since she had arrived in Norfolk, every effort to salvage me. My stubborn resistance though, my refusal to make friends with any girls of my age, well she had been at her wit's end when she had got rid of the books. She hadn't burned them all, of course, the others were being sold.

"First she stopped speaking and eating and now - this." She pulled off my bonnet to reveal my shorn head.

The doctor had put down his pen and sat back in his squeaky leather chair. He stroked his moustache.

"The dreadful effects of mis-education on a young lady's constitution are well-known in medical circles," he said at last. His voice had an authoritative resonance which suggested it was used to addressing lecture halls. "I have recently written a paper on the subject. It appears, Mrs Blunt, that your niece has a hystero-neurasthenic disorder."

Another burst of tears from my aunt.

"Don't fret madam, you have come to the right place. I have developed a treatment which cures young ladies most efficiently."

Across the tea and cake, Fanny was looking at me with sympathy.

"My husband is most discreet," she said, "and would be happy to attend."

I would never consult another doctor again - ever. I smiled at Fanny. "That's very kind, but I am only tired from all the travelling." I took a large mouthful of cold tea and put on a smile. "Now tell me more about your relief work. Do you and your husband go up to the Highlands often?"

"Oh no," Fanny replied, "we don't go there ourselves. Once we've raised the funds the money is sent to officers who arrange for the purchase of meal. Then the meal is delivered to the local land agents on the estates. The land agents run a work programme so the Highlanders can earn their meal."

"There must be other things they need beside meal though, clothing and such-like?"

Fanny stiffened, her mouth pinching. "It would be quite inappropriate to just give them money. Imagine if they wasted it. We have to be so careful with people's generous donations." She lowered her voice. "There is a shocking streak of laziness amongst some of the poor and those on famine relief are required to work an honest day to receive it. Can you imagine how disheartening it would be to raise all that money only to have it wasted on the un-deserving? Or even worse, the ungrateful?"

My heart lurched at the chilliness in her voice. "I do apologise Fanny," I said quickly. "I am sure that you have devised quite the best system for helping. In fact, I wish there was something I could do to help."

Fanny gave me a smile and went about finishing my cream cake. She broke off suddenly. "You know, it has just occurred to me that you could help. Just think, if the Highland Relief Board, the *Glasgow* committee, had the support and patronage of someone of your standing. A Baroness, well, imagine what we could achieve for the poor then."

I was flattered. I could do something to help those poor women trapped in that place. I saw myself, dressed in tartan, hosting a dinner at Armadale castle and making a speech.

"Oh, Fanny, I would be honoured," I said. "Tell me what I can do."

It seemed Fanny had already thought of exactly what I could do. I could come along with her that evening to a meeting of the board. She would call for me at five o'clock precisely.

Chapter Eleven

Sollas

When it was still dark, we got up, and fumbling for our clothes, and without breakfast, we set off towards Clachan for the April Fair. Da was helping to drive some of the village cattle and they had to get across the ford at low tide. Two years ago, the Spring tide was so high that the cattle had had to swim, the drivers sitting up on their backs. Mammy hitched the pony to the cart and we drove along behind, the early morning sky as pale as spilled milk over the sea. I sat up next to her and we watched the cattle splash through the low water, up over the wet sand, great snorts of breath rising from their shaggy faces. It's cattle now, Da said, that are the island's gold. The land might belong to Laird MacDonald, but the cattle belong to us. A lot of people were selling this year though, and the road was packed with carts, some said buyers had come from as far as Oban to get a good deal. I had heard Mammy and Da arguing about it the night before, whether or not they should sell, Mammy's voice, rising to a fierce whisper, Da's voice, a soft, low hum.

"Look, there's Auntie Fionnaghal," I said, pointing to a woman making tea on a fire beside her cart. Mammy's sister always came across from Benbecula for the fair. Aunty Fionnaghal had seven children, nine, if you count the ones carried off by tuberculous, and her oldest, Seonag, was getting married in the summer and was helping make the tea.

Mammy pulled up the cart beside them and jumped down. "Halo, halo," she said, hugging them.

Then they got straight down to business swapping news and gossip in Aunty Fionnaghal's cart as the warm steam from their tea rose in the cool April air. My cousins, Anne and Sile, sat squeezed together with me on the bench behind them. I was waiting for the chance to tell them all about the creature, but

Aunty Fionnaghal was telling about a letter that her neighbour had received from a cousin, who had gone to Canada.

"Five weeks it took them," she was saying, "five weeks in the bowels of the ship with no more than a two-foot-wide wooden plank keeping you off the vomit swilling about on the floor. Before they were halfway across all that was left to eat was dry ship biscuits with weevils and a mouthful of water each. They had smallpox on board too, so when they arrived the ship was quarantined for another four weeks and no one was allowed off. They had to stay below deck, in the dark with the smallpox, hoping and praying it didn't come to them."

Mammy made a "tsch" sound and shook her head. Seonag shivered.

"That's not the worst of it," Aunty Fionnaghal carried on. "They were promised money for setting up and clothing and provisions on arrival. That was what was agreed, before they left Barra, but there was nothing. The Laird never paid the Canadian authorities anything, not a single penny."

She sat back and looked at her sister. Mammy's face was white and she stared out towards the sea.

Seonag leaned in. "Tell Aunty Ceit what they did then."

Aunty Fionnaghal shook her head. "Most camped out on the dock under tarpaulin or in sheds whilst the authorities considered their plight. Some were accepted as paupers into the colony, others took to begging."

Seonag turned to Mammy. "What about you, Aunty Ceit? Have you thought about what you're going to do?"

Mammy shook her head and suddenly turned to look at me. "Morag, go and play over there in our cart. Off you go - and Annie and Sile too."

We sighed and dragged our feet. We were often sent away half-way through the conversation. We sat in our cart and watched the group of women, their voices lowered, deep in discussion. I wondered what a weevil was. My cousin, Anne, was four months older than I, which had always given her a superior edge. Her sister Sile was only five.

"I should probably have been allowed to stay in the cart with them," Anne said, glancing back to where our mammies sat. "My mammy said I am a woman now, because I've had my monthlies."

I looked at her blankly and she glanced at Sile. "You know," she said, "down there." She pointed to her lap and I nodded as though I knew what she meant. She might have the monthlies, whatever they were, but she didn't have a nice bonnet with grey trim like mine though. Hers was just plain and a hand-me-down passed through two older sisters.

She eyed mine jealously. "Where did you get that?"

Her smaller sister Sile tried to touch it with a grubby finger.

I jerked my head out of reach. "Mammy made it for me," I said, shrugging. I had wanted to tell them my news, about the creature, but now I didn't feel like talking, I was thinking about what Aunty Fionnaghal had said.

"Can I have some of your bonnets and shawls when you go to America?" Anne asked.

I flashed her an angry look. "I'm not going to America," I cried, making Sile jump away from me.

Anne gave a small smirk from beneath her plain bonnet. "My mammy said that Laird MacDonald is making everyone from Sollas go. Go to Langais or to America, and that they've got til Whit to get gone."

Why would anyone go and live in Langais when it was a marshy bog with not a single croft out there? Red Hugh's words rang in my ears. "Get out while you still have the chance."

"Did you not know?" Anne asked, watching me closely.

I remembered my best friend, Eilidh Morrison's, face too. Puffy from crying, getting onto the boat last year. Eilidh Morrison, down in the dark with smallpox and weevils. I looked down at my lap and I bit my lip. I would not cry in front of Anne.

"I'm not going to America," I repeated quietly and climbed down from the cart to find Da.

The spring day was bright and clean, but the chilly wind blew in off the sea and hollowed me out. My feet stumbled over the rough tussocky grass to the sale ring.

"I'm not going to America, I'm not going to America," I muttered numbly, searching in the crowd of men for Da.

Uncle Lachlan was after a couple of heifers and Da was inspecting a pair that had been brought in by Seamus MacRae on a halter. I went and stood beside him. Da was running his hand over their thick golden coats and down to their legs.

"Couple of fine heifers these," Seamus was saying, shifting from foot to foot. "You'd be craicte to offer less than five pounds for the both."

Da said nothing and moved to the other cow, his rough hands running deep through its coat to her warm downy under layer.

Uncle Lachlan watched Da carefully. "Five seems steep."

Seamus scratched his nose and shook his head. "What with the debts we owe and we want to gather a bit to take with us like –no – it's a good price." He folded his arms.

Dad stood up and rested his hand on the cow's back. "This one's going lame, Seamus," he said quietly, looking the man in the eye.

"What?" Seamus exclaimed, raising himself tall, his face reddening. "Never man. These are the picture of health, these heifers."

Da bent and lifted the cow's foot. "See, there," he said, pointing to a small sore between the cow's toe. "It's the start of foot wart. You've not been trimming their hooves properly."

"Auch Artair, It's a wee scab that's all, and It's healing up already. I'll tell you what, how 'bout four for the pair, now that's a bargain."

But Da looked at Uncle Lachlan and shook his head.

Seamus moved quickly between them. "Three pounds the pair then man," he offered desperately, tugging Uncle Lachlan's sleeve. "That's the best deal of the whole sale."

But Uncle Lachlan shook his head too and moved off after Da out of the ring.

"What am I to do?" Seamus called. "I've got my bairns to think of."

I ran to catch up with Da and held his rough, calloused hand in mine.

"Halo, darleich," he said. "Shall we see about some tea?"

We walked across the tussocks back to the cart. The wind was bringing in fine rain that settled on our hair like silver dew.

"Da, are we going to America?" I asked quietly.

He slowed a little and looked down at me, squeezing my hand.

"I don't want to go on a ship. I don't want to go to America, I don't want to sleep on the dock and eat weevils," I blurted out.

"Who's been telling you those stories?" he asked.

"Aunty Fionnaghal said that's what happened to her neighbour on Benbecula, and Annie said Laird MacDonald said we had til Whit to get gone." I wiped a salty trail of tears and snot across my sleeve.

"Aunty Fionnaghal," Da sighed. "Come on, let's go and find Mammy."

But he never said we weren't going.

We went home from the fair early, and I sat quietly in the cart beside Mammy. She had her thinking face on, her eyes squinting out to the sea. The drizzle had cleared and long evening streaks of pink and orange stretched out over the horizon.

"I think I'll take a walk up to the headland," Mammy said, putting a hand on Da's shoulder. He stopped the cart and she jumped down and strode away up the road. It was all Anne's fault, I thought bitterly, watching her go. She had spoiled the fair. But no, Anne could not really be blamed for just passing on news. It was Colonel Crawford with his shiny tap, tap boots and his brassy voice. But what could be done? I thought of Mammy, her face growing pale at Aunty Fionnalgh's story, and Da, his great heavy sigh as we had walked together.

I watched Mammy walk away towards the headland, to where my brother is. He was born too soon, two years after me, and is buried next to Granddaddy. I used to imagine that he was like a tiny green seedling, buried in the earth, but then I saw Mammy coming out of Moira's house last year, after she had lost the baby, something hidden in a bundle of clothes soaked in blood and I understood that babies are not like plants.

Da went to put the pony away and I walked on towards our croft. The village was strangely quiet and empty, most people were still at the fair. I should see about some supper, I supposed, and as I opened the door there was the charred smell of the tatties that Mammy had put in the embers to cook before we left. Standing in the doorway I saw that something wasn't right.

The milk pail lay empty on its side on the table and the lid was off the herring barrel. Stepping into the room, I saw the blanket from my bed was missing. The pale sheet beneath it glowed in the dim light. That's when I smelt it. The same ripe animal smell from the byre. The hairs on my arms stood up straight. There in the gloom, in the corner by Mammy's chest, something was crouching. I froze. I could not scream nor move. It was as though my feet were stuck in a bog, I could only stare and stare. All at once it sprung towards me, a shape half-covered by my brown blanket. I caught the flash of a large body as it pushed past me, an enormous head with pale staring eyes, then snarling and moaning it vanished out of the door. My legs were trembling so violently I could hardly stand and I turned and looked back into the street. The creature had disappeared and my blanket lay in the road. I ran and fetched it, then slammed the door behind me and leaned against it taking little gasps.

What would Mammy do to protect from evil? I looked around the room, my eyes moving from the table to the barrel to the chest to the table. My eyes rested on Mammy's wedding chest and my heart slowed. Mr Morrison's words came back to me. "Have faith, faith and hope." I went over to the chest and lifting the lid I took out the scrap of folded red velvet from Da's suit pocket. Then I ran out of the house, up over the sandbank, and down to the beach. The tide was on the turn, dragging the kelp back out to the ocean, each wave was a pewter-coloured swell and far out on the horizon were the last streaks of pink and gold. "Faith and hope, faith and hope," I muttered as I unwrapped the scrap of velvet and held the pearl in my palm. It gleamed in the gathering dusk. My heart see-sawed suddenly with doubt. But the mermaid had given this treasure to Mammy and that meant one wish. Was there any greater reason to use that wish than now? But how, I wondered, did you make a wish? Did mermaids have their own strange tongue? Eilidh and I had invented our own language once and had spent a whole day speaking it and once Cormac and I found a message in a bottle. The bottle was stamped "Dublin" and it had a scrap of paper whose ink had washed away.

I went down to the tideline, the wet sand sticking to my shoes, and looked out across the blackening sea. I looked at the pearl again, glinting in my palm. One wish, that's what you got. But what if you had more than one? All my wishes bubbled up inside me, for protection from the creature, for our village to be saved, to go to school once more. The tide foamed over my shoes, sucking at my feet as though pulling all my wishes out with it. Faith and hope, faith and hope I incanted then I lifted my hand and threw the pearl as far out as I could. It made the tiniest splash in the water.

"Help us," I whispered to the dark sea. "Please send us help."

Chapter Twelve

Glasgow

At five o'clock I was transported to the meeting room of the Presbyterian Church on Caledonia Road. I had not seen Godfrey since breakfast and the drawing room door in the hotel had remained shut. The porter had told me that they were not to be disturbed. In any case, I would be home by seven, Fanny assured me, but I rather hoped that he would finish early and wonder where I was.

The meeting room was laid out with rows of wooden chairs and the well-dressed ladies and gentlemen of the Glasgow Highland Relief Board were beginning to take their places. Fanny steered me to the front row and on the raised dais in front of us were four gentlemen who conversed in hushed tones.

"There's my husband," Fanny whispered, pointing to an older gentleman with silver grey hair. "The other gentlemen are Mr McAllen, one of the city fathers, and Reverend Scott from the Church of Scotland. The other is some minister of the Free Church." She wrinkled her nose. "It was thought we ought to include someone from their lot as so many Highlanders attend their church." Fanny turned in her chair to get a good view of incomers. She gave a little wave to a woman in a large moth-eaten fox fur, then indicated a grey-haired lady dressed in black who was taking a seat two rows behind. "That's Lady Stephenson, her husband passed away in January, but she is a very generous benefactor. Her husband owned an estate in Perthshire."

Now an elegantly dressed woman walked in on the arm of a younger man and Fanny lowered her voice, "Ooh, and look, there's Countess Dartford, she throws the most wonderful parties when she's up in Glasgow. That's her second husband –they say she wore the first one out." She winked at me.

Almost all the chairs were taken now and there was a pre-theatre-like expectancy about the crowd. Every now and then a pause settled upon the room, before little snatches of conversation broke out here and there again.

"Oh dear," Fanny muttered, craning her neck towards the door.

I followed her gaze to where a tall young man in a brown tweed suit and a deer-stalker hat was leaning against the back wall with his arms folded.

"Thomas O'Brady." Fanny cast him a sour look. "A newspaper journalist, Irish, and a radical, he's always stirring up trouble."

"What a funny hat," I whispered causing Fanny to giggle.

"Ahem." Dr Russell got to his feet and the hall fell silent.

"Thank you, Ladies and Gentlemen of the Glasgow Destitution Board, for attending this meeting. Reverend Scott will now open in prayer."

Heads were bowed along the rows and I stared open-eyed at my feet. I hadn't been raised a churchgoer. Grandfather said he had seen too many men blown to smithereens in the Navy to hold with all that.

"Thank you, Reverend Scott," Dr Russell said, now that the prayer was over. "May I say we are particularly delighted to be joined tonight by Lady MacDonald who has kindly undertaken to become a Patron of the Board." He gestured towards where we sat.

I sat up straight in realisation that he was referring to me. I half bobbed out of my chair in confusion, should I approach the dais? Fanny gripped my arm though and held me in place. There was a patter of applause and necks strained to have a look. Fanny smiled proudly, holding onto her catch, turning to nod and whisper, yes this is her, at other women who looked at us enquiringly.

"We shall now hear the monthly reports," Dr Russell continued.

Mr MacAllen, the city father, stood up and read out the figures. Three hundred fifty-six new immigrants had arrived that month from the Highlands and money that had been given to the poorhouse for their support. He read out more figures. Money raised, funds distributed across the Highlands for the purchase of meal. Finally, Dr Russell read out a letter of thanks from the British Government for the work carried out by the Board; by harnessing the generosity of the great British public, the Board had ensured that to date, not a single death by starvation in Scotland had taken place. The crowd murmured modestly.

"But what about the remainder of the fund?" a voice called out from the back of the hall. Eyes and necks swivelled to see. It came from the newspaperman, Mr O'Brady.

Dr Russell raised his eyebrows and it was all the journalist needed. He came down the aisle and standing level with me, he lifted off his ridiculous hat and with a small bow he addressed the gentlemen seated on the raised platform. I glanced up at Mr O'Brady. He was tall and lanky, not much older than I, and now he had removed his hat his hair sprung free in wild curls. There was the faint smell of tobacco on him and something else underneath, like the smell of a wet forest. The word that came to my mind was 'wolf.' Was it his green eyes, narrowed at the gentlemen on the dais, or his lean, easy stance? He stood watching Dr Russell intently, as though he were prey.

"As I understand it, sirs," he said, flashing a smile at them, "nearly half the money raised from the public remains in the bank untouched. I would very much like to know why this money has not also been distributed to the starving and destitute." His accent was captivating, full of soft vowels and a cadence I had never heard before.

There was an awkward pause. The city fathers looked at one another. The Church of Scotland minister got to his feet. "The call of destitution from the Highlands has been most benevolently answered, sir" he replied stoutly. "More munificently than any Highlander could expect. Is it right to provide them more lavishly with something greater than is their need? Who here would expect that?"

He looked about him and heads nodded. Who would expect that, they asked each other?

Another gentleman from the audience was on his feet now, emboldened. "To give more than is needed is to encourage indolence and laziness," he declared, "and goodness knows what stimulus the Highlanders need to exertion and honest work at the best of times."

"Hear, hear," people said. "Quite right."

Fanny nodded vigorously.

Dr Russell stood up. "Mr O'Brady, this committee takes its fiscal responsibility very seriously and what to do with the excess funds is a question that the board has been most carefully considering. We have read many detailed reports from the Highlands and it is our strong recommendation that the remainder of the fund is used for the purposes of assisting with the emigration of people to America where they can find a better life."

Mr O'Brady sprang forward to the foot of the dais and spun around to address the crowd with such speed that Fanny startled and grasped my arm. "A'ha," he cried. "Reports from the Highlands indeed. Reports no doubt written by the very landowners who wish to remove the people from the land. This is nothing more than a lightning strike into the heart of Scotland by her malevolent English masters."

Fanny rolled her eyes and shook her head. "Here we go," she muttered.

Mr O'Brady cast his gleaming eye over the silent crowd and clasping his hands behind his back, he paced up and down in front of them. "How many of you have visited the Highlands?" he demanded. "How many?" Who amongst you has seen the people eating their boot leather, their children crying from the pain of hunger? Who?"

There were no hands raised.

He wheeled about. "Mr Walker," he barked, making the minister from the Free Church jump. "I believe your church is in the Highlands?"

Mr Walker got to his feet hurriedly. "Aye, it is."

"And tell me, how many of the people are still hungry, still in want?"

The minister clutched his hat, shuffled his feet. "To be honest, most families are still struggling to feed themselves, most are still hungry on account of the famine last year."

Mr O'Brady ran his eye for a moment over the crowd and then turned back to Mr Walker. "And why is that, sir? Why are they still hungry despite the famine being over?"

Mr Walker said something inaudible.

"Speak up man!"

"For most it is the poor nature of the land they have been given, that cannot support sufficient crops," he repeated.

"Thank you, Mr Walker," Mr O'Brady wheeled around to face the audience. "What the people of the Highlands want is a decent chance to support themselves, a fair portion of land, enough for grazing and planting, not to be loaded onto ships and sent away over the sea."

Dr Russell got to his feet. "Now, now Mr O'Brady," he interjected, "this is not a court room, nor a lecture hall. I suggest you save your polemic for your newspaper column and allow us to continue our meeting."

The crowd silently watched this stand-off. Mr O'Brady seemed ready to spring up onto the dais and seize the doctor, there was such a fierce intent about him. But he only regarded Dr Russell for a moment then he turned, and with a loping gait, retreated down the hall. I caught the heat off him and the whiff of his outdoor smell as he passed me. I felt his gaze run over me briefly and I shifted in my chair. There was a pause as the door swung shut behind him, then the meeting continued.

Now the interloper was gone, there was plenty of indignant rebuttal of the Irishman's claims.

"The work programme has always been considered a fair and satisfactory method for apportioning famine relief," someone offered.

"Hear, hear," came the reply.

"Highlanders can't just expect hand-outs," said one.

"Quite right," said another.

"We can't take endless streams of immigrants," added the city father.

"Very true!" the crowd murmured. "Think of the disease they bring." The meeting was warming up.

"Who can expect any landowner to allow their tenants to sit on the land for free? Good land that could be used profitably for other purposes?" There was applause at this.

"Isn't emigration the most practical, humane and charitable solution?" People were nodding and clapping all around the room.

A vote was proposed. All in favour of the destitution fund being used for the purposes of emigration, say "Aye." I thought of the poorhouse, of those women trapped behind those black railings. I looked at Fanny sitting next to me, her face was shining with enthusiasm, her head nodding, her hands clapping. Hadn't Fanny crossed the Atlantic and found a purposeful and happy life in a foreign land?

"Aye," I said, "Aye."

After the vote was counted and the meeting formally closed there was tea and cake, organised by Fanny and she bustled off to oversee it. I listened to the hum of conversation around me, the rattle of cups and saucers, the scrape of chairs being cleared away. The members of the committee were each busy in their tasks. Dr Russell was sweeping the floor with an enormous broom. They all have their purpose, I thought, and what is mine? When Grandpapa died, my old life had died with it and since his death I had only felt the absence of everything, the bitterness of loss. I looked at Fanny stacking the plates. I had a friend now, something I had never had before.

"Excuse me, Your Ladyship," Dr Russell said as he swept the floor around me. Lady Maria MacDonald. My title had seemed ridiculous, as though I was pretending to be Queen Victoria herself, but perhaps it was time to start using what I had. I thought of the little girl and the dirty baby, unable to speak a word of English, standing in the muck, trapped in poverty. Perhaps when we got to the estate, I could do something about it? I felt a small, hopeful hum start up inside me and I went to help Fanny with the plates.

Chapter Thirteen

Sollas

Since I had thrown the pearl into the water, a veil of cloud had drawn in from the sea, covering Eaval hill and bringing rain that fell non-stop for a week, turning the road through the village into a squelchy, slippery bog. Still, there was always work to be done, and it was a waulking day. The women were coming to prepare the cloth for the bedspread they were making for cousin Seonag's wedding. Mammy had me sweep the floor and scrub the table, then sent me to the byre to fetch the bucket of maistir. Every night for three nights I had squatted over the pot, feeling the warm steam rise against my legs, and then had tipped the contents into the bucket ready for the waulking. The dye wouldn't fasten without it, and it was needed to soften the cloth, and now I carried the bucket carefully from the barn so that it wouldn't slop against my leg.

I liked waulking days usually, even though I had to mind the babies over on the bed. I liked sitting in the shadows, listening to the women talking, laughing and working the fabric in time to their singing. Today, though, the shadows made me jumpy, and the women worked silently around the table, their heads bent over their rhythmic thumping, the grey-green cloth tumbling through their hands. The sour smell of the maistir hung in our croft and caught in the back of my throat.

"Will you sing a song?" I called over hopefully. The singing was the best part. Sad songs, love songs, songs filled with nonsense words and sounds. Mammy would usually start by singing a line, and the others would join in with the chorus, the songs getting quicker and livelier as they went on. I was minding Aileen's twins and they were starting to get twitchy. They had been born early on account of The Hunger last October, and one was smaller and always had a green caterpillar of snot hanging down from his nose. I hoped Mammy might sing a song to take my mind off it, that and the other worry I had. After I had thrown the pearl into the sea, I had come home and straightened up the croft, but I had not said anything about the creature. I knew now that my parents were burdened with their own worries and I would not mention it to them, not now that I had asked the mermaid to help us. And once I had not told Mammy or Da, it was easier not to tell anyone, not Cormac, not old Ma MacNeill, I buried it inside me instead.

Mammy glanced at me. "I don't know if I'm in the mood for singing, darleich," she said, turning her face back to her work. She had opened the door to get rid of the smell of the maistir, and the grey light from fell onto her face making it look old and serious.

Aileen looked up. She had a thin, worried face and pale, straggly hair. "Auch, none of us are in the mood for anything these days. We're all just waiting for something to happen."

"My Seamus says they've got to serve proper notice first. The sheriff, Shaw, told us we'd be given enough time," Marseil MacRae replied confidently, wringing the fabric in her hands.

Mammy made her "tsch" noise and thumped the cloth hard. The others looked at her, but she did not look up.

Aileen stopped kneading the cloth. "Well, have none of you thought about it?" she asked them, looking around the pale faces at the table. "The offer?"

Cormac's Ma stopped waulking too, so that the cloth was pulled askew off the table.

Aileen went on. "After all, it's better than some. Tickets paid for, debts cancelled. My cousin away down in Barra had none of that and ended up in Glasgow with only a stitch of clothing on her back, blisters on her feet and nothing to eat." She paused and the women looked at each other, thinking of Moira no doubt, who was missing from the table. "Others on Barra were loaded by force onto ships and sent away across the sea," she continued. "Laird MacDonald is offering to cancel our debts and pay our passage at least."

"That's got to be better than what they've offered us here, I mean, can you imagine trying to grow anything in the bog over at Langais?" Cormac's Ma said, "there's a reason no-one builds crofts out there."

Marseil shivered. "I'm not living out there near a fairy circle."

Aileen nodded in agreement. "Aye and my sister in Lochmaddy had a letter from her brother-in-law who went over to Cape Breton last spring. He said there was land a-plenty, and good soil for growing too."

All eyes were on Mammy now, waiting for her to say something. She thumped the cloth down hard then looked up at them. Her eyes were bright. Her voice was stony. "Your words cut me to my heart, all of you. We have good soil here, the best in the Highlands even. And Aileen, do you really think that being offered free passage on a ship is any different from being forced from your home with the threat of fire? That is a lie and you are no more than a mule being tempted away by a rotten carrot if you believe it."

Aileen looked down and gripped the cloth, her knuckles turning white, her ears turning red. "Well what can we do, Ceit?" Marseil MacRae implored. "You heard Shaw, this isn't really an offer, one way or another they mean to get us out. And Whit is only a month away."

Even from my corner in the room I felt a shiver pass between the women.

Mammy spoke. "We have lived on these islands for generation after generation, your grandmother and her mother sat in the very seats we sit now. This is our home, our land. We won't be moved out because some Englishman has grander plans." She looked at the two women, her face was flushed.

The smaller twin began to cry and Aileen pushed back her chair and came quickly to pick him up. "I only mean we have to think of the bairns." She rocked the baby too fast, which made him cry even more. "What life can there be for them here? And for me especially, with Niall dead, one mouthful away from the poorhouse? The potato harvest -who is to say it won't fail again? I can't live through The Hunger again. I can't see my children suffer like we did. I can't, I can't." A tear splashed onto the baby's head and he stopped grizzling in surprise while Aileen herself began to cry freely.

Mammy pushed back her chair and came over to her, putting her arms about her shoulders.

"Shhh, shhh, shh" she hushed so that Aileen and the baby were rocked together. She began singing then, sweet and low, and one by one the other women lifted their voices too and the sound filled the dark croft and curled out of the open door into the village.

Chapter Fourteen

Glasgow

Back at the hotel, Godfrey was nowhere to be seen and the drawing room door remained shut. Upstairs in my suite, I took off my bonnet and looked at myself in the mirror. My dark hair was nearly chin length again and curled under my ears. I pulled it back, soon I would be able to get the maid to pin it and I could leave my bonnet in my room. I usually only gave my hair a cursory brush, but now I stood brushing it over and over until it started to shine. "Lady MacDonald," I said to myself in the mirror. Who was she? I wasn't sure yet, but on the steps of the hotel Fanny had kissed me on both cheeks and hugged me and I had vowed to hold a fundraising dinner just as soon as I could. I looked out of the window, but there was no sign of the fellow who had been watching the hotel earlier. Now I thought about it, it was very unlikely to have been the same man that Godfrey had been speaking to after all.

Downstairs the dining room was filling up, but our centre table stood empty. Seeing that I would be dining alone, I requested a side table for one away from the chandelier and the eyes of the other guests. Everything was suddenly beautiful, the candlelight catching the cut glass, the soporific hum of conversation, the weight of the thick linen napkin on my lap. I would even order a decanter of wine, I decided. The waiter filled my glass and I drank it quickly, then re-filled my glass. I watched a drop of red wine run down the outside of the decanter and remembered the way my blood had run down my arm into the bowl. Leeches had been the doctor's first treatment. I finished my wine and poured some more. I would not think about the doctor tonight, but the wine relaxed my guard so that memories came sliding back, one upon the next.

"It is simply a question of finding the right treatment," Dr Fortnum had told my aunt after three days of leeches had not obtained the desired results. I was weaker than ever, each rib visible, and I was still mute. Then came the ice-baths. Plunged into a tub of freezing water in my under-garments. Held under for ten seconds, twenty, thirty. The freezing water had drawn the breath sharply from lungs, but not my voice. I had been trapped in the diving bell for twice that long and I had not cried then. I did not cry now.

After a week the doctor suggested a different remedy.

"Pelvic massage," the doctor had said, taking off his jacket, "is widely recognised as an effective treatment for a hysterical disorder such as this." He wasn't speaking to me, but to his trainee, Dr Smith, who was attending the session. Dr Fortnum hung his jacket on a peg by the door. "If the patient will remove her outer dress and stockings and shoes and place them on the chair."

I did so hesitantly. I had learned that to comply in these treatments was better than being forced. I slowly undressed and draped my clothes over the chair by the fire, then I stood in my ivory petticoat, my arms crossed over my chest, my bare legs pricking with goose bumps in the sudden exposure. My teeth were chattering from cold and the anticipation of another freezing bath.

"Now lie down on the couch," Dr Fortnum said, pulling up a chair and motioning for Dr Smith to do the same. I could feel the cold, green clammy leather through my thin cotton undergarments.

"One can purchase a purpose-made table for this treatment, but I find the couch equally effective." This was to his assistant, of course, who balanced his notebook on his knee expectantly. Dr Fortnum looked down at me lying on the couch and I noticed that his moustache was waxed into a sharp point at each end. "Now, the object of the treatment is to induce paroxysm in the patient and thereby provide some relief from the hysteria," he said to Dr Smith as he rolled up his sleeves. "In this case our objective is to get the patient speaking and eating again."

"Could you elucidate on "paroxysm"?Dr Smith asked.

"Through the correct stimulation we are looking for to provide an outlet for the patient's emotions. A controlled outburst you might say."

"Akin to lancing a boil perhaps?"

"Yes, I suppose so. Now, some physicians apply the treatment beneath the undergarments, but I don't find this necessary." He placed his left hand on my stomach, his right hand felt cold through my petticoat, and I felt a shiver run up my legs.

"Relax, please," he said, his left hand pressing on my stomach, making me exhale in a long gasp. I screwed my eyes shut.

"There is no need to touch the internal organs, simply massage this region here where the pubic bone ends."

"How long does it take?" This from the trainee.

"Difficult to say. It can be anything from a few minutes to half an hour. Perhaps you would be so good as to keep an eye on the time on your pocket-watch."

"Is efficacy of the treatment related to age?"

"Not in the least, in fact I find the treatment to often be more effective in married or older women. Do try and relax now, Maria."

French verb etre: je suis, tu es, il est, elle est...

"Perhaps you would like to try?"

"I will be content on this occasion to observe."

"Very well."

The capital of Germany is Berlin, the capital of Italy is Rome, the capital of Russia is Moscow, the latin name for rhubarb is Rheum rhabarbarum.

"One's hand does get rather tired. The French recommend a douche method using water under high pressure, but that would require the right facilities."

The cotton of my drawers chaffed where the doctor rubbed.

After a while, Dr Smith spoke again. "And how will we know when the treatment has taken effect?"

"There is generally a rising of colour in the face and the neck, the patient will swoon and emit a cry or groan."

I heard Dr Smith scrape back his chair and I opened my eyes to see him peering down at me.

"There is a very slight pinkness in her cheeks."

"Hmmm. How long has it been?"

"Twelve minutes by my watch."

Dr Fortnum removed his hand. "It is interesting that after twelve minutes we have been unable to induce even the first signs of paroxysm. We might conclude that this indicates a very serious disorder indeed."

The two doctors stood over me with a frown.

"So, what next?" This was from my aunt, who was seated in the corner of the room. She stood up and came to join the doctors.

Doctor Fortnum turned to her. "I could suggest that a local midwife attempts treatment at home, most of them have some skill in pelvic massage," he said, rolling down his sleeves. "Of course, the most effective remedy for young women is marriage." He looked at me, still lying on the couch. "However, as the patient refuses to speak or eat I fear more extreme measures may well be required. I think a short admittance to a hospital is in order."

Now I bunched my napkin tightly in my fist and made myself focus on the dining room. I inhaled and exhaled. The room swam slightly in the blaze of the gas lamps. There was the gentleman in the natty cravat, there was the girl who looked like Elizabeth seated with her mother. I took a large gulp of wine, and then another. I would not think about Dr Fortnum and his treatments. I got up from the table and made my way unsteadily upstairs. I paused at Godfrey's door and saw that there was a faint light beneath the door. I gave a gentle tap and when there was no answer, I pushed the door open. The room was dim, the lamp on the desk turned low and there was Godfrey standing by the window. He did not stand directly in front of the window, but to the side, pushing the curtain aside only a crack as though he did not wish to be seen from below.

On hearing the creaking door, Godfrey dropped the curtain and turned around quickly. His face was pale and there were dark circles under his eyes.

"You didn't come to dinner," I said. My words were slightly slurred.

He went back to the window. "The meeting finished late with the trustees."

The room was slightly spinning. I put my hand on the desk to steady myself and saw the estate map spread out. I peered to look at it more closely. Circles and lines now slashed the landscape of

North Uist. "What are these markings?" I bent over where to a circle was drawn around the word "Sollas."

Godfrey turned from the window and glanced at the map. "The trustees have told me we must bring in our plan of improvements more rapidly. We must find solutions which are more profitable."

"More profitable than what?"

Godfrey took the map from the desk and began to roll it up. "Look, it is all very complex, Maria, and we shall be leaving very early tomorrow for the steamer."

It was a dismissal. "How rude," I exclaimed to myself, as I returned to my room, to be treated like a half-wit. I saw my journal lying on the desk. I had been making notes about our journey. I snatched up the pen and began to write.

"I must confess that marital relations hardly seem the therapy that Dr Fortnum was so keen to promote. Marriage seems nothing more than a series of stilted mealtimes punctuated by remarks about one's health. Each night I lie awake like a starfish in my cold bed, wondering whether or not there will be a husbandly tap at the door. And should my husband deign to tap, I am required to get out of bed and open the door whereupon we engage in a charade of politely saying goodnight on the threshold until, with a wild look in his eye, he comes into the bedroom. There he extinguishes the lamp so that I only catch the flash of a pale buttock, or his long white legs as he removes his clothes and I lie upon the bed. We then proceed to fumbling in the dark which is rather akin to a game of Blind Man's Bluff. Of course, from my visit to the sculptures I know about a man's anatomy, but I didn't expect it to be quite so —animate—changing from slack and pendulous to hard and urgent quite of its own accord! The whole act of love is a rushed affair- the sharp dig of his elbows, hips and knees - it strikes me as quite unsatisfactory. Once spent he will stay for a moment washed up on the pillow, his eyes half closed. Then he rises, plants an awkward kiss on my nose, dresses, and returns to his room leaving me, once again, alone in my cold bed."

I scanned my loopy, intoxicated scrawl, and felt a flush in my cheeks from writing such intimate details. It really was a silly thing to write and I would rip it out in the morning. I lay back on the bed watching the ceiling going round in slow circles, then with the lamp still blazing, I fell into a deep sleep.

* * *

But there was no time to rip the pages out. When it was still dark, Godfrey shook me awake. He was already dressed, or had he even undressed? He thrust a large carpet bag at me. "Put what you need in here," he whispered, "our trunks will follow later." I half sat-up, my head still fuzzy from wine. I was still fully clothed, I realised. He stood at the window looking out through the crack in the curtain as I stuffed my journal, a nightdress and my hairbrush into the bag. I glanced at him standing by the window, then added Miss Wollstonecraft's pamphlet too. Then we crept downstairs.

"Godfrey, why-?"

"Shhh!" he said with force. "We must be completely silent."

It was so early that there was not even a porter in the foyer and Godfrey drew back the bolts of the hotel door himself. He motioned for me to wait. He put his head out of the door, then signalled for me to follow. A cab waited outside. I saw him glance about the street as we got in, but it was deserted.

"What is the time?" I asked as we pulled away.

Godfrey reached for his pocket-watch and then he stopped.

"Where is your watch?"

"I must have left it at the hotel."

"Well we should return for it, don't you think?"

"No." His voice was resolute.

Grey fingers of dawn were creeping between the warehouses of the dockyard, but the cranes and winches for loading goods stood motionless. Was it five o'clock, or even earlier? Down at the dock the steamer was not there.

"We must be a little early," Godfrey said looking out at the empty quay. "We'll wait in the carriage. Why don't you sleep? Here, lean on my shoulder."

I rested my head on his bony shoulder. Even through his coat I could feel that it was tensed. He did not put an arm around me but sat straight like a pencil with his hands in his lap, twisting his signet ring on his finger. Thoughts staggered through my wine-thickened mind. Godfrey knew we were being watched. But, by who? Had we left in the dark to avoid being followed? I thought of the gentleman in the velvet coat watching the hotel. Did he have Godfrey's watch?

When I finally stood on the deck of the paddle steamer, *The Clansman*, I had a throbbing headache. I took big gulps of salty air as I gripped the thrumming handrail. The steamer cut smoothly through the water like scissors through a bolt of navy-blue silk. In the dazzling daylight our hurried departure from the hotel now seemed like a strange dream. How long had I slept? An hour or more? When I had woken passengers were already queuing to board. I looked up at the inky smudge of steam rose from the ship's funnel and watched a gull whoop and dive on its white wing, down to the sea and up away towards the dark mountains of Loch Hourn.

A few passengers stood out on deck too. A little way along from me was a young couple, newlyweds or sweethearts, by the look of the way their arms were intertwined. The gentleman was pointing to a round island that looked like a shoulder emerging from the water and beside it another that looked like a dorsal fin. "Look, *look,* there is Skye," I heard the young lady say, excitement in her voice, as though winning a game of eye-spy. The gentleman smiled and bent to kiss her tenderly on the cheek and I turned away feeling a cold stab of envy.

Godfrey was below deck playing cards, but nothing would induce me to go below deck, to be shut in, trapped in a metal hull. I looked to the horizon to where the black mass of Skye had appeared, the jagged Cuillin Mountains rising slowly out of the water across the sea.

A gentleman dressed in brown tweed with a deerstalker hat came out on deck and stood beside me. "Would you look at that view," he remarked.

There was something familiar about his voice and his hat. Glancing at him, I saw it was the Irish newspaperman, Mr O'Brady, from the Highland Relief Board meeting. I quickly looked away, hoping my face was hidden by my bonnet, but the sudden movement seemed to catch his attention and he turned to me.

"Excuse me, madam," he said, "You must forgive me, but I am sure that we have met somewhere before. Was it by chance at the Socialist Reform Meeting in Leeds?"

I looked up at him and his green eyes scanned my face. He was young, no more than five and twenty, his chin was unshaven and he had the smell of tobacco on him. "No, sir, it was not." I stepped away an inch. "We have not been formally introduced, but I saw you at a meeting of the Famine Relief Board in Glasgow yesterday. I am Lady MacDonald, Baroness of Sleat." It was the first time I had referred to myself out loud in this way and my voice faltered a little, as though I was telling a lie.

Mr O'Brady froze for a second and I saw a shadow of something chase across his face. Then he bowed and took off his hat so that his wild hair tumbled free. "Ah – of course – so, the Laird and Lady are returning to their castle at last. I am Mr Thomas O'Brady. What a pleasure to make your acquaintance."

I eyed him suspiciously, but Mr O'Brady's previous wolfishness seemed quite gone and he was smiling pleasantly. Still, I said nothing in return, and instead looked out over the railing to where Skye was looming. I could begin to see its colours now, a high brindled moor, dark green glossy woodland below.

"Are you here for a holiday, Mr O'Brady?" I asked at last.

He replaced his hat and shook his head, following my gaze. "I am not. I am on my way to catch a ferry to North Uist to write some articles for the *Inverness Courier*. And yourself, have you visited Skye before?"

I glanced at him. "This is my first time in Scotland," then added quickly, "but I have read so much about it. Scott's descriptions are absolutely spot on from what I've seen so far. It is a wild, romantic, rugged place." I felt my cheeks blaze, why did I need to show him that I was well-read for goodness sake? I bit my lip and clutched the handrail.

"So, you have read *Waverley* I take it, your Ladyship." I could see from the corner of my eye that he was smiling. "And what is your opinion?"

I felt a glow of pleasure that he had understood my literary reference, but for a moment I was taken aback. Not since Grandpapa's death had anyone asked me for my opinion on a book. "Why, it is a magnificent novel," I replied. "One of his best, I would say."

The steamer had begun to swing around now to navigate the shallow water and I glimpsed the castle before it was hidden again in the trees. Passengers were coming out on deck to watch our approach to Armadale. A woman with two young children squeezed in at the rail beside me, causing me to stand closer to the journalist. Beneath the smell of tobacco was that wild smell, of damp leaves and foxes. We were very nearly at the pier. It was no more than a wooden jetty sticking out of a rocky cove where a jumble of fishing boats bobbed on the wash from our incoming ferry. The children beside me were pointing down into the clear water and I looked down to where orange and green seaweed floated like hair.

Mr O'Brady spoke again. "And which of *Waverley's* heroines do you prefer, Rose or Flora?"

I glanced around to see if Godfrey had come out on deck. What would he make of me discussing literature with an Irishman? I half hoped he would see. "Why, I like them both," I said. "Though on balance, I would say Rose is my favourite. Flora is so passionate, but doomed. I wished Scott had given her a better ending than with those dusty nuns in Paris." There was a bitter ring in my voice that I hadn't intended. I looked away.

I could feel Mr O'Brady watching me and I glanced up to meet his gaze. There was a faint wolfish gleam in his green eyes. He inclined his head towards me. "But Flora burned brightly did she not; she gave herself to an important cause?"

I spoke with sudden feeling, my voice rising. "Cause? The rebellion was futile all along, she had no power, and she ended up incarcerated."

I saw with embarrassment that the force of my words had sent a fine dot of spittle onto Mr O'Brady's cheek. The woman beside me at the rail frowned and ushered her children away.

"Maria!"

I turned at hearing my name. It was Godfrey, at the far end of the deck, walking towards me through the crowd, putting on his top hat.

Mr O'Brady put his hand to his cheek, to where my spittle had caught him. "Perhaps to have fought and lost is a happier ending than a long, dull, domestic existence?" he said, softly, his voice a smoke whisper. Then he tipped his hat, turned, and disappeared off through the crowd.

Chapter Fifteen

Sollas

I left the women behind at the waulking and went out into the village. It felt as though the tide was rising rapidly inside me. I ran up over the sandbanks and down to the beach, the mizzle wetting my face. The mist hung over the sea, so that I could hardly see Cod Point, and the sea lapped weakly at the shore like grey bathwater slopping in the tub. I picked up stones and began throwing them in, one after the other, they made small, useless splashes. A week it had been since I had made my wish and thrown the pearl in the sea, and nothing. Nothing at all.

"You need to throw them flat," a voice said.

I jumped and turned around, a pebble ready to throw at whatever it was that was standing there in the mist. It was a tall stranger, with a funny hat, standing a little way up the beach. He spoke the Gaelic with a strange accent.

He came closer and picked up a pebble. "Here," he said. "Watch this." He bent his knees and flicking his wrist, let the pebble fly so that it skimmed across the water, bouncing four, five, six times.

I bent eagerly for a pebble too.

"It needs to be as flat as possible," he said.

I tried to throw it as he had shown me, but it only bounced once and disappeared beneath the surface.

"Bend your elbow more, here, try again." He came and stood beside me and handed me a flat stone. He was very tall, taller than any man in Sollas, and dressed like a gentleman in tweed.

I did as he told me, cracking my arm like a whip, and the pebble bounced three times, leaving three circles in its wake.

"Well done!" he said, "You've got it."

He watched as I tried again, reached four then five, then six.

I heard a shout from the dune, and through the mist I could just make out Cormac standing there. "Halo, Morag," he called, I've been looking for you."

I ran towards him to collect more pebbles from further up the beach. "Here, come and look at this." I showed him my new skill and he bent quickly to pick up stones to copy me.

"Where d'ya learn this then?" he asked at last.

I looked about me, but the stranger in the funny hat had gone.

We stayed on the beach practising our skimming until the wet mist made our hands too cold to hold the pebbles any longer then we walked back up through the village together. I stood at the door of our croft and listened. Mammy was laughing and there was a man's voice too. I opened the door and saw that the waulking had been put away, but there, sitting in Da's chair was the stranger from the beach. Mammy was sitting across from him in her own chair and was laughing.

"Come in, Morag," Mammy said. She smiled and tucked a loose curl of dark hair behind her ear. "This is Mr O'Brady."

He sat, Mr O'Brady, with his strange tweed hat in his lap, drinking tea from our best china cup, the one that still had its handle. Without his hat I could see that he was younger than Mammy or Da and his hair was curly and as wild and springy as heather. Even sitting down he was tall, his knees sticking out from the chair, his booted feet sticking out towards the fire.

"We've met already." He smiled, his Gaelic tinged with that strange accent. "Morag is an expert stone-skimmer." I fancied he winked at me then and I blushed and fiddled with my sleeve.

The door opened and Da came in behind me, shaking his jacket. He looked in surprise at the gentlemen sitting in his chair.

"This is Mr O'Brady." Mammy said. "Mr O'Brady, my husband, Artair MacDhomhnaill."

Mr O'Brady got quickly up from the chair and shook Da by the hand vigorously.

"Mr O'Brady is a newspaperman from the *Inverness Chronicle*, he wants to find out what is going on here, to write about it in his paper," Mammy said.

Da raised his eyebrows.

"So I've been telling him," Mammy said, tilting her chin, "telling him about it." She glanced at me, "telling him about the school closing."

Da hung his jacket on the peg. "Please have a seat, sir," he said to Mr O'Brady, gesturing to his chair, but Mr O'Brady refused.

"On the contrary, sir, you have been working all day, you must have it." The two men stood over the empty chair looking at one another and Mammy quickly stood up too and poured some tea for Da, so that now we all stood like cattle in a byre looking at one another.

"I'm most grieved to hear about your troubles," Mr O'Brady said, shaking his head. "Most grieved indeed."

Da took a gulp of tea and said nothing whilst Mammy lifted the lid of the crowdie on the table, stirring the white cheese with the wooden paddle.

"I've told him how you've been to see Colonel Crawford," she said, glancing at Da. "How he'd refused to listen to you, to your suggestion of improvements. This was back in March, before the meeting."

"Injurious," Mr O'Brady said, shaking his head again. "You know, of course that Crawford is no longer a colonel, he was cashiered by the crown, for his enormous gambling debts." He looked from Mammy to Da, glanced at me. "Why he still uses the title 'colonel,' I do not know."

"Well, well," Mammy said, tapping the paddle against the bowl, "that is not a surprise, that little -"

"Ceit," Da said. "Whether that is true or not, he is still the factor on this estate." He frowned at Mammy and set his cup on the table and looked at the stranger standing with his hand on the back of his chair.

"It's not him you need to appeal to, in any case," Mr O'Brady said looking at them both, "It's Laird MacDonald."

"Aye," Da said, "and he's away in London. He's not been seen since last October and there was all that trouble with his brother."

"No," Mr O'Brady said. "He's here on Skye. I met his wife, Lady MacDonald, earlier today. He's at the castle."

Da's eyes brightened then he looked downcast again. "I don't know. His father, maybe, but this one- we don't know much about him, except for that he keeps himself down in London."

Mr O'Brady leaned forward and tapped the back of the chair. "He is still clan chief, he can still be reasoned with. If we collect a petition of names, present it with your plan of improvements, too. That's what we need to organise. We need to submit it directly to Laird MacDonald himself."

There was a crackle in the room like static before a storm, I felt it, like a shiver up the back of my neck. Mammy's eyes flashed, her hands hovered over the cheese. She looked at Da, and Da looked at Mr O'Brady. "And why do you wish to help us, sir?"

Mr O'Brady drew back, his eyes narrowed a little. "I have my reasons. The MacDonalds did my family an injustice many years ago, one that cannot be put right. But your family, sir, I can help them."

Mammy looked at Da, her eyes shining in the gathering dark of the croft. "Why not stay for something to eat, Mr O'Brady."

After we had eaten, and the cattle had been shut up, Mr O'Brady sat on the narrow bench at the table whilst Mammy and Da sat in their chairs by the fire. I sat on the bench beside him and showed him my slate and chalk, and he showed me a game called Tic, Tac, Toe which I beat him at four times. Then he took out some tobacco and a pipe and offered some to Da too, who fetched his pipe from the chest. My heart skipped a beat as Da opened the chest lid, thinking suddenly of the mermaid's treasure that was gone from the pocket of his suit. But he didn't notice it missing. Anyway, perhaps it had been answered, I thought, looking at our guest, stretching out his legs, tapping his pipe and complimenting Mammy on her cheese.

"Which part of Ireland are you from?" Da said, settling in his chair and pressing a pinch of tobacco into the bowl of his pipe. He passed it to Mr O'Brady to light.

"Please, call me Thomas." He lit Da's pipe from the candle beside him. "I'm from Donaghadee originally, though I moved to Belfast."

"I must say, Thomas," Mammy said, glancing up from the mending on her knee, "you speak the Gaelic awfully well."

He lit his own pipe and gave a puff on it, "Ah well, my Mother spoke Scots Gaelic, and my Grandmother too." He took a strand of tobacco from his mouth. "Her mother was from Skye originally."

"From Skye?" she asked. "And what took them over to Ireland?"

"You might not ask what took them to Ireland, but who," he said, then clamped his mouth around his pipe.

The peat in the fire hissed and spat and Mammy looked up sharply, her needle hovering above the shirt she was mending. Mr O'Brady held her gaze and then he looked into the fire.

"The Ship of the People," she said, her voice a smoke whisper.

Mr O'Brady nodded and Da gave a cough and took the pipe from his mouth.

Mammy leaned forward and touched him on the knee. "I'm so sorry," she said.

"What?" I asked, looking at them, "what are you so sorry about?"

Mammy looked at Mr O'Brady expectantly, and he looked down at me, sitting beside him.

"My mother's grandmother was a MacAllister from Skye. This is eighty years ago. She and her people had lived there for centuries in the village, working the land, the same as you do here. The estate passed to the new Laird MacDonald and the first thing the new clan chief did was take a census of how much money his land was making him. Turned out it wasn't enough."

Mr O'Brady shifted on the bench and rested his elbows on the table behind.

"First, he raised the rents, double, then triple, but people didn't have the money to pay. So, he thought of another way." He sucked on his pipe and looked into the fire. "It was the middle of the night when they came, with torches and irons. My great-grandmother was eleven years old. They pulled her father out of bed and beat him with a stick, then bound him in irons, setting fire to the thatch. Then they forced the family out onto the road, tying the women and children with rope to where the other villagers were being rounded up too. Down to the sea they were forced to march, men, women and children, by torchlight and the light of their thatches burning, to where a ship waited."

"The SS William," Mammy said.

"Aye, the SS William. Bound for the colonies, where, it turned out, the tenants had already been sold as labourers by Laird MacDonald." Mr O'Brady stared into the fire and said nothing more.

"But it didn't get to the colonies," Da said, resting his pipe on his knee. "Was it shipwrecked, Thomas, in Ireland?"

Mr O'Brady looked up. "Shipwrecked or not, I don't know, but there was a dreadful storm. My great-grandmother and the rest of the villagers were locked down in the hold, pitching and rolling for two nights out at sea, the whole ship creaking and groaning as though it would be ripped apart. When they made land at Donaghadee they were all forced off and locked in a nearby barn."

"And then what happened?" I asked. "To the people locked in the barn?"

He smiled suddenly and squeezed my arm. "Well," he said, "luckily someone heard cries coming from the barn and they went for help. The justice of the peace was called for and seeing their desperate condition he ordered shelter and food to be provided."

"Did they all go home, back to Skye?" I asked.

Mr O'Brady looked into the fire, the orange glow cast on his face. "No, I'm afraid they did not. They had no money, and besides, their homes had been destroyed. Kind folk gave them shelter and they found what work they could in Donaghadee, but they never came back."

"And what happened to the crew, I wonder?" Da said, putting a peat on the fire. "And the captain?"

"I don't know, scarpered I think," Mr O'Brady said. "But what I do know is that the MacDonalds were never brought to justice for what they did. For selling their own people."

"Until now," Mammy said, stabbing her needle into the shirt on her knee.

Mr O'Brady had been offered a bed at Mr Morrison's house, and I was allowed to stay up until he went. After he had gone I lay in my bed looking up at the dark thatch above me, thinking about our strange visitor. From over in their bed, I could hear Mammy's voice too, whispering excitedly like a mouse rustling in the thatch, and Da's voice, every now and then, like a creaking beam. I heard Mammy laugh, a girlish laugh as though she was being tickled, and Da shushing her, then they went quiet, as though they were concentrating on being very quiet. I turned in my bed, covering my face with the bedsheet, breathing in the unusual smell of pipe tobacco that still clung there. Please help us, I had wished down on the beach, please send help, and a week later, Mr O'Brady had appeared like magical driftwood brought in on the incoming tide.

Chapter Sixteen

Armadale Castle, Skye

The castle was like a picture that a child might draw. It was a traditional old stone keep with crenulations and arrow slits and then, in a flight of fantasy, a huge Georgian wing had been added on to one side with colonnades and large glass windows. Godfrey's father had extended it, Godfrey had told me back in London and there had been no expense spared. The long driveway curved up through beech and conifers and between the trees were glimpses of wet sand and coves, the distant flash of the sea.

I glanced at Godfrey sitting beside me, but his eyes were cast down onto his lap and his expression was grim. He had spoken with enthusiasm of the castle, the views, the boyhood adventures he had had here, yet now it was as though he dreaded seeing it again.

"It's just as you described," I said to him, "the planting, the way the trees are laid out. Look, there is the stone bench that you told me your mother put beside the little brook."

He looked at his hands and twisted his signet ring on his finger and would not look to where I pointed.

"Are you not pleased to see it all again, Godfrey?"

He glanced up at me. "I fear it will not be as I remembered it."

"Things from childhood rarely are. They are generally smaller," I reassured him. "Although perhaps that is not the case with a castle."

The trees and shrubs gave way to a gravel approach and there was the magnificent green lawn that I had seen in the painting. It rolled away from the castle down towards the sea. A large dog was coming slowly across the grass towards us with a stiff-legged gait.

110

"Things are different here now," Godfrey said suddenly, "they are not the same since my parents died. There have been some changes and you might find that-"

The carriage had drawn to a halt and there was a furious barking at the door. Godfrey got up and jumped down onto the driveway. He knelt down and buried his face in the dog's side and his hat was knocked aside as the beast, a deerhound by the looks of it, greeted him. I heard him lavishing praise upon it, then he let it lick his face as he rumpled its grey ears and muzzle. I stood on the carriage steps, breathing in the cold sea air and watching this display of affection silently.

"This is Ella," Godfrey said when eventually he stood up. "She was my best friend here." He retrieved his hat. He had gravel dust on his trousers and his hair was tousled. The dog barked once more and set off across the drive. Godfrey looked where it had gone, towards the castle, where five or six people waited at the top of the steps by the entrance. Godfrey's face was grim once more as he replaced his hat. He brushed off the dust from his knees. "Right. Let's go and meet the staff."

I looked at the short row of people arranged at the top of the steps like odd socks. Surely this wasn't all the staff? We had had more than this in Norfolk.

"Duncan," Godfrey called, raising his arm in greeting.

An elderly-looking man in an old butler's suit stepped forward from the head of the line and looked down at us from the top step. He said nothing until we were level with him.

"Your Lordship." His greeting was a gruff cough and he gave small bow, almost a shuffle.

"May I present my wife, Lady Maria MacDonald of Sleat," Godfrey said.

So, this was Duncan. He was much older than I had imagined, and he had rheumy, slightly bulging eyes, like a trout. I thought of how Godfrey had told me how Duncan had played cricket with him on the lawn and had helped him to make a wooden sword. It was hard to reconcile with the dour old man who barely greeted us. He cleared his throat.

"Your Ladyship."

"I have heard so much about you," I said, but Duncan only continued to look miserable. Perhaps his health is poor, I thought.

"This is Maigdh," Duncan said, indicating a thin girl standing beside him in a brown dress. He glanced at Godfrey, a scowl on his face. "She's the maid now."

Maigdh gave a curtsey and mumbled hello.

Besides her was a boy, for doing the errands, and beside him four men who were in charge of work in the gardens and on the estate.

A thin young man with ginger hair stepped forwards and shook hands vigorously with Godfrey. Hello, Godfrey," he said, "It's been a good wee while. I've been taking good care of Ella."

Godfrey blushed, extracted his hand and clasped them behind his back. "Yes, Baligall. Very good. And it's Lord MacDonald now, you know."

Baligall looked down at his boots. "Yes, Your Lordship."

The small line of people shuffled their feet.

"Right. We'll go in now then," Godfrey said. "Duncan, please show Lady MacDonald to her room."

I stepped into the enormous entrance hall. This must have been where the guests had waited for Godfrey to cross the threshold that Hogmanay when he had been given his signet ring. Now it offered a cold welcome. The light was dimmer than outside, and it was cooler too, and I felt a damp chill on my face. A peculiar smell hung in the air that was hard to place, as though smoke and tallow oozed from the walls. A grand marble staircase led away upstairs and from the vaulted ceiling hung a crystal chandelier, gathering dust.

"This way, Your Ladyship."

Duncan had lit a smoking lamp. He indicated, not up the main staircase, but to our left, through an archway and into a passage whose ceiling was low and walls were bulging and un-even.

"Where are we going?"

"I will show you to your room. It is in the old castle."

Up a cold stone flight of stairs we went, the tread of each step was worn smooth, from generations of MacDonald feet. I am the next in a long line of Baronesses to climb them, I thought, as I went up the uneven steps behind Duncan. He grunted and muttered in his own tongue and the smoky lamp cast shadows on the wall of the dark passageway. I followed him into a wood-panelled room with a four-poster bed and a small, mullioned window deep-set in an alcove.

I went to the alcove and opened the small stiff window, the ancient glass warped in its frame. The view was onto the back of the castle, onto a mossy lawn surrounded by dark conifers that rose steeply into rhododendrons and more woodland behind. Over the lawn hovered a cloud of midges and I drew back into the room to find that Duncan had gone. I went out into the passageway and peered back the way I had come. It was eerily quiet, not even the ticking of a clock could be heard. In the other direction the passage continued to an archway, and ducking through it, I saw that I had re-joined the new castle wing, coming out at the top of the grand staircase above the entrance hall. Surely it was much quicker to get to my room this way. Duncan must have taken me deliberately up the servants' stairs.

I heard footsteps below and saw Godfrey come into the entrance hall dressed in boots and an outdoor jacket, the dog at his heel. I had the impulse to call down to him, but then I hesitated. With Godfrey outside this was my chance to look for the library. I watched the heavy door shut behind him as he left the house then I hurried down the main stairs. The first room I tried was an airy drawing room where bright light poured through the large windows catching the shafts of dust which floated in the air. I looked about me. It was sparsely furnished and a small walnut writing bureau stood in one corner. On some of the walls there were square yellow stains where paintings must once have hung and beside the window was a large blackened scorch mark. I went to the window and saw the room looked out over the rolling green lawn that went nearly right down to the sea. I could see as far as a rocky point. This must have been where Godfrey had swum out to as a bet. There was Godfrey now, heading across the grass with the dog, and I watched until he had disappeared into the woods before moving on. I tried the next room and the next, but these rooms were covered in dust sheets, their paintings missing, and their fireplaces un-lit.

The whole place had the air of having been shut up for some time, and I thought of Godfrey's apprehension as we had arrived. How sad it must be to come back here with all his childhood memories when the castle looked like this. No wonder he had headed straight outside. I crossed back past the main staircase and ducked back into the old castle once more. The gloomy passageway continued beyond the stone stairs that Duncan had led me up, and I opened the door to find a small oak-panelled snug. This room, at least, looked lived in with two worn leather sofas and a peat fire smouldering in the hearth. Over the stone fireplace hung a large stag's head, and its glassy eyes watched me as I closed the door. Next to this room was another and as I flung open the door I gasped. I had found it at last, the library. It was smaller than the library in Notting Hill, but lined with shelves from floor to ceiling. It was not in wonder though that I gasped, but in bitter disappointment. Every shelf was empty. I remembered that awful day when I had gone into the library in Norfolk and seen the shelves stripped bare. Now I went around this room and traced my finger along the empty shelves. I inspected it, it was clean of dust. Books must have very recently stood here and must surely still be somewhere in the castle.

"Duncan," I called, walking down the passageway towards the back of the castle.

There was no reply. I tried a door and discovered it was a boot room with the smell of wax over-jackets and shoe polish. Riding jackets and tweed hats hung from pegs and a variety of stout boots and riding boots stood in a line beneath them. I thought of my hikes over the Norfolk broads in a pair of comfortable boots and realised that I would need some better footwear for going outside. Most of the boots were old, their leather cracked and dull, but here were a pair whose chestnut leather gleamed and I sat on a wooden stool to try them on.

"M'Lady?" Duncan stood in the open doorway, in an apron, holding a silver teapot.

Red-faced from pushing my foot into the boot, I stopped and looked up at him. "Ah Duncan, yes. I'm just trying on these boots, but I wanted to ask you about the books."

Duncan came into the boot room, bending to peer down at the boots. "These are his Lordship Alexander's boots," he said, frowning. "You can't use these."

I stopped, one foot half in and out of the boot and looked up in surprise. "Well surely he won't be needing them today?" I said, "as he's not here."

Duncan straightened and glared coldly at me. "These are not your property. They are the property of his Lordship."

His words hung between us and I put down the boot and stood up.

"Perhaps, then, you would be so kind to lend me a pair of my husband's boots?"

"I don't believe we have any, save for the pair he has on," Duncan said, bending to straighten the boots I had just been trying. "Master Godfrey wasn't one for the outdoors and he didn't keep a spare set here."

The mention of London reminded me. "Actually, I came to find you to ask you about something else. The books. From the library, where are they?"

Duncan curled his lip and looked down at the teapot in his hand, then turned away, muttering.

"What was that?"

"I said the books have gone, Y'Ladyship." He turned and looked at me. "They've been packed away, ready to be sent away to auction with everything else." He spat this last word out.

A wave of panic came over me, was I too late? "Well, where are they now? Are they still here?"

He cradled the silver teapot to him like an injured bird. "You'll have to ask Master, I mean, *Lord* Godfrey if you want them."

* * *

Later that evening, I sat at one end of the long dining table and Godfrey sat at the other. The table could have seated twenty comfortably, but we sat at either end, like salt and pepper, alone with our plates of lamb and potatoes. The evening light fell through the tall windows causing the carved fireplace and the vaulted marble ceiling to glow white. Only the candelabra on the table were lit, the two great crystal chandeliers hung darkly between us. I must ask about the books, I really must, I told myself. Besides that, I hadn't forgotten my promise to Fanny to arrange a fundraising dinner. I looked down the table to where Godfrey had finished eating. He was now slicing off meat from the leg of lamb beside him and feeding it to the dog who sat drooling at his feet. I laid down my cutlery.

"I was wondering," I called down, "perhaps we shall arrange a dinner party."

Godfrey dropped some meat for the dog and looked up. "What was that?"

I raised my voice and my exasperation bounced off the ceiling in a dim echo. "I said, perhaps we should arrange a dinner, here at the castle."

Godfrey looked puzzled, glanced around the great dining room, at the empty marble alcoves. "Who would you invite?"

"I found a guest list in that bureau in the drawing room, entitled 'summer luncheon.' Obviously, it doesn't need to be a huge affair, but a few local guests, there was a Lady MacAllister of Broadford and-"

"She definitely won't come."

"Well who then? You suggest someone. You told me about how your parents had wonderful parties here and I was thinking we might do the same."

Godfrey looked down at the dog and frowned. "I think you might be right," he said slowly, "perhaps a dinner is just what we need to show them who is in charge."

Fortified by this small victory, I crept on towards the subject of the books. "I was having a look round the castle. Would it not be better for us to take bedrooms in the new wing where it is so much lighter?"

"Is there something wrong with your room?"

I thought of the damp view onto the mossy lawn, but said nothing.

"My room has always been in the old castle, ever since I was a boy. I thought it was better that our rooms were opposite one another. The room you're in was originally Alexander's."

I held my breath. Wondered about straying into the forbidden territory of Alexander, an icy lake, thinly covered with snow. Dusk was shrouding us both in shadows at our separate ends of the table, I could no longer see his features clearly. The light from the candelabra was a yellow puddle on the cloth.

"Won't Alexander need his room, if he should ever come to stay?" I asked as lightly as I could.

"Ha." A snort from the other end of the table. "He won't be coming, believe me."

"Why not?"

"He promised to never have anything more to do with this place."

The carriage clock chimed the hour quickly from the mantelpiece.

"And why is that?"

I could see Godfrey playing with the knife at his end of the table. The ivory handle gleamed in the dim room. Eventually he said, "You might as well know, Alex is a thorough bastard. A very bitter individual and he hates me."

I thought of the telegram: *after what you have done!*

I heard Godfrey's signet ring clink against his glass and saw him take a long draught of wine.

"Why does he hate you?"

"He blames me for our mother's death and his own misfortune."

"But why does he blame you for her death?"

Another gulp of wine, then he said, "It was her heart, the physician said. But Alex couldn't accept it. We had argued the night before her death, you see, and he was sure that was what had killed her."

So, Fanny had been right.

You'll pay for it.

I hesitated, not wanting to reveal that I had read his telegram. "Do you think that Alexander is dangerous?"

"Dangerous? Ha."

"Godfrey, I think we were being watched at the hotel. There was a gentleman, but I didn't see his face. He was watching the hotel." He had your pocket-watch, I wanted to add, but I didn't. "Is that why we left in such a hurry? To avoid him?"

Godfrey was quiet for a moment and then he finally said, "Alexander is no threat."

"But can you be sure? You said yourself he was a bitter fellow."

"Maria, believe me, the situation is in hand."

My heart was beating fast, this was surely the time to speak up. Mention the books, mention them, tell him about last

117

summer. "I have something I'd like to raise with you." I could feel a pulse in my throat. Scraping my chair back, I went to his end of the table. The words came rushing out. "I would like the books that were taken from the library."

"Maria."

I spoke quickly. "No, Godfrey, you have told me something about Alexander and now I want to tell you something too. I know my aunt told you about last summer, about what happened with the doctor and all that, but I'm quite well now and I want you to know it is all in the past." I knelt down beside his chair and the dog thumped its tail and thrust his wet nose in my face. I put my hand on Godfrey's arm and looked at him. "Please," I said.

He looked down at me. Half of his face was in shadow, the other illuminated by the candelabra. He pushed back the brim of my bonnet with both hands and looked at me. It was the first time that we had looked at each other in such a way and he put a cool hand on my cheek. For a moment I thought he was going to lean in and kiss me.

"I was given the report that Dr Fortnum wrote," he said at last. "I know about your illness."

I felt my cheek growing hot in his hand and I dropped my gaze to my knees.

"I am your husband now. I have to protect you, and if a physician recommends that-"

"No! Dr Fortnum doesn't know anything."

"You were sick, Maria."

"No." I pulled my face away from his hand. "I was grieving for my Grandfather who raised me."

"It sounds like a very dubious sort of upbringing to me. No company, no church, being exposed to all sorts of reading material from a very young age. Thank goodness for your aunt's arrival."

"My aunt just made everything worse. She tried to force me into all sorts of things, like-

"Like spending time in the company of other women? Like wearing stockings? I've read the report, you know."

"She burned my books!"

"You were extremely ill. Books were making you worse."

"No, it was nothing to do with books."

"It seems that it was everything to do with them to me."

He got up and stood over me as I knelt before him on the floor. "I cannot in good conscience allow you something that would do you harm. If you were an alcoholic, would I ply you with gin? Why no."

"Books are not gin. How ridiculous."

He bent down and in a sudden movement he pulled my bonnet. The ribbon caught around my throat and choked me as he ripped it from my head. I knelt on the floor, my short hair exposed, coughing.

"Because of books, Maria, you hacked off your own hair, you refused to speak, you starved yourself and then you were admitted into an asylum."

A hundred words sprung to mind, a host of counter-arguments. All quelled with that one word. I looked down at the dining room floor, remembered the cold stone floor of the asylum through my thin cotton dress as they had held me down with the tubing.

"We don't want that to happen again." There was something flint-like in his tone which made me look up at him, but it was too dark now to discern his features. He put his hand out to help my off my knees. "Please, Maria," he said. I looked up at him for a moment, then got to my feet. He brushed my dress for me and patted me on the arm. We don't need to think of the past anymore. We will have our own family." He glanced at my stomach. "God knows we need an heir."

I thought of how he tapped on my bedroom door, his earnest nightly endeavours and I clasped my hands over my stomach tightly and stood up straight.

"And we will open the castle, organise a dinner, have people over, that will be a thing to look forward to, won't it?" He went on. "I know I have been preoccupied with things, but look, how about we take a turn around the lawn before it gets properly dark?"

I smiled stiffly. "I think I am coming down with a headache, I'm afraid."

And with that I went upstairs and I locked my bedroom door.

Chapter Seventeen

Sollas

It was May, and the colours of the fallow machair began to unfurl like a faerie banner. Creeping buttercup and yellow-rattle wove together with ox-eye daisies and white campion, and tiny dog violets and rare marsh orchids appeared, dotted about like finely stitched faerie embellishments. The days were long and light now, at dawn the grasses were full of the song of larks, and at dusk with the call and dart of corncrakes.

Since Mr O'Brady had come to the village the weather had held, day after day of high, fine blue weather, so that the summit of Eaval hill could be seen all day long. There was a holiday feeling despite the work to be done. There was peat to be cut and dried, a job the whole village turned out for, voices calling and laughing over the peat banks, our hair and faces kissed by the sun as we cut the rich dark slabs for drying in stacks. The first of the potatoes were ready too, hard little tatties that we boiled on the fire outside and ate in their skins, tossed in fresh butter. One evening, Cormac's Da, Mr MacIver played his fiddle and Mammy and Aileen led the singing until it got dark.

There had been no more sign of the creature either, as though the arrival of Mr O'Brady had chased it away. For three days Mr O'Brady went up and down the village collecting names for his petition, followed everywhere by a crowd of children. For he had magical pockets and could produce from thin air a rare-looking feather or a piece of blue sea-glass which was considered the most precious amongst children. As for me, I walked ahead of the children, at Mr O'Brady's side, allowed to carry his knapsack and was entrusted to re-fill his pen with ink from the square bottle whenever was needed. Up to a front door we would go and knock politely, or call out halo and go around the back. And there Mr O'Brady would explain his purpose, the collection of names to present to Laird MacDonald, along with Da's plan of improvements, which showed, quite clearly that, with only a little more land, a profit could handsomely be made and the rents paid up. To the men he was courteous, to the women he smiled, and everyone nodded and agreed and scratched their name or put an X on the parchment.

In the evening, Mr O'Brady would sit out on the sandbanks with his pipe overlooking the sea and tell the children tales from Ireland, of great serpents that lived in caves, and of a handsome hero, Finn, who we already knew about from the stories we had on our island. "But did you know?" Mr O'Brady said to the children gathered about him, "that Finn was stolen away from his true love by the faeries and taken to the underworld?" I shivered, thinking of the creature, wondering where it was now. Was it sleeping somewhere in the underworld too?

"There was no way out for Finn," Mr O'Brady was saying, shaking his head, "except for this." He picked from the coarse grass beside him a green clover, with three small leaves. "Finn's true love, you see, had given him a magic clover as a keepsake. He held up the clover for us to see. "But Finn's clover had four leaves, not three." He pointed to each leaf of the clover in his hand. "Each leaf of the clover represents something different: faith, hope, love – and the fourth leaf is for luck." His eyes glittered. "The very next night, as luck would have it, a fairy had left the door to the underworld open and Finn was able to escape and be free."

One by one the children would be called indoors until even Cormac had to go in. Then it was only Mr O'Brady and me sitting together in front of the darkening ocean listening to its steady roar. This was what I cherished above all else, the smell of his pipe smoke, the feel of the cool sand as I ran it through my fingers, and the opportunity to ask him all my questions. For Mr O'Brady had travelled, not only to Skye and to Ireland, but to London. And it was these tales, of clock towers reaching to the sky, of great cathedral domes, and shop windows filled with every edible fancy, that now captured my imagination the most.

"And can they really fashion a flower out of sugar?" I asked, thinking of the taffy Da once brought back from Lochmaddy for my birthday. It was oh so sweet, but a brown sticky lump wrapped in paper.

"Yes, of course. They look quite real. Pink roses and violets, buttercups – all perfectly edible, on top of cakes."

"What sort of cakes?"

"Cream cakes, chocolate cakes, some cakes with five or six different layers of fruit."

I felt my mouth water. "And have you seen the River Thames?" I asked, thinking of our geography lesson with Miss MacAllister.

"Why, of course, it is a great wide river, almost as wide as-," he puffed on his pipe and looked out at the sea to where the tide was right out, "-from here down to the water."

"But how do people get across?" I puzzled. "Is there a boat?"

He smiled. "Sometimes by boat, but mainly by bridges, great bridges with huge arches."

He looked at my puzzled face then reached down on the slope of the sandbank and drew a bridge with five arches in the sand. "This is like new London Bridge, it was finished about ten years ago, but there are many others."

I heard Mammy calling me and sighed. I wanted to stay out here with Mr O'Brady all night, until the stars rose and faded again, asking my questions. I stood up and brushed the sand from my dress and went inside, to lie in the smoky darkness with visions of bridges and sugar petals dancing in my head.

The next morning, as the weather was still so fine, Mr O'Brady declared he would like to visit Langais to see for himself the land that had been offered instead of Sollas. I was allowed to go with him to show him the way. It was a whole day's walk there and back across the moor and we formed easy company, Mr O'Brady striding along and I trotting beside him. I would point out things of interest, where berries could be found, or a nest of grouse chicks. He told me things too, of a place called Africa where there are enormous animals with huge ears and long necks. And of how every week, more and more interesting treasures are brought back from all over the Globe, and how they were making an enormous building in London called the British Museum to put them all in.

We skirted round the bottom of Eaval hill and stopped on the rise on the moor to look at the view. From here we could see back the way we had come, across the moor, past the peat banks, down to the rigs and the crofts and to the wide machair beside the sea. Ahead of us, towards Langais, the landscape was wilder, and dotted closely with lochans and dark stretches of bog, so that we gave up speaking and watched our steps as we continued on. When I saw the southern Lochmaddy road ahead of us, I stopped by the loch.

"This is Langais," I said.

Mr O'Brady looked about him, at the barren land pitted with peat bog and dark pools. It was more water than land, clumped with sedge grass and rocks. He pressed his toe in the ground, watching the water bubble up around it, though we had had no rain for a week. Then he bent down and pulled back the rough sedge grass that showed rock and bog beneath. "You couldn't grow an oat out here." He stood up. "What about up there," he pointed to where the land rose on the other side of the road and a heap of stones lay on the small round summit of Benn Langass.

"That's Barpa Langais, where ancient folk lived, and beyond it is Pobhull Finn, where Finn had his fireplace."

We walked towards it and climbed the rise, stopping at the top by the heaped stones where the bog became heather again. Eaval hill looked wrong from up here, like a letter written back-to-front. It was so quiet too, without the sound of the ocean. Only in the far distance was the line of the sea by Locheport. It would be strange to live here, I thought, on the wrong side of the hill, without the sound of the waves, without the machair. Mr O'Brady refilled his canteen from the stream and I looked at the circle of stones. I suddenly had the impulse to tell Mr O'Brady about the creature. I watched him bent over, filling his bottle, and turned the words over in my mouth.

"We had a creature in the village," I said eventually.

He looked up from filling his bottle and cocked an eyebrow at me. "What sort of creature was it?"

"I was the only one who saw it," I could feel the colour rising in my cheeks. "It was pale, with a big head, and staring eyes. And it smelled awful too. I saw it first in the dark by the peat stack and then I found it hiding in our croft."

"And did it take anything?" Mr O'Brady said, standing up straight and looking at me.

"Da's oilskin and some milk from the table."

123

"Not a faeire then, but some other creature, because faeries won't take milk themselves."

I think I loved him at that moment that he did not, for one heartbeat, disbelieve me. He passed the canteen to me to drink from.

"What do you think it was?" he asked.

I handed him back his canteen. "Old Ma MacNeill said it could be a changeling or some such, seeing as we found the shells from wild bird's eggs." I thought of that strange face, the staring eyes. "But I don't know."

"And what about your mammy, what does she say?"

I frowned. "She doesn't know that it was in our croft." I flashed him a warning look. "But she said we have more to worry about than monsters."

Mr O'Brady laughed, but then his face was serious again. He looked out towards the moor and the loch. "Aye, your mammy is right. We'd better be getting back."

We walked back in easy silence and then when we were on our side of the hill and could see Traigh Iar beach again, Mr O'Brady inclined his head towards me. "They said my older brother was touched by the faeries, because he had a leg that did not grow like the other. It was shorter and bent. They said that my mother must have not watched him properly as a baby, that the faeries came in and twisted his little leg. People in our village feared him, they thought he had the sight, you see. He grew up friendless and became a priest in Belfast."

"And does he believe in faeries still?"

Mr O'Brady smiled. "He believes in God now, and the devil."

He stopped and kicked a rock half-hidden in the grass. "You know, Morag, Mr James Hutton from Edinburgh believed that the earth is always changing underneath our feet, that this rock, perhaps, was once right down there in the sea."

"Well who put it up here? Was it giants?"

"Nobody put it here, it moved, slowly, over time, on its own."

I looked at him doubtfully.

"There is another Scotsman, Mr Lyell, who believes that the earth is more than three hundred million years old." He looked

124

at my blank face. "Do you know what one million is? It is counting to ten thousand, one hundred times."

My mind boggled at the thought of trying to reach such a number, I hardly ever had cause to count beyond one hundred, much less to reach to a thousand. We were coming near the peat banks now, and I could see Mrs MacIver was there, cutting peat with her iron.

"So you see, there may be another explanation to your creature, beyond faeries, I mean," he said.

* * *

The next day, Mr O'Brady's list of names was complete, the plans were finished, and it was time for him to go. The sun drew a veil of cloud across itself at the prospect of his departure. He had entrusted me with his bottle of ink and pen and a sheaf of paper so that I could record for him what went on whilst he was away. A small crowd stood on the road beside the schoolroom to bid him farewell.

"I shall be back within a week, all being well," Mr O'Brady said, swinging his knapsack onto his back. "Morag here is going to keep an account of things in my absence."

"God speed, Mr O'Brady," Mr Morrison said, shaking him by the hand. "We shall be praying for your endeavour."

Mammy stepped forwards and smoothed her hair. "Good luck, Thomas." She looked as though she wanted to say something else, but patted his arm instead.

"Thank you for your hospitality, Ceit." He smiled then shook Da by the hand. "And yours too, Artair."

"Don't forget to mention the twelve rigs for cloverage," Da said, "that's very important."

Mr O'Brady nodded. "Rest assured, I will not forget. And I will mention that I have been out to Langais and that it is totally unsuitable for cultivation."

He looked down at me, but I said nothing and instead walked with him a way up the road, my steps light and quick to match his long-legged pace. There was so much more I wanted to say to him, but it felt as though my mouth had been stuffed with bog-cotton. The sky had properly clouded over now and the wind had got up. The road began to curve away from the coast, heading over the moor towards Lochmaddy. From away in the heather, I heard the long desolate call of a curlew and my hands tingled, for it was an ill-omen for a journey. We stopped at a small rise in the road, where the village was nearly out of sight and I had the sudden urge to throw my arms about him and cling to his coat.

"Well, I think we shall say good-bye here." He turned to face the open road ahead.

I nodded, mutely, then blurted out, "You will come back, won't you?"

He gave his easy laugh, but I was suddenly seized by desperation, and a fear that he would never come back.

"Promise me, promise me you will."

He ceased his laughter then and nodded seriously. "Of course I will, Morag, of course. I promise I will come back. I'm going to show you how to be a journalist, aren't I? He stuck out his hand. "We'll shake on it, how about that?"

I took hold of his hand then and he folded mine in his and shook it solemnly, a promise sealed.

"Good-bye then, Morag," he called, striding away and I stood and watched him until he had vanished over the rise.

I turned away, back to the village, my feet felt like lead boots. From the rise in the road, the village looked in miniature, the small crofts beside the rigs, the schoolroom like an empty matchbox. And beyond it, the ocean, wide and empty, nothing between us and America. I heard a cart behind me, coming fast and stepped aside into the heather. It was Alasdair MacInnes, provisions clinking and bumping in the back. When he saw me, he drew the horse up hard.

"Who was that gentleman on the road, back there?" he demanded. But I looked at the village and said nothing. He shrugged and following my gaze, grinned slyly. "All packed, are we?" He leered. "Three more weeks 'til you're out."

I could smell his rotten breath from where I stood, he had been drinking in Lochmaddy by the whiff of him. All my heartbreak at the loss of Mr O'Brady turned to an icy river.

126

"We're not going anywhere," I said, folding my arms. "Mr O'Brady is helping us and he's off to see Laird MacDonald right now, so there."

He leaned back then in his cart and grinned. "Mr O'Brady, so that's who it was." He spat onto the heather, his gob nearly catching my dress. "Thank you for the information, the colonel will be wanting to know that." Then he clicked the horse on with his tongue and snapped the reins over its back.

"I'll be seein' you soon," he called over his shoulder as he went.

Chapter Eighteen

Armadale Castle, Skye

I kept my bedroom door locked each night now and put my pillow over my head when I heard my husband's tap. Instead of being angry, Godfrey looked at me hopefully each morning over breakfast, enquiring about my health, glancing at my stomach, as though there would be news. Ha. My monthly courses were nearly due but let him think it if he liked. With each night that my door remained locked he grew more tender, accompanying me around the grounds, pointing out his mother's careful garden design, though I was not the least bit interested in plants.

"What you need, Maria, is a hobby," Godfrey said as we took a turn around the front lawn overlooking the sea. "My mother was a terrific gardener, she said it gave her time to think." We came to a stop in front of a border of flowers. There were some tall pink ones and some blousy looking white ones. "Perhaps you can take on one of these beds." He glanced shyly at my stomach. "Whilst your condition allows it of course."

I turned away and looked out across the Sound where the ferry looked like a model boat.

* * *

One morning he showed me his camera, which was much more interesting. I had seen a demonstration before at the Polytechnic. It was a wooden box with a short brass telescope that stood upon long legs and he took my photograph positioning me on the main steps of the castle entrance. He presented the plate to me afterwards. There I was in a high collared dark dress, my hair scraped severely away from my white face. *Lady MacDonald, May 1949* he had written on the back, as though I might forget. Perhaps I might, for I did not recognise the lady in the photograph. It could have been his mother. There had been a mix-up at the hotel and our trunks had been mislaid. In the meantime, I was forced to wear what remained of Godfrey's mother's dresses. It was a choice between extravagant evening wear or her gardening clothes and wherever I went an odour of mothballs followed.

I felt like one of those steam powered automaton machines from the Polytechnic. Automatically I dressed, ate, walked around the castle grounds. Just like the days at the hospital, stumbling in circles as I was walked twice a day around the gravelled yard. I dreamt of it now, that redbrick building in Lambeth where Aunt Caroline had taken me when the doctor's pelvic treatments failed to induce me to speak or eat. Down to the lower floor of the hospital where the smell of drains and camphor hung in the air and a small window looked out onto a sunless yard. Upstairs in the hospital was a maternity ward and the wail of babies drifted down.

There was nothing to do though, I realised, except stumble on and hope that somehow, through good behaviour, I might convince Godfrey that the doctor had been wrong. Godfrey had set a date to invite guests to dinner and I had received a letter from Fanny full of helpful tips and advice for making it a success:

Good food and fine wine are the key," Fanny wrote, *"in order to stimulate a sense of benevolence and charity. Just before dessert is served give a small speech about the need for famine relief. Remind guests of their Christian duty to help the poor, but don't lay it on too thick! You can follow it up with the wives once the gentlemen have retired. After all, it's us women who really hold the purse strings!*

This seemed doubtful, I thought. I had not seen so much as a penny since I had got married, everything was put on account. Not that I had any money of my own, for it had all passed to Godfrey now. As much good as it had done me. I sat reading Fanny's letter at the walnut bureau in the corner of the drawing room. The desk must have once been Godfrey's mother's, for in the drawer I found a heap of old guest lists and notes of functions and parties, along with planting plans for the gardens. I dutifully copied out an old menu. A salmon mousse, roast beef, marzipan fancies. I sat back and looked about the drawing room. This bureau would be much better over near the window where it would overlook the sea.

I got up and began to drag it across the room, trailing a thick train of cobwebs and dust. One of the bottom drawers did not sit straight on its runners and something had fallen behind it. Pulling open the drawer and stretching my arm inside I could feel that something was wedged there. It felt deliciously like a book. I struggled to pull it out, wiggling and pulling it until it was free. I looked at it with bitter disappointment, it was only a bible. Godfrey's mother's name was written in faded blue ink on the inside flap. I picked it up and went along to give my menu to Duncan. He was scrubbing potatoes in cold water in the kitchen. He held the list with his wet hand, blinking at it with his rheumy eyes.

"You want me to cook all this?"

"Er well, no, these are just some suggestions of course".

He blinked. "Smoked salmon mousse?" He looked up at me. "Mousse?"

"I copied it from a menu that I found in the bureau in the drawing room."

Another stare. He put the list down on the wet draining board and went back to his potatoes. "That was a long time ago when there was money," he said. "We had a chef in those days, not French mind you." he curled his lip at the thought. "And servants a plenty too." He shook his head. "It's just me and Maigdh who do the cooking now."

I watched as the words on my list began to slowly dissolve on the draining board. I would try a different tack. "I believe you used to have the most wonderful parties here."

Duncan inclined his head, grunted, continued to scrub the potatoes.

"Like the Hogmanay ball. Godfrey has told me all about it."

Duncan stopped scrubbing then and fixed me with a piscatory stare. "Did he?"

"Oh yes, the music, the food, the whisky. The ring hidden inside the bun."

His eyes widened. "He told you about that?"

"Why yes, of course."

Duncan shook his head. "He nearly burned down the castle."

130

"What?"

"The way the fire caught the curtains. Could have been a lot worse than smoke damage."

I laughed. "We must be talking about different things. I'm talking about when the signet ring was hidden in the black bun."

"Aye," Duncan said, "Godfrey was crazed about it. Snatched up the juniper branches used for the saining and set it ablaze, then went running through the castle like he was possessed. It caught the curtains in the drawing room and nearly burned the place down."

I thought of the large scorch mark I had seen beside the window. Why on earth had Godfrey become so wild? It was hard to imagine given his usual composure. It must have been the whisky. Unless-

"Are you sure it wasn't Alexander who set the place on fire?"

"Alasdair?" Duncan looked puzzled. "Now why on earth would he do something like that?"

"Well he's rather wild isn't he? Prone to outbursts?"

Duncan shook his head and I watched the water drip off his scrubbing brush into the sink. My menu had completely disintegrated. "Alasdair was a good lad."

From out in the hallway, I heard Godfrey shouting. "No. I will not see him. On any account. And I want him off my property, right now."

I went to the kitchen doorway and saw Godfrey walk into the snug. Baligall was hurrying out towards the main hall. From the hallway I listened. Baligall was saying something to someone, then the heavy front door slammed close. I put my head round the snug door.

Godfrey was standing by the mantelpiece and he looked up, frowning. "Ah, hello," he said, smiling quickly. "I was rather thinking we might go out to the ruins of Knock castle as the weather is so fine. Duncan's prepared a picnic. If you're up to it, of course?"

Again the quick glance at my stomach.

I opened my mouth to disabuse him of his hopeful notion, but I closed it again as Baligall came into the hall behind me, loitering as though he had something to say.

"Go ahead and fetch your things," Godfrey said to me, "and I'll call for MacAllen to bring the trap."

But as I was half-way up the stairs, Godfrey came into the hall and called up to me. "I'm so sorry, my dear. Something has come up and I may be some time. Why don't you go to Knock on your own? Baligall will tell MacAllen to keep an eye on you."

I went upstairs to my room, throwing Godfrey's mother's bible onto the bed. I thought of Miss Wollstonecraft's pamphlet that I had hidden at the bottom of my carpet bag. I had not had the heart to read it recently and would take it with me. As I took it from the bag that lay beneath the mullioned window a movement outside caught my eye. There was someone standing among the trees at the back of the castle. What were they doing? I peered through the ancient glass. Yes, there was someone there in the shadow of the conifers and they seemed to be gouging one of the trunks with a knife. I struggled with the latch to open the window to get a better look. The window was swollen and warped and when I finally thrust it open, I recognised the velvet coat immediately.

"Hey!"

He glanced up and turned away. I hurried out of my room, downstairs, along the passage, past the boot room, and out onto the back lawn. He was gone, of course. A raven cawed mockingly from the gloomy conifers. I went across the soggy lawn, the damp moss soaking my feet, to where the man had stood. The trunk had been carved with the letter A. The smell of pine rose from the freshly cut initial. He was here then, Alexander. I looked up through the conifers to where the garden rose steeply and became dense rhododendrons. There were a hundred places to hide. Was he watching me? A pigeon burst noisily out of the undergrowth and my heart leapt into my mouth. I turned and half ran back towards the castle, pine needles clinging to my wet slippers.

MacAllen, the buggy driver was waiting in the hall, so I fetched my things and we set out along the coast road towards Knock castle. We passed a group of long, squat crofts with smoke rising from the thatch. Behind the crofts, two women were working in a plot of land, bending and digging, their sleeves rolled up. One of them straightened up and shielding her eyes in the sun, waved to the buggy and MacAllen waved back.

"My sister," MacAllen said.

He began to sing a Gaelic tune that had a mournful quality that played on my nerves. I kept glancing behind me, but the road was empty. The letter A carved with a sharp knife. *You'll pay for it.* I shivered. "I want him off my property," Godfrey had shouted, then, "Sorry my dear, something's come up." What was he going to do?

Up ahead was the green ruin of Knock castle now reduced to a stub of its walls. I jumped down from the trap and looked out across the expanse of the sea that glittered all the way across to the brown, velveteen mountains on the mainland. A little boat with a white sail was becalmed out in the Sound.

"You might as well visit your sister whilst I picnic here," I said as MacAllen unloaded the hamper, parasol and picnic rug.

MacAllen shook his head and protested, but I was insistent, oh to be alone for just an hour. I carried the hamper and blanket and parasol over the grass, to a hollow beside the ruins and settled myself down on the rug amongst clumps of sea pinks. Duncan had packed the hamper with cold lamb chops that were congealed thickly with fat. Instead, I pulled out a punnet of raspberries and put one in my mouth. Its tiny hairs brushed my tongue then it burst with ripe sweet flavour. There was not a soul around. Being some distance from the road, I took off my bonnet and ruffled my short hair. My slippers were still wet from the grass and I kicked them off and then with a glance around me, took off my stockings too. I gave a happy sigh. Who could enjoy grass after all without feeling it between the toes? Propping the parasol at a certain angle, I found I could lie back with my face in the shade and my bare toes left to bake in the sun. The blanket was so warm and soft beneath my fingers and the heat and the hum of a nearby bee made me drowsy. Sleep slowly sucked me into its tow.

"So, you have found a perfect spot for a picnic I see."

I startled violently, knocking the parasol over so that it rolled off down the grassy slope. I looked up. It was Mr O'Brady. He stood above me, grinning a wolfish smile. I jumped to my feet, retrieving the parasol, the spiky grass prickling my bare feet, my bare neck felt hot and I tucked my hair behind my ears. Mr O Brady was dressed in his tweed walking suit, his jacket flung over his arm and his top shirt buttons undone, the ridiculous deerstalker on his head. He watched me flapping about with some amusement. I sat back down on the picnic blanket, crumpling my stockings hastily into a ball and pulling on my slippers.

"Mind if I join you?" the journalist asked casually. "I've come over from North Uist and I'm done in."

Without waiting for my assent, he sat down beside me, took off his deerstalker and reached into his knapsack for a flagon of water. I could feel the heat radiating off him and caught a feral whiff of sweat. His dark curls were tamped down with sweat and I watched him take the cork stopper from his bottle and take several long gulps. His throat swallowed and water splashed down his chin wetting his shirt. My hands dangled awkwardly in my lap and I reached for the raspberries and stuffed a couple in my mouth. Their tart-sweet flavour exploded in my mouth.

He put down his canteen and picked up the *Rights of Woman* where it was lying in the basket.

"Ah, the formidable Miss Wollstonecraft. You know, I rather suspected that you might read a book of this nature." He looked at my hair and my hand rose self-consciously to my bare neck. I felt a glow spread in me. There it was again, that dratted need to impress him.

He opened the first page. "I haven't read this particular volume, but I am acquainted with some of her views. Did you know she went off to France, alone, to see the revolution for herself? And that she travelled unaccompanied around Sweden with her daughter? She was quite the adventuress."

"Did her husband not object?"

He cocked an eyebrow. "Miss Wollstonecraft was not married until the very end of her tragically short life. She had several passionate affairs though, and even a daughter by one of them, but she lived mostly alone." He flashed me a smile, his lips were wet. I looked away.

"She did get married eventually," the Irishman said, frowning at the pamphlet in his hands. "I suppose you could say it was marriage that finished her off, for a year after she was married she died in childbirth."

He looked up at me. "Perhaps my frankness has shocked you, Your Ladyship, and I if so then I apologise."

"I can tell you that I am not in the least bit shocked, Mr O'Brady. Quite the opposite. I am in admiration."

He laughed and stretched out his legs and crossed his feet. He handed the pamphlet back to me. His hands were weathered and brown and they brushed mine. He leaned back on his elbows on the rug.

"Now, tell me, what do you think of Miss Wollstonecraft's principles on education?"

I looked at his easy smile, the way he posed the question merely as a theory for us to discuss. He knew nothing of smouldering books, the long, clammy, white fingers of Dr Fortnum, or the asylum.

"Principles are a fine thing, Mr O'Brady," I said, picking a sea pink and flicking its head off across the rug. "But they can sometimes be rather difficult to keep hold of in the face of reality."

He suddenly sat up, looking at me intently, his smile gone. "Principles are sometimes the only thing we have left to hold to."

I felt suddenly exposed sitting so close to him like this. Beneath his unbuttoned shirt, I caught sight of curls of dark hair on his chest, and I was aware of my naked thighs, free of their stockings, sticking together in the heat beneath my dress. I stood up and stepped off the rug away from him, the grass cool on my feet. There were grass seeds clinging to my dress and I busied myself with brushing them off, then turned to look at the view. The sky was clouding over now and a light breeze had picked up. Across the sea, clouds were banking on the hills, casting them into shadow.

"It is a magnificent view," I said to fill the silence, glancing at Mr O'Brady.

He was shading his eyes to look up at me, then he looked out towards the sea too. "I think landscape is overrated personally," he replied. "A hill is always a hill, no matter where you go. I passed a group of tourists just a little while ago "oooing and ahhing" over the blue sky and clouds. They had come all the way from Oxfordshire believe it or not, just to admire the very same sky they live under all year round."

I gave an over-loud laugh, a sort of honk. "That sounds rather facetious to me, Mr O'Brady," I said, in relief at being once more on safe ground. "A change of scene does people the world of good you know, that's why people come – to experience a change from their everyday lives."

He stood up quickly beside my then, only two feet away. His face had utterly changed, gone was the easy smile, the cocked eyebrow. The cloud had cast his face into shadow, narrowing it and making his features sharper. "With respect, what do you know about everyday lives, Your Ladyship? From the comfort of your castle?"

"It is not my castle."

"And yet you live there."

"I have only been here for a few days and I can assure you it is far from comfortable. What business is it of yours anyway?"

Mr O'Brady stepped closer and I felt something like fear run through me, only hotter. "It is of the most pressing and urgent business, Your Ladyship. Lives are dependent on the decisions that are made there."

I felt a fleck of rain on my face, or was it his spittle? I stepped backwards, away from him, my heel struck a piece of buried wall behind me. "I can assure you that I am the very last person who has any bearing on those decisions. It is nothing to do with me."

"And yet as a patron of the Relief Board you voted for emigration."

"To help the poor."

"Believe me, that will not help them at all."

The grassy ruined wall was behind me, and I would have to turn and clamber over it to move any further away. I lifted my chin and looked at him in the eye. "Look, Mr O'Brady, why don't you take this up with my husband?"

"I've tried to see him, but he'll not give me an audience." He let out a great sigh, his face suddenly downcast. He turned back to the picnic rug.

I felt drops of warm rain on my neck. I was suddenly overwhelmed by Mr O'Brady's disappointment and to be its author. Up on the road, I could see MacAllen was arriving with the trap. Before I had time to think, I heard myself say, "I'm holding a dinner in two days. Why not come and speak to him there? Tuesday, eight o'clock."

Mr O Brady turned and grinned at me, but I could see MacAllen already coming across the grass towards us. I looked about me at the rumpled blanket and the way my bonnet and my stockings were all flung amongst the picnic things. Mr O'Brady stowed the canteen back in his knapsack and replaced his deerstalker on his head. I turned and reached down for my bonnet, concealing the crumpled stockings in my hand. Mr O'Brady looked up and gave me a complicit smile, but I fastened my bonnet and hurried up towards the road, avoiding the enquiring eye of MacAllen.

"I'll see you on Tuesday then. At eight o'clock," Mr O'Brady called, raising his arm in farewell.

What had I done? And yet my heart was beating very fast and I watched the journalist until he had disappeared out of sight.

By the time we reached the castle, it was raining hard and I went to my room to change. I put Miss Wollstonecraft's pamphlet beneath the mattress. I felt flushed from too much sun and my body was shivering from the cold rain. I stripped off my outer dress and went to the bed and lay face down in my petticoat. I felt enervated, there was a hum in my head. I pressed my mouth to the pillow, feeling my own hot breath on my face. I breathed in through my nose and out through my mouth just as Dr Fortnum had once instructed. I banished Dr Fortnum from my mind. Instead I imagined that I was in Norfolk in the meadow down by the river with Mr O'Brady. My stockings were crumpled beside me and my hair was loose around my shoulders. He was reaching across the rug, feeding me raspberries, popping the soft red fruit into my mouth so that the juice ran down his fingers. I felt a strange prickling in my breasts and a dull ache in my belly thinking about it. I saw him reaching, not for the fruit, but for me instead, kissing me hard with his hot mouth, pulling me towards him. Now his warm, juice stained fingers were inside my dress, my petticoat, running up the inside of my bare thigh, tugging at the edge of my drawers.

Lying on the bed I put my hand there. My fingers found a pulse beating in a small fleshy cleft, hot and ripe. I felt a growing sensation, like an oncoming sneeze, and then a deep shudder went through me and I groaned into the pillow, falling into a deep sleep.

Chapter Nineteen

Sollas

It had been four days since Mr O'Brady had left for Skye and we all tried to get on with life as best we could until he returned. The fine spell continued, and as the weather got hotter, our croft became suffocating, for we still needed the fire for cooking. There was a restlessness in me too, like the ceaseless incoming and outgoing of the tide, and I could not concentrate on my chores. I over-churned the butter so that it was curdled and picked dandelions instead of sorrel for the soup. Faith and hope, faith and hope. From waking 'til sleep the words were on my lips and I took up my own strange rituals and looked everywhere for signs. At daybreak, I would wake with a damp sweat on my forehead and go down to the sea to stand on the shoreline and skim pebbles into the water. Three circles in a row meant he was coming in three days, four circles for four. I would leave gift offerings on the tideline, a rare flower, a pebble as round as the pearl had been. I would scan the water for a splash or the sign of a fin, but nothing except the guillemots and terns answered me. I was not even sure any longer what it was I hoped for, only a return, a return of Mr O'Brady and his knowledge.

I shunned the company of the other children, and of Cormac, who called for me daily. The knowledge that Mr O'Brady had shared with me had opened a gulf as wide as the Thames with no bridge between us. I drew great arched bridges in the wet sand with my finger, and tried to count to one million, losing myself before I had reached the first thousand. Mammy watched for Mr O'Brady's return too, I saw. She choose to work in the rigs nearest the road and her movement was like a wave, bend, dig, look, bend, dig, look, her dark brown hair tied back from her face in a kerchief. She took to going on her own long evening walks, up to the headland, out across the moor and she burned the bannocks more often than usual. Every evening I sat at the table and recorded the events of the day, just as Mr O'Brady had told me to do, in English. There was not much to report, a new calf, the tatty harvest.

Worry nibbled me about the fact that I had told MacInnes of Mr O'Brady and his plan, and about what MacInnes had said. Three weeks, three weeks until we were out. It was two weeks now, but I didn't tell anyone about it. I wrote it in my journal though, in English, away from Mammy and Da's eyes.

Every morning from first light, the hammering and breaking of stone could be heard from over the moor as the men worked on the committee road. It frayed my nerves, the ring of metal, the cracking and splintering of rock.

"For pity's sake," Mammy exclaimed at breakfast one morning, "why should we still build that damn road when we don't even need the meal this year?"

Da looked up from his cup of tea, startled to hear her cussing, but she went on, "we need a road going nowhere across the moor even less than we needed a tower in the middle of a marsh." She was talking about Scolpaig tower out on the loch that Granddaddy had built in the famine of '36.

Da who had quietly endured our dark moods that week simply said, "better to finish what you started." And pulling on his cap he left the croft.

At lunchtime, Mammy had me take him some food. I set out, glad of the long walk over the moor, thinking of how I had walked this way only a few days before with Mr O'Brady. "Thomas," I whispered to myself, feeling a delicious thrill at the daring of it. My toes hurt in my shoes, my feet were growing and I could see a tiny hole where my nail was rubbing through. Up ahead was a cloud of white dust hanging in the air where the men were building the road and I could hear the clang and chime of their tools. It was started two years before, in The Hunger. The factor had decided that a road should be built across the moor, though it started nowhere and led nowhere. Still, all the men had to help if they wanted meal for their families. Eight hours of work for one cup of meal for each person in the household, that was the rule set by the Famine Relief Board. It was Mr MacInnes who oversaw the work. Colin McCuish collapsed one afternoon with exhaustion and had to be carried home. He was as light as a feather, Da said, and I imagined him floating in the air like dust from the classroom. The men of Sollas told the story of how at the end of the day, Da went to collect Colin McCuish"s portion of meal for him, but MacInnes had refused to give it. Rules were rules, he'd said and Mr McCuish hadn't finished his eight hours. Da had stood firm, the men said. He had reminded MacInnes how his own family had helped the MacInnes in the famine of 1836, when their family had nothing to eat and his mother had been fainting from hunger. MacInnes had blushed to his roots then and handed over the meal without another word.

I sat with Da a while in the heather while he ate the bannocks I'd brought him, the sun beating down on us, the white stone glaring in the heat. As I headed home, my neck was prickling from the heat and when I reached the machair, I thought how nice it would be to lie in the tall, cool grass. I lay back watching the tall grasses swaying a little in the breeze. Here, the whole world was in miniature. A tiny spider was clinging to a stem, one leg outstretched and three ants toiled across a sorrel leaf, carrying the husk of a dead beetle. I thought of how Mr O'Brady had told me what he had seen in a place called the British Museum that they were building in London. It was a thing called amber he said, brought back from the East. It looked like a blob of honey, but it was hard, like a rock, and caught inside it was a winged insect trapped forever in flight.

Something caught my eye and I sat up to see. There in the grass amongst the sedge and saxifrage grew clover. There, as green as a jewel, was a four-leafed clover just like the one Mr O'Brady had told us about in his story. Its veined leaves trembled at my touch as I counted the leaves to make sure. Faith, hope, love and the fourth for luck. As I picked it by its stem the breeze shook the grass and I fancied it was Mr O'Brady speaking to me, whispering, "Faith and hope, faith and hope, Morag". I put the leaf carefully in my apron pocket and stood up out of the grass, my heart soaring in me like a lark.

Cormac was walking along the road towards the village, and he looked in surprise to see me suddenly appear from out of the machair.

"Morag," he said, "you look- well- you look grand."

He blushed and I saw that his hair had gone blond in the sun and there was a strip of sunburn over his freckled nose. I fell into step beside him and we walked in silence together. Besides the outlying rigs, two older boys, Murdo and Angus, were throwing pebbles at crows to keep them off the crops. They had both long stopped going to school, which I was glad of, as they would often snap your chalk, or tip you out of your chair, given half the chance. I glanced at Cormac beside me, wondering if we should go another way, but it was too late, they had seen us and Murdo hopped over the rigs and blocked our way, looking at us with his small hog eyes.

"Wanna play spit dare?" Murdo asked, throwing the last of his stones away and turning to this new sport instead.

I glanced at Cormac, it wasn't really an invitation. He was looking down at his feet, chewing his lip.

"Or are you chicken?" Angus asked from beside him, poking Cormac sharply. "Playing with wee girls." He nodded in my direction.

I scowled at them both. "I'm not a wee girl and I'm not a chicken either."

Cormac glared at me to be quiet, but my blood was up.

"I'll play your stupid game," I said crossly, scowling at Cormac too.

Angus dropped Cormac's shirt and he and Murdo conferred for a moment. Murdo turned and grinned slyly. "You have to take something from the haunted crofts." They both spat on the ground in front of us to issue the challenge.

I looked at Cormac. That was the name we gave to the crofts that had been abandoned last year, near Malacleit. They were next to Dunfel bog and we were forbidden to go there.

"That's too far," I said.

"That's too far," Murdo mimicked, "It's not too far y" wee softie."

Cormac gave a great weary sigh and spat on the ground to accept the dare. Now it was sealed there was no going back.

"We'll be following ya to check ya do it" Angus called behind us. "You know the rules."

The sun blazed down on us as we walked up to the road and trudged out of the village towards Malacleit, neither of us talking, until the crofts came into sight. Blackhouses, the English called them, and I could see why, their windows were dark and dusty and the thatch was rotting through. We had been told many a time not to go inside them in case a roof collapsed, and looking up at the first one, I saw a large crow pull at some of the loose thatch and flap away with it in its beak.

"I hate these crofts," I said suddenly to Cormac.

He had his head down and his hands in his pockets ahead of me. He stopped to look at me in exasperation. "Why do you hate them? They're only old crofts."

"No, they"re not, they were somebody's homes. Eilidh Morrison was my best friend and her Ma had the best singing voice on the whole island, and all those others, our people gone, gone – forever."

"Auch, you *are* a wee girl after all," Cormac said crossly, "crying over some crofts." He was mad at me for accepting the dare, I could see, and with reason, we both knew the rule.

He went to the first croft and pushed open the door, it was loose on its hinges and fell half off, then he went inside. I stood at the threshold, my eyes squinting from the sudden change from light to dark.

"Cormac?" I couldn't see anything. An old-smoke smell crept out. "Cormac?" My voice was rising shrilly.

"There's nothing here to take," his voice came back. "It's empty."

We went to the next croft, and then the next, but they were all the same, nothing had been left, except the bare stone walls and the packed floor. In one croft, the thatch had been ripped half-off by the wind and the rafters were like the ribs of a dead sheep.

"What about up there?" I asked. Further on, away from the road, was a croft that stood on its own. Unlike the others, it had its back to the sea and faced the moor instead.

"That's where old Mr MacAulay lives," Cormac said.

"I don't know an old Mr MacAulay." I frowned

"Auch, you do. He's from Clachan, but moved out here after his wife and son ran off to Glasgow and left him."

"That wasn't MacAulay, that was MacKenzie, and his wife ran off to Harris, not to Glasgow."

He shrugged. "Well, anyhow, he lives there now, ashamed to show his face, my Da said, after his wife and boy left."

"Are you sure?" I asked, looking at the thatch, it had grass growing upon it, and there was no smoke rising. We walked up behind the croft, and my hands began to tingle. Coming round the side of it, I saw that there was no peat stack by the wall, no tools, or signs of life, and all across the ground was scattered fish bones, and broken eggshells of different colours.

"I think we should go back." I grabbed his arm, but he shook me off.

We went up to the door and stopped in front of it. It was old and splintered, and someone had nailed a clumsy wreath of brown dead grasses and feathers to it, and beneath the wreath something dried and brown was smeared. I looked up at the small dark window beside the door, covered in cobwebs.

"Cormac, don't."

But Cormac put his hand on the latch and opened the door an inch, and the stench hit us, that vile, animal smell that I had smelled before, came barrelling out of the dark. We gagged and Cormac shut the door quickly and turned to retch, his hands upon his knees. I pressed my sleeve against my mouth, and glancing up at the window, I caught for the briefest of moments, something pale staring back at me.

"C'mon," I said, my feet tripping over the debris, grabbing Cormac by the arm. He caught my panic, and we both turned and ran, back to the other crofts, down the road. Cormac slowed then to a walk, but I kept running, my feet would not stop.

"Morag? Morag?" Cormac called to me, his breathless voice was like the caw of a crow behind me.

As the first thatch of Sollas appeared, I stumbled to a stop. My hair beneath my kerchief was soaked through, and sweat ran down my temples. I looked at Cormac's red face, coming along behind me, his chest heaving for air.

Up ahead on the road came Murdo and Angus, grinning at us.

"We saw you running, you couple of softies," Angus said.

"And empty-handed too," Murdo said, "which means one of you has to fight us."

Cormac turned to them, unable to speak. He opened his hand and showed them. It was an egg-shell that he must have scooped off the ground. Their faces fell in disappointment.

"That was lucky for you," Murdo muttered. They turned away back to the village.

Luck. I put my hand in my pocket and pulled out the four-leaf clover, it was a little squashed, but still had all its leaves.

"Look," I said to Cormac. "I found this in the grass, just like the one Mr O'Brady told us about in the story. Four leaves for luck." I held it on my open palm and it quivered a little under his hot breath as he admired it. I put it back in my pocket, faith, hope, trust, and luck, it had protected us from whatever was inside that croft.

"Da said I could be in the shinty this year now I'm fourteen," Cormac said as we walked towards home. "He's gonna make me a shinty stick soon."

We had a shinty competition every year at Whit, all the young men from Sollas playing against the other villages on North Uist.

"Will you come and watch me?"

I dragged my thoughts away from the abandoned croft and thought instead of how the lasses would sit on the sandbanks, cheering for their sweethearts, as the men tossed the ball high over their heads, the hollow tap of the shinty sticks as they tackled one another. I started to laugh, but I saw how he glanced hopefully at me, how his cheeks had reddened at asking his question.

"Auch, I don't even think there will be a shinty competition this year, will there?"

"Yes, there will. Mr O'Brady has gone to see the Laird, hasn't he? So there will." He jutted out his chin and walked ahead.

From behind us, we heard hooves and turning around we saw a lad with a broad rim hat and a leather satchel trot up behind us on a pony. "Do you know Artair MacDhomhnaill?"

I shaded my eyes with my hand. "Aye, he's my Da."

He opened the satchel and handed me an envelope, with my Da's name on it. "This has come across from Skye on the steamer," he said passing it to me and my heart soared as I recognised the handwriting at once.

144

* * *

When Da and the other men came home from working on the road, their hair and faces white from stone dust, they found a fair crowd waiting outside our croft to hear the contents of the letter. Mammy was at the very front. Da took the envelope and covered it in white fingerprints as he fumbled to open it.

"You read it, Morag," he said quietly, for his reading wasn't very good.

I looked at the hopeful faces before me. Mr Morrison, Mrs MacIver, Old Ma MacNeill, and the rest of the village. My hand touched the clover in my pocket as I lifted my voice to read.

"Greetings, Artair, Ceit and Morag, and the rest of Sollas also-

"I thought I would write to you with the most promising news: I have secured an audience with Laird MacDonald on Tuesday evening of this week where I will present both the petition and your plan of improvements at a dinner. I have had the good fortune to make the acquaintance of Her Ladyship Maria MacDonald, and I believe she is a person of sympathetic nature. I feel hopeful that she will support your cause and add her voice in persuading the Laird about these matters. I will of course write and keep you apprised and hope to return to you soon."

With warm regards,
Thomas O'Brady."

Chapter Twenty

Armadale Castle, Skye

At the top of the main staircase, I paused. There was a man's voice, followed by sudden male laughter, echoing in the entrance hall below. My stomach knotted, was that him? I caught my dim reflection in the windowpane at the top of the stairs. I was wearing an evening dress made of MacDonald tartan that had belonged to Godfrey's mother. It was very frumpy, I thought, looking at my image stretched in the bowed glass. What would he think? Maigdh at least had pinned up my hair so that I was without a bonnet at last. I peered down the staircase. I had not told Godfrey yet about the extra guest for dinner. Since the day of the picnic he had been out on the estate all day. Hopefully Mr O'Brady would just blend in.

"There you are." Godfrey was at the bottom of the staircase, standing with three other gentlemen. None of them him. I carefully came down the stairs under their gaze. The marble floor had been polished so that it shone brightly in the lamplight. "May I present Lady Maria MacDonald, my wife." Godfrey was wearing a high collared dinner suit that was slightly too large for him, and his cheeks were flushed and his grin loose, as though he had been drinking.

I looked at the three men in front of me and he turned to them. "This is Colonel Crawford, the factor on the estate in North Uist and this is Mr Shaw, the sheriff-substitute from Lochmaddy."

The third man, I saw, was Baligall who Godfrey did not bother to introduce.

I made to curtsey, but the colonel grasped my arm. "No, no, you don't curtsey to us," the colonel said, taking my elbow. He was a tall man with a veined red nose and pale, blond hair brushed thinly over his head. He spoke with a neatly trimmed English accent. "Well perhaps to me, although I rather imagine

146

house trumps rank, what?" He gave a hoot of laughter and turned to Godfrey.

"The colonel and I were at Eton together," Godfrey said by way of explanation.

"I've known Godfrey a long time," the colonel said. He put a proprietorial hand on my husband's shoulder.

I looked at the other two gentlemen. Baligall looked as though he had scrubbed his neck with a brush, it was so pink.

The sheriff, Shaw, frowned silently into his bushy beard. "It's a pleasure to make your acquaintance, Lady MacDonald," he said with a bow. He had a soft Scots accent. Baligall said nothing, but only jiggled his foot on the marble floor.

"And will the ladies be joining us soon?" I asked, looking at their small circle.

This provoked a sharp laugh from Crawford. "Ha! MacDonald, have you invited ladies, you devil?" He turned to Godfrey and punched him in the arm, Godfrey reddened and rubbed the spot where he had been hit, frowning at Crawford.

"These gentlemen do not have wives," he said to me.

"More's the pity, they might liven up the evening," the colonel replied. "Though women are a damn nuisance sometimes of course." He looked around at the other gentlemen for their agreement. "Do pardon my language, your Ladyship, present company excepted, I'm sure." He looked at me, and I saw that despite his bluster, his eyes were a strange frosted blue.

The colonel turned to the sheriff. "Shaw, didn't you have a wife once?"

"She died, Colonel, some eleven years ago."

"Ahh. Well, proves my point really." He was holding court now and turned to Baligall. "What about you Baligall, no lassie that takes your fancy?"

Baligall turned as pink as a radish and started up with a fit of coughing.

"Godfrey, is this everyone?" I whispered. I thought of the fundraising speech that I had been practising, not to mention the other thing.

"Well, yes. Lady Cavendish has sent her apologies, she is unwell and it turns out the Montagues and Stephensons are down in London until July."

The clock began to chime eight.

I turned hastily to him. "I must tell you Godfrey, I have invited-"

"Get this man some water," the colonel said, slapping the choking Baligall on the back. "Or better still, some more wine."

We entered the dining room where the ornate crystal chandeliers blazed and the cutlery and the glasses, laid out for a dinner for twelve, gleamed in the light. Over the mantelpiece hung the MacDonald coat of arms, the gloved fist. Through the tall windows the sky was a lilac dusk with the dark indigo sea visible beyond. The colonel ordered the party to gather at one end of the table. Godfrey at the head and the colonel placed himself at Godfrey's right hand. I took a seat beside the colonel facing the door. The door opened and I held my breath, but it was only Duncan. His collar had been stiffly starched and was tightly buttoned so that his face seemed to bulge over the top. He was followed by Maigdh carrying a great tureen of soup, her forehead in a sweat from the steam. I glanced at the clock, five past eight, where was he?

"Your grandfather was a Navy man, so I read in his obituary," the colonel said to me.

"Yes, he passed away last year." It was always a surprise how grief could appear out of nowhere and knock me sideways. I looked down into the soup that Maigdh had served, large chunks of potatoes bobbing about in thin cream.

"And left you with quite a fortune. Lucky old Godfrey, I didn't think he'd pull it off."

I looked at the door. Mr O'Brady wasn't coming, after all. "Sorry?"

"I've never been to Norfolk," the colonel was saying now. "Plenty of other places, mind you, like Egypt."

I had read a monograph about Egypt. Grandpapa and I had wanted to visit.

"And what was Egypt like?"

"Hot. Saw the pyramids though, carved my initials on a wall. My little mark on history." A bark of laughter, another slurp from his soup.

"Was that with the Army? That you went to Egypt?"

"What? Hm? No, the Army didn't suit me it turns out. I decided to come up and give Godfrey a hand."

I saw that Godfrey was speaking to the sheriff in a hushed tone. Was it about his brother? 'The situation is in hand,' Godfrey had said. And since the day of the picnic there had been no further sign of him.

"What's that you're saying, Shaw?" the colonel asked. "What are you muttering into his Lordship's ear?"

"Just some business about the estate, Sir."

"Ha! Well, you know my opinion, MacDonald. A strong arm and a clenched fist, that is what is needed. Nip it all in the bud."

I looked from Godfrey and the sheriff to the colonel.

"With respect, colonel, as an officer of the peace, I can't condone the use of violent force," the sheriff said.

The colonel set down his glass, looked at Godfrey, and turned his gaze on Shaw. "You've got to remember who you are dealing with. Violence is what they understand."

I thought of the knife, the *A* carved deeply into the trunk.

The sheriff's mouth was a frown within his beard and he shook his head. "There are other ways than violence," he said.

The colonel snorted and refilled his glass. "What is the total rent arrears on the estate now, Godfrey?"

Godfrey shook his head, stared gloomily into his wine. "Somewhere in the region of £3000 the trustees told me last month."

"Exactly. Hopeless situation. Something needs to be done."

"Well actually, Colonel," I said, seeing a sudden opportunity for my speech, "I am a patron for the Highland Relief Board and we are fundraising to assist the poor. Perhaps I might ask you gentlemen for a donation."

The three men stared at me and the carriage clock on the mantelpiece quickly chimed quarter past. It had come out a wrong, a little too direct. I looked at Godfrey, he was frowning at me, not frowning, glowering. His lips were a narrow line and there was a tic in his cheek. "Maria, this is wholly unacceptable."

"Fundraising for the poor?" The colonel stared at me. "Fundraising for yourselves would be a better idea." He gave a cold laugh.

149

"Colonel, I really must tell you that the needs of the poor are-"

"Maria!" Godfrey's voice was whip-like and I flinched. The door opened, but it was only Duncan, once again. Thank goodness, it really would be the last straw now if-

"There is a gentleman in the hall asking for Her Ladyship," Duncan announced. He looked at me sourly. "An Irish gentleman."

The men around the table looked at me. My stomach lurched. Could this evening get any worse?

"And," announced Duncan, "He wants to discuss the business of the estate with Your Lordship."

Godfrey stood up. "Maria, what is the meaning of this?"

I tilted my chin. "I invited Mr O'Brady here as a guest to dinner. As a guest."

The colonel got to his feet, scraping back his chair. "We'll see him off. Shaw, you're the sheriff, you lead the way."

Shaw got to his feet and I did too, so that only Baligall was left sitting at the table with his spoon still in his hand.

I shall speak to Mr O'Brady myself," I said. "I invited him here after all."

"No." Godfrey put a hand on my sleeve, his face was pale now. "Who knows what he wants? Duncan, was he armed? Raise the groundsmen and fetch the dog from the stables."

"For goodness sake, Godfrey," I said, shaking off his hand. "Mr O'Brady was invited for dinner, that's all."

I pushed past Godfrey into the hall. There he was. My stomach did a somersault. He was standing in front of the large glass hall window, his deerstalker under his arm, his wild hair tamed by some hair-oil.

"Your Ladyship." Mr O'Brady gave me a bow and an easy smile as though we were good friends. I stepped towards him, my heart dancing in my chest.

"What is it you want here?" Godfrey said, coming out into the hall behind me. The colonel and the sheriff were with him.

Mr O'Brady looked at Godfrey over my shoulder and I noticed him stiffen. "Lord MacDonald," he said, but he did not bow. I should congratulate you on your remarkable fortune on inheriting the estate."

"This is trespass," the colonel said, his voice raised. "Sherriff arrest this man, he is a known troublemaker, he's been stirring up the tenants. Arrest him for trespass and disturbance of the peace."

O'Brady smiled and opened his palms. "This is not trespass, sheriff, and I certainly do not intend to disturb the peace. I have an invitation to dinner from Her Ladyship." He smiled at me again.

"I invited you here for dinner," I said, quickly glancing at Godfrey behind me. "Nothing else."

Mr O'Brady's smile faded and I felt a shrinking inside.

"I simply wish to present a petition to your Lordship, on behalf of your tenants." He reached for his knapsack and began to untie it.

"Stop him," the colonel urged. "He may have a knife or a pistol."

Mr O'Brady gave him an injured look and took out a parchment and unfolded it. He held it out to Godfrey. "The tenants wish to present a plan of land improvements to better feed themselves and to make a profit to pay the rent. It is drawn up by one Artair MacDomhnaill and there is a map and notes to accompany it."

The colonel stepped forward and snatched the parchment from Mr O'Brady's hands. "Now, look here," he said, "these tenants owe £3000 to Lord MacDonald. It's absurd to suggest they should get any land, they're not bloody farmers, they are kelp workers and now the kelp-work has gone."

"And I would remind you that it is his Lordship who now owns this estate, not you." O'Brady growled.

Godfrey stood in the hall, his hands dangling by his side, looking from the sheriff, to the colonel, and back to Mr O'Brady.

"For decency's sake, you are now these people's clan chief, their Laird," Mr O'Brady said to him. "They look to you for protection. Act in good conscience. Your Ladyship, you agree with me, do you not?"

I was standing between Mr O'Brady and Godfrey. I looked over my shoulder at Godfrey standing behind me, then turned to Mr O'Brady standing in front of the window.

"Well, I certainly-"

But whatever I was going to say was swallowed up as something was lobbed through the window behind the Irishman. The glass shattered over us and Mr O'Brady sprung forwards and covered me with his arm, so that my face was pressed for a moment into his armpit. Glass splintered and skittered around us across the marble floor. Then everything was still and Mr O'Brady released me. Standing up straight, I was reminded of one of Godfrey's photographic plates. Godfrey, the colonel, and the sheriff were stood in a frozen pose, beyond the reach of the broken window. I looked at Mr O'Brady. He had a cut on the side of his face and blood trickled thickly from it. There was a fine diamond-like sprinkle caught in his curly hair. By his feet lay a rock, the size of a fist.

There was sudden commotion. Godfrey was yelling for Duncan, the colonel was shouting at the sheriff, the sheriff was laying his hand upon O'Brady, and I was led away upstairs by Maigdh, glass fragments scattering in my wake. Upstairs to my room, where I was helped out of all my clothes and my hair was washed clean with jugs of water. A low ache had spread from my back to my stomach and down my thighs and as my drawers were heaped upon the crumpled tartan dress I saw that they were stained with blood. I sat at the dressing table in my nightdress and saw that my hands were trembling. There was a tiny glass cut on my forehead, already crusted over. I thought of the rock, like a fist, lying on the marble floor.

What had happened to Mr O'Brady? I thought of his bloodied face and the glass caught in the curls of his hair. I had been too slow to speak, but even now I wondered what I had been going to say. I blew out the lamp, climbed into bed and stared up into the dark. There were footsteps in the hall and the bedroom door opened. Godfrey appeared with a lamp in his hand. His face, underlit, was hollow and he had a newspaper under his arm.

"My God, Maria. Are you alright?" He sat on the bed beside me and placed a tentative hand on my stomach.

"Where is Mr O'Brady?"

"Under arrest. He has been taken to Broadford for questioning."

"Arrest? What for?"

"Criminal damage, of course."

152

"Surely you don't think he smashed the window, do you?" I put my hand on his arm. "It was Alexander, I'm sure of it."

Godfrey did something strange then, he laughed. Then he shook his head. As though his brother was the most unlikely suspect in the world. He looked at the newspaper in his hand. "Mr O'Brady has been running a campaign against me in his newspaper since I inherited this place. It may well be that my brother put him up to it of course. In any case, the Irishman has been stopped now. Here, this is his latest article."

He handed me the paper and by the light of the lamp he was holding I saw it was the *Inverness Courier* dated the previous day. Beneath a piece on cattle prices I read.

A Time to Decide
From your correspondent on Skye
Only yesterday, I came across the newly married Lady MacDonald cheerfully picnicking on a feast of raspberries beside Knock Castle. She was only two miles from where the desperate inhabitants of her estate are still struggling with the effects of starvation and deprivation thanks to the pitiful and pernicious land policy of her husband.

On enquiring if she had observed the suffering of her tenants, she said that she had not– too many picnics one imagines! This same lady was recently observed in Glasgow by yours truly to vote for a policy of forced emigration. Let us hope that it is not too late for a pricking of conscience. Can this lady act for the good of the people and take a stand against the tyranny of these shameful landowners?

There was a hot tumble in my stomach at the thought of the picnic rug and the raspberries, then a cold, hard stab at reading Mr O'Brady's words. I stared up at Godfrey sitting beside me on the bed. His face was grim. My mouth opened and closed like a fish hooked out of the sea.

"You met with this journalist for a picnic? Alone?"

"No. Godfrey, really, he just turned up."

"But you had already met with him in Glasgow?"

"I didn't meet him, he happened to be at the Famine Relief meeting, I had no idea-"

"You're right, you have no idea what's going on here, Maria, no idea at all." He stood up and went to the dressing table to light the lamp there. Its flare illuminated my clothes that lay in a heap beside it.

I looked down at the newspaper again, the words were like a hard slap on the cheek. *Too many picnics?* Really! I glanced up at Godfrey and saw he was bending and examining something. I saw in embarrassment that it was my blood-stained drawers. He stood up and looked at me in concern.

"Should I call a physician?" he asked.

"It is only my monthly courses, as normal."

He stared at me. "You are not with child then?"

There was a crestfallen look on his face and I felt a small wave of sympathy at how his hopes had been dashed.

"No, I was never-"

He sank onto the bed next to me holding the lamp. I saw there was despair on his face. "And yet, you sought to make me believe that-"

I tilted my chin. "I never misled you. You believed it yourself."

"But you locked your door every night. Why would you do that, if not?"

I looked at my hands. "I want the books," I said quietly.

"What do you mean?"

"Until I get the books there will be no child."

He scoffed and held the lamp closer to me. His face was now full of scorn. "Listen to yourself, Maria. The books? The books! Don't you see how much we need a child?" His voice was desperate but instead of fatherly tenderness, his face was pinched with anxiety. "It turns out a child must be born before your inheritance money can be touched."

His voice came out in a strangled sort of tone. So, that was it. I remembered his vigorous nightly efforts. The lamp swayed dangerously in his hand and its wick guttered and dipped and gave a smoky blaze, heat blasting through the glass. He stood up.

"No matter. It's too late."

"What's too late? Where are you going?" I asked.

He went to the door. "To London. I have arranged for you to stay at the colonel's house on North Uist whilst I am away. You will take the ferry to Lochmaddy and stay there until my return. You will be safe there."

"Safe from who?"

But he did not answer.

"Safe from who, Godfrey?"

But he had gone and I heard the key turn in the lock.

Chapter Twenty-one

Sollas

Three days before Whit the hot weather broke and a squall blew up over the ocean bringing in a wall of rain. It pounded the thatch until it found its way in then it ran down the beams, dripped onto the earth floor and the beds and made the fire sizzle and hiss. All around us the rain made a sort of awful music, hitting the metal pail, the chamber pot, the wooden bucket with different speeds and discordant notes. Our croft was hot and dark and suddenly it seemed too small, confined as we were like animals, pacing back and forth. Since we had received Mr O'Brady's letter our hopes had soared, but now packed in together, they mouldered.

Da stood in the open doorway, it was late afternoon, but it was as dark as evening and he watched as the road became a running river of mud with straw and debris floating past in slow eddies. He had packed sacks with sand and had laid them at the threshold, but still the water seeped in with long dark fingers. "Should have replaced the thatch when we had the fine weather," he said, sucking the air between his teeth and glancing up at the roof.

Mammy was lifting the herring barrel onto the table out of the wet. "Summer rain. It'll pass soon."

It was Wednesday now, a day after Mr O'Brady said he was having his meeting with Laird MacDonald and he had not returned. It did not look likely that he would in this weather either. My fingers went to the clover in my pocket, faith, love, hope, luck. He would surely be back within a day or two.

From the open doorway, we heard the clatter of hooves on the road and I jumped up to see. A rider was coming down through the village on a pony, throwing up water and muck as he passed. His hat was pulled down low over his eyes, his oilskin jacket wet through, but I could tell by the thin, small look of him that it was not Mr O'Brady.

"Halo," Da called to the rider. "Can we offer you shelter?"

The rider pulled up his pony and wiped the rain from his soaking face, squinting as more water dripped from the brim of his hat. I could see it was the lad who had brought letter from the steamer.

"You're Ian's lad from Lochmaddy, aren't you?" Da said, peering at him.

The boy nodded. "I'm Niall. I'm on an errand to the colonel's house to fetch him his things." He glanced up the road. "I mustn't be late."

Mammy came to the door too. "Well, step inside until the worst of this rain has passed at least," she said.

Da went to put the pony in the byre, and the lad sat on the bench at the table and dried his hair and his face on a piece of sacking. Mammy made him some tea and cut him a thick slice of brachan and we sat listening to the dripping getting faster until Da came back.

"I haven't seen your father, Ian, for a long while," Da said, taking a seat by the fire. "Is he well?"

"Aye," said the lad, then added with pride. "He got promoted to harbour master. There's a new steamer now, so business is good, and we're going to have a tall ship call into the harbour soon."

"And what brings you out here?" Mammy asked, poking the fire and sitting back in her chair.

The lad swallowed his bread. "There was word from the colonel that he needed things fetching over to the mainland. A spare pair of boots, three best shirts and his regiment trousers."

Mammy narrowed her eyes. "On the mainland is he? And staying over there a-wee while?"

The boy leaned forward. "He's gone to Inverness they say, to see the Justice of the Peace. On account of the Irishman."

We looked at one another and back at the lad. A rushing feeling, like pins and needles came into my face.

"Do you mean, Mr O'Brady?" I whispered, his name getting stuck in my throat.

The lad shrugged. "I don't know his name. Only that he caused a disturbance at the castle and got himself arrested." He drank his tea in a hot slurp.

I felt my face turn hot, then cold again.

"Arrested?" Mammy stood up, her hand to her mouth. "Arrested for what?"

"Criminal damage, that's what I heard," the lad said. "He's been taken to Inverness castle, to go before the justice there."

"And you're sure about this, are you?" Da asked, I could see the tendons standing up in the back of his hands as he gripped his chair. "You're sure that it was an Irishman who got arrested?"

The lad nodded earnestly, looked at my Da. "Aye, because when my Ma heard about it she said, "never trust an Irishman." They'll likely serve him with transportation seeing how it was the Laird's property that he damaged - that's what my Ma said."

Mammy made a noise like steam escaping from the kettle and dropped to her chair, her hand still to her mouth, and I held tightly to the back of Da's chair, feeling like I was standing on a bank of shifting sand.

"It could be a different Irishman," I blurted out, "It can't be Mr O'Brady, it can't."

Across from me, Mammy was staring into the fire as though she could see something in the smouldering flames. She was nodding slowly, her eyes flicking back and forth. The rain's drumming into the buckets and pails starting to slow. She looked up at the boy suddenly.

"A tall ship?" she asked. "You said a tall ship is coming soon to the harbour at Lochmaddy?"

"Oh, aye. On its way to America. It'll be the first that's ever stopped here on North Uist. We're expecting it soon."

I remembered Mr O'Brady's story, the one about his great-grandmother being taken away. He had been sitting in the very same spot where the harbourmaster's lad was sitting now when he told it.

The lad stood up and set his cup on the table. "Well, looks like the rain has eased," he said, watching how the drips in the pails and pans had slowed. "I'll thank you and take my leave."

We went to the door and watched Da walk out to the byre with the lad to fetch his pony. I saw that the rain had cleared as quickly as it had come in. Steam was beginning to rise from the thatch of each croft, the river of mud in the road was slowing to a thick slurry. When Da came back he closed the door and stood looking at us.

"We ought to tell folk," he said to Mammy. "People need to know."

Mammy lifted her chin and folded her arms. "We've not been served notice yet, Artair. The sheriff promised notice would be given and we haven't had it."

"Ceit," Da said. He gripped her by her shoulders. "What can be done? Mr O'Brady is in the gaol in Inverness castle and the Justice of the Peace there is a known friend of the colonel's."

Mammy stood very stiffly like a timber plank.

"We haven't had notice," she said again, staring at him.

"A ship bound for America is on its way," Da said, his voice rose suddenly. He stared at Mammy. "Auch!" The sound he made was violent, as though he'd hit his finger with a hammer and it made me jump. He dropped Mammy's shoulders and turned away, then opening the door, he picked up a sandbag and hefted it out into the road where it landed with a splash, then he went out after it, slamming the door behind him.

I lay on my bed, my face turned to the wall. I felt like a crab shell that had been scooped empty by gulls. Pulling out the clover from my pocket, I lay looking at it, it was so thin and dry now, and it had browned at the edges. Slowly I pulled off each leaf, faith, hope, love and luck and scattered them onto the floor.

Chapter Twenty-two

The Little Minch

Just after dawn the colonel loaded me into a buggy, bound for the postal steamer to North Uist. My carpet bag was thrown in beside me. Then he climbed into the buggy and sat opposite me with a flintlock pistol on his knee.

"Is that your Army service gun?" I asked. With its long wooden barrel and brass butt cap it was very like Grandpapa's Navy Service pistol.

But he said nothing. He kept his hand on the pistol and his eye on the road, for all that he could see there. Mist had drawn in overnight and I could not even see as far as the sea. I looked at the flintlock. I had had the task of cleaning it. Powder, ball, patch and primer, Grandpapa had made a song to the tune of *Ring-a-Roses*. The words came back to me. *Load the powder in the gun /Wrap the ball up in its patch / Prime the flash pan then you can/ pull the trigger, bang!* There was a line missing somewhere, I thought, but what was it?

The buggy bumped along the rutted road and my thoughts lurched along too. "It's too late," Godfrey had said in that strangled voice. What was too late? And what had driven his sudden flight back to London in the middle of the night? And where was Mr O Brady? My stomach did its double somersault, first hot then cold. His words still stung, *too many picnics!* The window, still broken, had drawn the cold mist into the hall this morning. I could not imagine that Mr O'Brady would resort to violence and surely the sherriff would see that too. And anyway, I thought, glancing at the pistol on the colonel's knee, the threat was still out there. It was Alexander, I knew it. Godfrey had laughed when I suggested his brother had smashed the window, but I knew what I had seen. The man with the broad shoulders and the velvet coat was Alexander and he'd been following us from London. *You'll pay for it,* the telegram had said. And now I knew he had a knife. Godfrey said himself that he was prone to outbursts and violence. "Violence is what they understand," the colonel had said. I eyed the pistol on the colonel's knee. Something nagged me though. It was Duncan's comment about the Hogmanay Ball. He was adamant it was not Alexander who had nearly burned the castle down. "Why would Alexander do something like that?" The butler had seemed genuinely puzzled. "A real charmer," Fanny had said when she had met him at the fundraising ball.

We came to a sudden stop as we reached the harbour at Uig. The rain had properly set in and a small crowd of people huddled on the dock waiting for the postal bags to be loaded onto the steamer before they could board.

"Wait here," the colonel said.

Rain hammered against the carriage window as I watched the colonel push through the crowd and go up the gangplank.

Two men were slowly carrying a heavy-looking crate between them towards the steamer. As they negotiated it towards the gangplank another man pushed past them, causing the rear man to stumble and drop his end of the crate. He did not even stop, this fellow, to apologize, but pushed his way roughly through the crowd, as though in a hurry. He wheeled around, looking about him. I froze. The man in the green velvet coat. I darted back away from the window, but not in time. The carriage door was wrenched open.

"Where is he?"

His broad shoulders filled the doorway and his velvet coat was sodden. It was not Alexander. His accent was coarse. And when he lifted off his hat to lean into the carriage, I saw that this man was older, perhaps nearly forty. He had dark hair that was receding and an unshaven face with a nose that looked as though it had been broken at least once before.

"Where is he? Your husband?"

I stared at him and when I did not speak, he opened his coat and pulled out a knife. It was such a natural, fluid movement that I had no doubt that he would use it.

"He's gone to London. He went this morning."

The man cursed. He thrust the knife towards me and the mouldy odour of his coat rose off him like a wet dog. "Tell him:

161

two weeks until Mr Brentwood collects." He had a deep cut above his lip that made his sneer more dreadful. I looked at the knife. There was something crusted on the blade. He glanced over his shoulder then opened his coat to stow the knife. His waistcoat was missing two buttons and I caught the glimpse of a gold pocket watch chain. Then he put his hat back on and slammed the door leaving my heart thudding in my chest. Less than a minute later it was opened again.

"Come on," said the colonel. "Time to go."

The colonel loaded me onto the postal steamer, but he did not board himself. He had business in Inverness, he told my curtly, and would return within a week. Then the anchor was lifted and the harbour wall began to vanish in the rain. "The weather is too foul to stand on deck," the crewman told me and though I protested, strongly, I was forced below where I clung to the handrail at the bottom of the stairwell and refused to move. It is a question of being close to a stairway, Grandpapa had said, on not drowning in the event of a wreck. He had been blown up twice during the war. Panic at being shut in rose in me like bile. I could feel a scream expanding in my throat. Sweat pricked my forehead and I felt my whole body turn clammy under my clothes as the steamer groaned and toiled across the Little Minch. The pitch and yaw of the boat and the smell and throb of the hot engine turned my stomach inside out as bags and baskets slid one way and then the other across the rusted steamer floor. I shut my eyes and tried to collect my thoughts, but each heave and sway sent them rolling into one another. There was only one point that I could hold onto. The man with the knife had not been Alexander. I clung to it as the steamer churned its way across the rolling sea.

Chapter Twenty-three

Sollas

We were woken by a dreadful hammering at the door. So sudden and violent that we all jumped out of bed in fright and stood trembling before it. Light from a flaming torch was flickering through the small window and again came the pounding on the door. We looked at one another, Da standing uncertainly with his hand on the latch.

"Artair! Artair!"

Da opened the door and Mr MacIver, Cormac's Da, was standing there, a flaming torch in his hand. "It's Seamus MacRae. He's been attacked."

Da pulled on his trousers, and we ran out into the road, where we saw, by the light of his torch, Seamus sitting with his back against the wall of his croft, his wife, Marseil, knelt beside him. He had a rag pressed to his cheek that when he lowered it revealed two long, bloody scratches as though he'd been slashed by a claw.

Da knelt beside him. "What happened, Seamus, what happened?"

The torchlight caught an unhealthy sheen on Seamus" forehead, his mouth was working, but no words came out.

"I just found him," Mr MacIver said. "I heard a sort of moan and I found him, out in the road." Mrs MacIver was there now too and Old Ma MacNeill was coming across the road with her stick.

"He only went out to water the veggies," Marseil said kneeling beside her husband. She looked up at us, "you know, to take a pee."

Mammy bent and touched Seamus" forehead. "He's so cold," she said, then to Seamus" wife, "help me get him inside, Marseil, by the fire." Between them they lifted Seamus to his feet and took him away to our croft.

"It's the work of a beast," Ma MacNeill said as Seamus was helped away.

Cormac's Ma shook her head. "It is the devil's work more like." She made the sign of the cross. "Beware, your adversary the devil, as a roaring lion, walketh about, seeking whom he may devour." That's what it says in the Book of Peter."

From across the road, her front door opened and Cormac and his brother and sister peeped out. "Cormac, fetch Mr Morrison," she called. "And you wee ones get back indoors".

"I know where the creature is," I said, "I know where the creature is hiding."

All eyes turned to me then and Mr MacIver swung his torch round to see me better.

"It's hiding in the old crofts at Malacleit. Where old Mr MacKenzie lives."

"MacKenzie?" Da frowned. "Do you mean that chap, MacAulay, from Clachan, whose wife ran away and left him?"

There was some debate amongst the men as to who he was, for he had no kin in Sollas, whether he was a MacAulay or a MacKenzie, whether the wife had left him, whether he had gone to America with the rest from Malacleit or not. They agreed, aye, he must have gone, for he had not been since.

"Are you sure about this, Morag?" Da asked severely. "This is no light matter."

But I looked at him seriously, "I promise Da, I swear. Cormac and me, when went up to the croft, there was something hiding in it. I will swear on cold iron," then looking at Mr Morrison who had just arrived, added quickly, "or even The Bible."

"Better not to swear at all," Mr Morrison said looking at us. "But rather to go and take a look into this ungodly business."

Then a party was formed. Mr MacIver and Mr Morrison bearing torches and my Da carrying a peat iron. I led the way. Up the road we went, it was still claggy from the earlier rain, and the air had a clammy feel. Overhead, the clouds scudded back and forth across the moon and no-one spoke, though I fancied Mr Morrison was muttering a prayer under his breath. Past the empty crofts of Malacleit and then on to the one with its face turned towards the moors.

"It's up there." I pointed towards the dark outline of the croft.

"Submit yourselves to God. Resist the devil, and he will flee from you," Mr Morrison said, swallowing. He lifted his torch higher.

Mr MacIver led the way with his torch and Da behind him his peat iron. I held his other hand, feeling it slipping and sweaty in mine. Up to the door we went, just as Cormac and I had done before, our feet crunching over shells and bones. The strange, dead garland that was nailed to the door fluttered in the night breeze. Even without opening the door we could smell it, the awful animal reek stealing out through the wood.

Mr MacIver looked back at Da and put his finger to his lips and Da dropped my hand. He took his peat iron in both hands and nodded. "Stay here," he mouthed to me. Mr MacIver reached forwards and opened the latch, and the smell rushed out at as they rushed in, coughing and gagging. The men tucked their faces inside the collars of their shirts and cast their torches about so that shadows leaped across the walls. I peered in behind them. By the orange torchlight I saw that the croft was ramshackle, crates and rubbish lay everywhere, there was only a large wooden chest against the wall, the outline of a bed in the corner and a broken chair that stood by the dark hearth. Everywhere, everywhere, was that awful smell.

"Look," I said coming into the croft behind Da, pressing my hand against my nose and mouth. There on the back of the chair was our oilskin for covering the peats.

"Dear God!"

Mr Morrison's voice came out as choke from the corner by the bed. "Get back, Morag, don't come near."

But it was too late. In the light of his torch I saw what lay upon the bed. A rotted body, its face mostly gone, the yellow of a skull, hair still clinging to it. Mr Morrison stumbled outside, choking, his hand to his mouth, leaving the two other men staring.

A tiny movement came from the big chest that stood against the wall. The lid of the chest began to slowly open. The torchlight caught two narrow eyes watching me. My scream drew the creature out. It threw back the lid and leapt into the room moaning and shrieking.

Mr McIver raised his torch and Da spun around and swung the peat iron, but it missed. The creature was as big as a man with a huge head and a gaping mouth which uttered a terrible shriek.

"Morag, shut the door!" Da shouted.

I slammed the croft door shut behind me. Da dropped the peat iron and caught the creature by a flailing limb, but it was strong and it wrestled with him trying to bite and scratch him. Their struggle sent them crashing into Mr McIver who dropped his torch and in its final flare, I saw the creature break free. The croft was now in total darkness. Everything extinguished save the dead smell and the creature's terrible howls.

"Da," I whimpered.

"Shhh, stay quiet."

The creature had fallen silent too and I shrank back against the door, my ears straining in the dark. Where was it? A sudden moan. It was only feet away. Now I could feel the heat from its body. I stuffed a fist into my mouth to stifle a scream. Out of the dark a long white limb reached towards me, its skin pale and hairless. It had bony fingers and each nail was long and yellow and encrusted with filth. I felt their cold touch run across my face and through my hair as it searched for the door latch. The creature brought its face towards mine. It had a human head, large and misshapen. Its cheeks were hollow and there was distress in its staring eyes. The creature gave a low moan, one of pain, and beat its head with a fist.

"Pa-pa," it said, pointing to the bed, "pa-pa."

It moaned again and rocked, beating its head.

"Da," I said softly, "come quietly. I think it is afraid."

My Da and Mr MacIver crept out of the dark behind it. They put their hands upon the creature's shoulders and although it moaned and flinched it did not fight anymore. I opened the croft door and we went outside.

Dawn was already breaking far out to sea. In the grey light I could see it was not a monster, but a strange-looking boy of fifteen or sixteen. He was nearly naked, covered in filth with a misshapen head and matted, pale hair. He sat on the ground covering his head with his arms and rocking back and forth.

"We'll have to call on the sheriff about this matter," Mr Morrison said, mopping his face with his handkerchief. "Do you

166

think this boy killed Macaulay, or Mackenzie, or whoever that is inside?"

I shivered, imagining spending so many nights in the dark with that rotten stench. Da had been kneeling by the boy and now he stood up. "I suspect that man was the boy's father," he said.

He had tied the lad's hands with a piece of rope that he had found inside and as we set off back towards Sollas he followed along behind making soft moaning sounds to himself. I looked at him properly as the light came up. His body was emaciated and covered in dirt and his clothes hung off him in tatters. His skin all over was white, his eyes, wide and staring, and his head was strangely bulging at the back. It seemed loose on his neck so it bobbed about as he made his strange noises and loped along with a strange gait.

"Don't forget, Artair, that he attacked Seamus, we mustn't forget that," Mr MacIver said.

Da stopped. The boy nearly bumped into him. He looked from Mr MacIver to Mr Morrison. "We don't know what happened to Seamus, he probably startled the boy, that's all." He looked at the boy who was shivering now. "It is best if we spread no stories about him until we know what's happened. We will put him in the byre and I will ride to Clachan and see if he has kin there."

The boy seemed content enough to be led to the byre. He had slept there before, after all. Da gave him some milk and the boy drank thirstily, the milk dribbling down his chin like a child. Then Da fetched the pony's bridle and rode away to Clachan.

Weariness suddenly fell on me like a cloak of lead and I stumbled towards my bed.

* * *

I woke late. The sunlight was already falling through the window onto the second plank of the table and I blinked, trying to remember why it was I was in bed at such an hour. It came rushing back to me the awful news about Mr O'Brady, the attack, finding the boy.

Our croft was empty, but I could hear Mammy's voice from outside. "A letter will have to be sent over to Harris," she was saying.

"If she's still there," I heard Da reply.

I opened the door. Mammy and Da had brought their chairs outside and were sitting in the warm sunshine against the wall of the croft.

"Halo, darleich," Mammy said, looking up at me and I squinted at her in the bright light.

"Where's the crea- the boy?" I asked.

She pointed to where he was squatting in the road looking at some pebbles.

"His name is Peter," Da said. "Peter Mackenzie."

The boy looked up at hearing his name, then went back to looking at his stones.

"Is he not dangerous, then?" I asked. He had been given a bath by the looks of it, and clean clothes, and his hair, now washed, was a wispy white.

"I don't think so, unless you surprise him in the dark, like Seamus did."

"How do you know what his name is?"

"Because," Da said, yawning, "I rode to Clachan to find out. Although it turns out he has no kin there, they all went to America. His mother left the boy and his father a few years ago and went to Harris, so they say."

"Poor thing," Mammy said, watching Peter. "First to be left by his mother, then to have his father die."

"But why is he so - strange?" I asked, as Peter tapped two stones together, cocking his head.

"He was born like that, so they said in Clachan," Da said. "His parents kept him indoors and he was hardly ever seen. People thought he brought a curse if they saw him."

Mr Morrison was coming along the road and he stopped when he got to us. His mouth was a small, straight line and he did not give his usual cheerful greeting. "I have some bad news, I'm afraid. I've been up to Lochmaddy to see if the sheriff can come down and deal with the body." He looked at Peter. "But he's away on the mainland."

"Auch," Da said, glancing at the boy. "We'll go up there and see to it ourselves then."

"And we'll look after the boy for now," Mammy said.

168

Mr Morrison took off his black brim hat and held it in both hands, looking solemnly at them.

"That is not the bad news that I'm here to deliver," he said. "The reason that the sheriff and Colonel are not here is because they are in Inverness. They are set to return with the constabulary. To begin the evictions by force."

Chapter Twenty-four

North Uist

All night long the rain fell. It drummed upon the slate roof and leaked into my dreams. I was in the diving bell again and the water was pouring in around the door. The green water rose rapidly past my knees, my chest, around my neck until with a final tiny gasp of air I was drowning. My hair streamed in front of my face as my hands scratched and banged at the glass door. Everything in me urged me to take a breath, but I knew that I must not. Breathe, my body said, breathe. No! my mind said, but its certainty was slipping. There was a sudden jolt as the bell began to be pulled from the depths.

I woke up panting for air. It was so dark that I could not even see my hand in front of my face and it took a while for my heart to calm. I lay awake listening to the nearby roar of the ocean and thought of the terrible journey across from Skye to North Uist. At Lochmaddy I had been conveyed by covered buggy from the port and cold water leaked through the hood and dripped down my neck. It grew dark as mile after twisted mile we toiled along a rutted road to a house where a rough-looking man with stumbling English met me on the threshold with an oil lamp. The girl who did for the colonel was asleep, he'd said, showing me to my room, but I'd be seen to in the morning.

I fell asleep again and when I woke the light was seeping through the curtains. The rain had stopped. Sitting up, I saw that the room I had been given was sparsely furnished with only a desk and chair and a single chest of drawers. The floorboards were bare and when I got out of bed, they creaked under my feet. I went to the window and pushed the curtain aside. The house was perched on a small rise of land and was surrounded with crops that rippled like a green sea in the breeze. Beyond the property a rough narrow road wound away through flat brown moorland. The moor was studded everywhere with small boggy pools which caught the early morning light. In the distance there was a single hill, made mountainous by the flat landscape around it. It was shaped like a dark fin breaking through water. I shivered, remembering the man with the knife. 'Two weeks until Mr Brentwood collects."

I turned from the window. My dress was flung over the chair and was still damp from yesterday's journey. Salt from the sea-spray had dried in white crusty circles upon it. I went to the carpet bag that Maigdh had been instructed to pack for me seeing as our trunks from the hotel had still not turned up. It was an odd assortment that she had chosen. Mainly nightdresses as though I were an invalid and would be spending the day in bed. She had only packed one of Godfrey's mother's dresses. Pulling it out I saw that it was an evening gown of dark green velvet with pearl buttons on the sleeves and a matching pair of velvet slippers. For some reason she had also packed Godfrey's mother's bible that I had found in the walnut bureau. Perhaps she thought me in need of religious comfort. And perhaps I was, I thought, glancing out at the half-drowned landscape. I am marooned here in this house, on this island. Even Miss Wollstonecraft had abandoned me, for the *Rights of Woman* had been left at the castle. I suddenly saw my days stretching out, one after another like a string of rosary beads. Round and round I would go like circles of the asylum yard. Four days, I had lasted at the hospital, before the rubber tubing had induced me to eat and speak once more. My voice had been reduced to a cracked husk.

At the bottom of the carpet bag Maigdh had packed a letter that had arrived just before the fundraising dinner. I had not opened it before. The small, anxious handwriting told me it was from Aunt Caroline. It seemed apt that she would write at this low ebb. I ripped the letter open.

Dear Maria,
I trust that you and your husband are in good health.
I write to you about a rather sensitive issue. A few days ago, I received a letter from the Buckshead Hotel in Glasgow. It seems that they found my address inside your travelling trunk and they wrote to me, having had no reply from yourselves. It appears that you left the hotel without paying your bills. As well as items

relating to your stay, there is £300 in card chits. I am sure that this is simply an oversight on your husband's part and will be rectified quickly. I have let the hotel know accordingly.

    Your Aunt,

    Caroline Blunt

    P.S: The hotel informed me that your trunks are being kept at the Buckshead until your account is settled.

I felt my cheeks redden. *You left the hotel without paying your bills.* I thought of our hurried departure from the hotel under the cover of darkness. The way Godfrey had quietly drawn back the door bolts. And our trunks were not lost, as Godfrey had told me, but they were being kept by the hotel. He had lied.

There was a small tap at the door and a young girl appeared, no more than fifteen years old. She reminded me of a rabbit with her large brown eyes and soft brown hair wisping from her cap and spoke in hesitant English. "Would you like some tea, Your Ladyship?"

"No, thank you," I said, quickly folding up the letter. "Thank you, er-?"

"It's Hilda, Ma'am." She bobbed quickly, her eyes fell on the open carpet bag. "Shall I put away your things Ma'am?"

"It is very quiet here," I said as I watched Hilda fold the nightdresses and place them in the drawers. "Is there no clock? I haven't heard the hour strike."

"The master doesn't like noise," Hilda replied, stroking the fine velvet dress. Her fingers faltered. "We must all be quiet."

No clock. My days would be timeless, as well as endless. "Who was the man who let me in last night?"

"That'll be MacInnes, Ma'am." I saw the girl's lip tremble at his name. "He helps the colonel." Her fingers tightened on the velvet dress. "Did the colonel not return with you?"

"No, he did not. He said he would return within a week."

I saw the girl exhale. I glanced out of the window and watched the clouds scudding over the moorland. Oh to be outdoors.

"Is there somewhere I may walk, Hilda?" I asked suddenly. "A garden or something?"

172

"There's no garden," but then she added, a little uncertainly, "but perhaps we could take a turn in the trap seeing as the master's not here."

I put on the green velvet evening dress, seeing as my other was still damp from last night's journey and the alternative was a nightdress. As I went downstairs, I noticed the austerity of the colonel's house. There were no curtains on the landing windows and my feet echoed on the uncarpeted wooden staircase. Halfway down there was a large stag's head mounted on the wall.

"He shot that himself, the master did," Hilda said from behind me.

It stared at me mournfully and I quickly moved on. Downstairs the rooms were empty, save for one and it seemed as though all effects had been placed here. There was a large, fine, rug in the centre of the room, two leather wingbacks placed by the fire, and a small settee which had, I noticed, the same fabric as those in the castle. I looked about me with a sudden glimmer of hope, but there was not even a bookshelf.

Hilda indicated a drop leaf table by the window, set for one. "The master takes his meals in here," she said. The view was out over the gravel drive and the crops.

The girl returned from the kitchen with a bowl of porridge and I picked up my spoon. It was made of silver and stamped with the MacDonald coat of arms.

"Why does the colonel have MacDonald cutlery?" I asked Hilda who came to clear my bowl.

"It was all sent over Ma'am when the colonel arrived, on account of the colonel having come up from London so quickly without any belongings." She bit her lip. "I was sent over too." I could see tears welling in her eyes.

"From the castle?"

"Yes, Ma'am. My uncle said I shouldn't go, but I had to." A tear dropped onto her dress. "Seeing as the colonel doesn't speak the Gaelic and I was the only one who could speak English." This came out in a rush, blurred with tears.

I frowned. "And who is your uncle?"

"Hugh Duncan. He raised me since my parents passed." At the mention of her uncle and her parents the girl began to cry, her small face crumpling. She sniffed and wiped her eyes with the back of her hand.

I thought of Duncan's sour demeanour, the way he had banged the plates. I passed the girl my napkin. So that was why he was so unhappy.

There was a knock at the front door and Hilda's face brightened. "That's Ian, he's brought round the buggy to take us to Scolpaig, Ma'am."

The buggy took us along the coast road and Hilda sat up beside me pointing things out. Corncrakes hiding in the grass, a marsh harrier gliding over the moor. The rain had cleared but despite the blue sky above us more clouds were building out over the sea. The tide was in and only a strip of meadow studded with pink and yellow flowers separated us from the waves that crashed and foamed. I thought of my aunt's letter. £300 in card chits. Were there other debts too? The man with the knife: *Mr Brentwood will collect.* I thought of the paintings, the books, the furniture all stripped from the castle. Godfrey's look of despair that I was not with child. I suddenly thought of Alexander's telegram: *You'll pay for it.* What if it wasn't a threat, but a refusal to loan Godfrey money?

"Hilda," I said suddenly, "did you ever meet Alexander, my husband's brother?"

"Alasdair, you mean? Of course."

"Why do you call him Alasdair and not Alexander?"

"My uncle taught him the Gaelic when he was wee, and that's what he's called here."

"So, they were close, your uncle and Alexander?"

"Yes Ma'am. My uncle used to make him wooden swords and play cricket with him on the front lawn."

"Like with Godfrey."

Hilda frowned. "No, ma'am, not with Godfrey. He didn't like the outdoors."

I opened my mouth to correct her, but we were passing a man, dressed in a black coat and hat standing amongst the wildflowers with a sketchbook in his hand and Hilda called, "Good-day, Reverend," as we bumped past. "That's Reverend MacLean from the Church of Scotland in Sollas," Hilda explained. "He loves orchids."

A tower came into view. It was an octagonal stone tower built on an islet out on a small loch with a small causeway partly submerged by the tide.

"What is that tower?" I asked as the buggy came to a stop.

Hilda said something to the driver and his answer ran on and on in Gaelic. "It's Scolpaig tower, Your Ladyship," Hilda said. "The local men built it during the famine of 1836."

The driver had pulled off the road, onto the soft grass bank overlooking the tower. He jumped down from the buggy.

"What is it for? A hunting lodge or something?"

"No, your Ladyship, It's not for anything. It was for meal."

"To store meal do you mean?"

"No. It was in exchange for meal. The men had to build it if they wanted meal for their families who were starving."

I looked at the tower standing by the loch. So solid and yet so purposeless and useless. A folly, I thought, like me.

"Should we picnic here?" Hilda asked. She was pressing the grass with her toe doubtfully, watching water bubble up around it.

The driver bent to examine the ground, then walked about the buggy, cursing in Gaelic. The back wheels had completely sunk into the waterlogged ground. He climbed up and drove the horse forward, but the wheels spun and sprayed mud, causing it to sink deeper into the bog. The clouds were thickening over the sea now, and the promise of blue sky had gone. I felt the first spit of rain blown in the breeze. Hilda and the driver stood together discussing what could be done. He was pointing up the road, she was shaking her head.

Eventually, she looked at me. "There's no way Ian can get the buggy out on his own, Your Ladyship. But Sollas is only a mile or so down the road, we can go there and get help. We should perhaps go with him, or we'll be soaked."

The rain was beginning in earnest now, darkening my green velvet dress. Ian was unhitching the horse from the harness. He said something to Hilda and she looked uncertainly at me and my feet in their thin silk slippers.

"These roads aren't made for your slippers, Your Ladyship, they'll be ruined. You could ride on the horse, I suppose."

"Don't worry," I said, remembering harvest-time in Norfolk and the Clydesdales who pulled the carts of hay in the fields behind Grandpapa's house. "I have ridden bare back before."

The driver led the horse by the bridle so that it was level with the buggy then we set off up the road towards Sollas.

Chapter Twenty-five

Sollas

It was the day before Whit, but there were no garlands of flowers, no songs, nor the shinty competition. Several families left when they heard the news about the constabulary, their possessions hastily loaded onto a cart. Others said that the constabulary wouldn't come until notice had been served, but everyone was waiting. It was like a game of Grandmother's footsteps, waiting for that pounce on your back. Some of the men had started a watch, up on the hill overlooking the road. Others said, what for? But it was better to see it coming, Da said.

It had rained all night, but had dawned bright and the clouds moved quickly across the sky. I wanted to go down to the beach, but Mammy said, no, stay close. She and the other women were digging the tatties from the rigs, gathering them in. Dig, dig, plunk, plunk, plunk into the bucket. Two or three women digging, another one standing, looking out up the road for any sign. But there was nothing.

Da came back from the watch at lunchtime, his eyes were bloodshot from looking and looking. He said after a while it led to a certain madness, when your mind started telling you that there was something there: the flash of a wing could be the shiny button on a uniform, the pound of the surf, the heavy crunch of boots.

Even Peter kept his own strange watch. He had taken a liking to three particular pebbles and he crouched in the road, rocking back and forth, clinking them in his hand and talking to them in his own language. When Da and the other men had gone up to the croft to see about the body, Peter had followed them, watching. After that he became calmer and less prone to his wild shrieking. He slept each night in the byre and ate his food outdoors, he could not be persuaded to come into a croft for anything. At first, folk were afraid of him and would not cross his path. Nor would they put their cattle in the byre in case he turned the cows dry. The first day, Old Ma MacNeill followed him about the village sprinkling salt on him, but Mammy made her stop. It was a waste of salt. Slowly though, people got used to him. He was incredibly strong and when he could be persuaded to, he could heft a barrow of kelp twice as fast as another man. He would surprise folk with strange gifts too, a bunch of wildflowers, a piece of fool's gold from up on the moor.

The morning of Whit dragged slowly into afternoon and the sky clouded over. Despite the watch, there were still the chores to do. Out in the machair, I pressed my head against the cow's shaggy side as I did the milking. My thoughts rested on Mr O'Brady, thinking of him in the gaol, all alone. Would they allow him his pipe, I wondered, and his hat? I felt the first fat drops of rain down my neck, then the smell of cold rain rising from the warm earth. Within a minute the rain had begun to come down hard and I stood up and covered my pail. Glancing up the road, I saw three figures, two on foot and one on a horse, coming along from Scolpaig.

"Good-day," one of them called as they drew nearer. It was the girl from the colonel's house, Hilda, her apron and cap were soaking wet, but I did not return her greeting. I could not, for words had escaped me. For there, sitting upon the horse, just as I had always pictured her, was the princess I always drew. She wore a velvet dress, green as my four-leaf clover had been, and where her dress had ridden up her finely stockinged calves could be seen, her neat ankles finished in velvet slippers. Others had seen the strangers approach too, and were hurrying in from the rigs and the village. Mammy was among them.

"The buggy is stuck fast in the bog at Scolpaig tower," the man with them explained. "I can't shift it and I need someone to give me a hand."

At once people began offering help, turning towards their crofts. Others stood, still staring, up at the princess sitting upon the horse, her bonnet and dress bedraggled in the rain.

"This is Her Ladyship, the Laird's wife," Hilda said to Mammy in a low voice. "She's staying with the colonel."

Mammy glanced up at her, then she wiped her hands on her apron. "Her Ladyship better get in from the rain, before her fine clothes are ruined."

Hilda led the horse into the village and up to our door where Mammy helped the princess down. Her feet squelched a little in the mud and she looked down sadly at her slippers.

"Come inside," Mammy said opening our front door and the princess stood in the doorway, looking about her.

"Oh," she said, and her mouth made a perfect O shape when she said it. She sneezed loudly which made me jump, pressing a hand to her mouth and nose.

"It is the smoke," she said. Her English was the loveliest thing I had ever heard, like sweet angels singing.

Her bonnet was soaked through and her velvet dress too and she sneezed again and began coughing.

"Please – have a seat, here by the fire, and I'll make some tea," Mammy said, offering her the chair by the fire.

The princess sat down and I sat on the bench where I could look at her closely. She had taken off her bonnet and the damp curls of her short dark hair were plastered to her white neck. She put her hand over her nose and mouth and I saw that on the cuffs of her dress were two of the most beautiful buttons I had ever seen, winking in the darkness like tiny shells on a night beach. Mammy crouched by the fire and warmed the tea; she hardly cast a glance at our visitor. The princess looked about her and I saw it through her eyes. A dark smoky croft with a few sticks of furniture and a packed earth floor.

"Most of what you see the villagers have made themselves from driftwood and the like," Hilda said, in English, to fill the silence. "The mattresses are made of seaweed and heather."

"Oh," said the princess and began to cough again as the smoke blew up from the fire towards the thatch.

Mammy set out our two cups. One had a missing handle and the other, the best one, was chipped in two places.

"What is she doing here in Sollas?" Mammy asked, nodding towards the princess.

Hilda was standing by the door, looking out for the buggy. "She was sent across by Laird MacDonald."

"Sent?" Mammy said sharply. "On what business?"

"I don't know, Mrs Macdomnaill. I only know that she has been sent over by the Laird."

I looked at the princess who was dabbing her streaming eyes. Sent. She was sent, I thought. I touched my pocket out of habit. Mammy handed the princess our best teacup and I saw how swollen and worn Mammy's hands were against the soft hands of the princess.

"Mr O'Brady said that he was certain that Lady MacDonald would help us," I said.

Mammy narrowed her eyes. "Why would she be sent here now?"

"Is that Gaelic that you are speaking?" the princess asked suddenly.

"Oh yes, Your Ladyship," Hilda said in English, "but Morag here can also speak English, can't you, Morag?"

The princess turned her lovely pale face towards me, squinting a little in the smoky gloom to see me better.

"Come here, Morag," Hilda said.

I came and stood before them, looking down at my bare dirty legs.

The princess looked at me.

"Oh, but she is so thin," she exclaimed. She drew back a little and supressed a shudder and I wished the floor would swallow me up.

"Well times have been difficult," Hilda said, "what with the famine and no work as such. Come on now, Morag, let's hear something in English, what about reciting something from The Bible?"

I began to recite Psalm One in a trembling voice. My English sounded coarse and rough as brambles to my ears, my accent thick. I struggled on, the princess swallowed and her eyes glazed a little.

She gave a little nod. "Very good," she said weakly, she took a sip of smoky tea, "do you know anything that isn't relig...."

But she didn't finish because, quite suddenly, the princess was very sick, all over her lovely green dress and all over the floor. I jumped back to avoid it splashing on my toes and the princess leant over and retched and retched like a dog. The cup slipped from her hand and fell to the floor, smashing in two. When she was finished, sick and spittle hung from her chin and all down her dress.

"Oh, oh, I'm so sorry," she said and big tears sprung from her eyes.

"We should change her dress - at least the outer dress – she can't stay like this," Mammy said, going to her wedding chest. "Here, we'll give her one of mine." She pulled out her Sunday best dress, charcoal grey from the trunk. I've always loved that gown, but now it didn't seem good enough to mop the floor with.

The princess refused at first, but then agreed, allowing Hilda to help her. Underneath her cotton petticoats were so white that they glowed in the dim light of our croft.

"I'm so sorry," she kept saying, "so sorry."

We heard the clatter of the buggy arrive and Mammy bundled the princess's dress up and handed it to Hilda, and we watched them pull away.

Mammy picked up the pieces of broken cup and scrubbed the floor and then she put some tatties on to boil, as though the visitors had never been there. I sat in the chair by the fire, where the princess had sat. Everything was upside down and strange since her visit.

"Do you think it's a sign, Mammy?" I asked at last.

She was chopping greens very fast at the table and she looked at me.

"A sign of what?" she asked.

"A sign from Laird MacDonald," I said. "A sign that Laird MacDonald has changed his mind about putting us off the island."

She scoffed and began chopping again.

"But why would the princess be here otherwise? I think It's a sign."

Mammy stopped chopping and looked at me seriously. "Firstly, she's not a princess, Morag. She is an English lady, that's all. And as for a sign, have we not learned with Peter to be careful with signs?"

She opened the door to throw away a pail of dirty water, but my hand touched my pocket. Faith and hope, I thought. Faith and hope.

181

Chapter Twenty-six

North Uist

I sat up in bed staring at the maroon curtains that had been drawn across the window. My brain felt loose and my mind was jangling from the day's events. Fearing I had caught a chill, Hilda had sent me to bed and brought me a cup of tea. It brought back the flavour of the earlier, hot smoked tea and the events of the afternoon. The blackhouse filled with stinging smoke and that ripe animal smell. The language they spoke, like music. The girl, Morag. I thought of how she had stood, in rags, reciting Psalm One, her voice rising and falling in the gloom. Staring at the curtains, my thoughts began to dart like swallows, until I could hardly trace them. Suddenly I knew what I would do. I got up and went to the desk and began writing.

Dearest Fanny,
I have been to visit the village of Sollas today and I know what I must do: I must teach the children English. Education is my calling, Fanny, and I must answer it. These poor, famishing children are living in the direst of circumstances, but I shall teach them to speak English so that they will be better equipped for their lives in America."

I stopped writing and sat back, seeing that in my haste my hand had smudged the words. I had felt so thwarted this past year, so frustrated that all my education had been for nothing, but now purposefulness surged through me. And it would show Mr O'Brady, too, I thought. "Principles are sometimes the only thing we have left to hold onto," he had said. Well this would show him that I was a woman of principle, like Miss Wollstonecraft. Perhaps I would write a pamphlet called *Educating Highland Children: An Experience*. Mr O' Brady could publish it in his newspaper. Reflecting on it, Mr O'Brady had only written the truth about me in his article. I *had* sat on the picnic rug eating raspberries and I had not thought about the famishing Highlanders. But now I had visited them in the homes and seen their plight and I was going to help them. I should thank him wherever he was now, which was probably back at his desk at the *Chronicle*, having been given a caution by the sheriff. I leaned over my letter again, but then I thought of Godfrey. My pen hovered over the paper. What would he think of my plan? I had a sort of shrinking feeling, but he could hardly object, seeing as he had lied to me about the trunks, and the debts too. I would take the moral high ground. Which made me think, I would pay a visit to the reverend and borrow some books.

The next morning I instructed Hilda to find me a pair of stout boots and we set out on foot towards the reverend's house which stood outside of Sollas. The sky was grey and overcast above us, but the clouds were high enough not to bring rain. I looked at the waves rolling in and back out again on the beach beside the road. In the cold light of day this was how I felt too, propelled forward by ambition and sucked backwards by doubt. I summoned the voice of Miss Wollstonecraft in my mind which buoyed my spirits and the stone house of Reverend MacLean appeared on a small rise of land outside the village.

An elderly housekeeper showed us into a dark parlour that smelled of yesterday's fish supper and we sat down on hard wooden chairs to await the reverend. I scanned the small bookshelf. There was a volume of poetry by William Wordsworth and *A Journey to the Western Islands of Scotland* by Samuel Johnson, along with several books on horticulture. The door opened and Reverend MacLean came in. He was a tall, thin man with a mop of white hair.

"Your Ladyship," he said, bowing, "What a pleasure and an honour to have you call. I was in the garden. I am attempting to grow bearded lilies in the lea of the house. Wonderful, fertile soil you see, and I am curious at what else might be persuaded to grow. Are you a keen gardener yourself?"

I shook my head. "I am not the slightest bit green fingered, I'm afraid."

The reverend's face fell. "Ah shame. The previous Lady MacDonald was a wonderful horticulturalist of course, splendid gardens at the castle, magnificent. She loaned me a book once in fact." He glanced guiltily at the bookshelf. "Is it a social call, your Ladyship, or something of a spiritual matter that I can assist you with?"

"Not spiritual, reverend, but you might say educational."

"Ah?" His white eyebrows twitched as the housekeeper brought in a pot of tea.

"I have a plan to re-open the school you see – here in Sollas."

His eyebrows shot further up his forehead. The housekeeper rattled the cups in their saucers and gave a sharp, dry cough. "Really? Do you think that is wise? Given the – uncertain times people are living in?" He looked from me to Hilda, and back again.

I frowned and reddened, but pressed on, in fact I had already thought of this, had prepared a small speech. "Uncertain or not, I visited Sollas yesterday, and the children are in desperate need of education and I shall answer that call."

The reverend frowned. Perhaps he took this to be a slight on his own ministry. He looked at Hilda who was studying the patterned rug with great interest. He looked back at me. "The villagers are in need of a great many things, Your Ladyship, but the re-opening of the school-"

"Do you not think education is a vital tool? To serve them well in their futures?"

"The islanders are a stubborn people," he said. "What will serve them well and what they choose are often entirely different things. You must be aware of what a…" he paused, "precarious situation they are in?"

"Precarious. Hmm."

"I only mean, it is better not to stir them up," the reverend continued. "There is strong feeling and well, it may be taken as some sort of sign if the school is re-opened."

"I only wish for you to speak to them, Reverend, to encourage them to send their children to me and to perhaps borrow some books."

The reverend clasped his hands and looked at the teapot. He sighed. "To tell the truth, my influence here is limited. Most are not in my congregation. They are part of the Free Church, run by a Mr Morrison from the village. It is perhaps he that you should speak to."

I put down my tea and rose at once. "I will go and speak with him now. If you would be kind enough to tell me where he lives."

The reverend got to his feet hastily too, still holding his tea-cup, and his tea sloshed over the side. "Might I be bold enough to ask what His Lordship makes of this plan?"

I looked at him squarely. "His Lordship is in London presently."

"Not on account of his health, I hope?"

"No, on business. Good day, Reverend."

But at the gate I turned to Hilda. "Why would my husband be in London for his health?"

"He was often ill as a child, Ma'am, and in need of a specialist physician so he was sent down to school in London when he was seven or eight. We didn't see him for many years."

"But he came up in the holidays?"

"No, Ma'am. Godfrey stayed down in London and his mother went down to see him once a year."

A chilly breeze had got up and was sending the clouds scudding across the sky.

"What do you mean, Hilda? Godfrey told me he spent his childhood here. What about when he swam out to Ardmore point for a bet?"

"That was Alasdair, Ma'am. I was only a wee bairn, but I remember it. Godfrey had a weak chest, he never would have swum. Anyway, he wasn't here, he was away in London."

The light broke through the clouds and fell upon the grey sea then it vanished again. I gripped Hilda's arm. "What about the Hogmanay ball then, when Godfrey's father gave him the black bun with his signet ring hidden inside it?"

Above us a single gull swooped, calling and crying.

Hilda shook her head. "It was Alasdair who got the ring. It was Alasdair."

The reverend's front door opened and he came out with his gardening gloves in his hand. When he saw us standing by his gate he stopped. "Everything alright, Your Ladyship?" he called.

I dropped Hilda's arm and raised my hand to the reverend. "Go back home, Hilda. We will talk about this later."

I marched briskly away from the vicarage. My stout boots clipped the loose stones and sent them flying along in front of me. Hilda was mistaken about the bet, about the ball. She was young and seemed a nervy sort. But it would be hard to confuse the two brothers, wouldn't it? And she didn't seem like a liar, whereas Godfrey, well, he had already lied to me once. But why had Godfrey pretended to have grown up here, I puzzled, when he had really been sent away? Why would he put himself at the centre of those stories when they had happened to his brother? "A thoroughly miserable time." That's what he'd said about school. I remember how he told me he had lain awake with his precious map, hundreds of miles from home. I felt a small wave of sympathy for him then. I thought of the day I had met him. 'It's all mine now," he had said about the estate. But as I walked towards the village the small wave began to grow into a cold current of fear, remembering how his hand had been so hard and cold.

Behind the crofts there were women out in the fields, digging, and behind the houses a group of children were following cattle through the meadow beside the sea. I came to the schoolroom opposite the stone church and found it unlocked. It was a small rectangular room with rows of desks and a small stove on the back wall. A chalkboard hung on the front wall behind the teacher's desk. I could make out the word, "earth" that had been rubbed out. I stood with my hands on my hips, imagining the seats filled with children before me. What would I teach them first? English of course, so they could understand me. And then science. I would get them to build a working telegraph model just as Grandfather had done with me.

There was a noise at the door and I turned to see two faces looking curiously in. One was the girl, Morag, from the previous day, the other a taller, sandy-haired boy.

"Come in," I said, beckoning them.

In they came and I saw in the light of the schoolroom how pale they both were, their eyes large in their pinched faces. I could smell the peat smoke in their hair. I perched on the edge of the desk and looked at them both.

"Now, I know your name, you are Morag. But what about you?"

The boy blushed and looked at his feet.

"His name is Cormac, Ma'am. Cormac MacIver," Morag said. "but his English isn't very good."

I smiled. "Well, that's alright, because I am going to be your new teacher."

Morag looked at me, her eyes widening. She said something to Cormac in Gaelic and he looked at me in wonder too.

"The school is going to open again?" Morag asked. I saw the girl's hand reach into her apron pocket.

"Yes." I said, standing up. "From tomorrow, in fact. Do you think that you can tell all the children to come along?

Morag nodded. "Yes, Ma'am." She looked at Cormac again and then she stepped forward. "Excuse me, Ma'am." She looked at the floor then up at me shyly. "Did Mr O'Brady send you?"

"Mr O'Brady?" I said in surprise.

I looked down at the girl. Her face was lifted hopefully up at me. I thought about it. Was it his call to action that had stirred me? "Your Ladyship agrees don't you?" he had asked me in the entrance hall. Well, finally, this was my reply.

"Yes, I suppose you could say that in a way, he did."

Morag looked at Cormac for a moment. What was on the girl's face? Triumph? Excitement? Then the children turned and ran out of the schoolroom together and I could hear their excited voices all the way down the road.

Chapter Twenty-seven

Sollas

I lay awake in my bed until the light reached the edge of the table then I took my shawl and crept out of our croft. The rain had passed and everything looked washed clean, each blade of grass and each flower sparkled in the light, and the sky over the sea was a pale, fresh blue. I ran up over the sandbanks, the breeze catching my hair and whipping it across my face. The tide was out and the kelp lay glistening on the patterned sand. I ran down to the water's edge looking out at the sea, to where guillemots and gulls were bobbing about on the waves. I thought of how I had thrown in the pearl. It seemed like such a long time ago, though in truth it had only been a few weeks. Now my wishes had been answered: school was starting again today.

Mammy hadn't believed me when I had told her the news that the school was re-opening and that it was Mr O'Brady who had sent Lady MacDonald to us. She had scoffed, but I had insisted and in the end she had gone over the road to ask Cormac. Yes, Cormac had said, it was true. So Mammy made me repeat exactly what Her Ladyship had said, about how she was opening the school again and that it was Mr O'Brady who had sent her. I had to repeat it again for Old Ma MacNeill who stuck her head around the door, and then Marseil MacRae and the other neighbours who quickly crowded into Cormac's croft.

"I told you, Ceit, that if they meant to get us out they would have served us with a notice first," Marseil MacRae said from the doorway, her eyes glittering at Mammy.

"But what of the news of the constabulary? What about Mr O'Brady who is still in gaol?" Mammy asked. "We've had no word from him."

"All we know about the constabulary or Mr O'Brady is what that boy said from Lochmaddy. It's probably just harbour gossip," Marseil said, folding her arms.

"An Irishman was all that harbour lad said, and there are plenty of Irishmen, aren't there?" Old Ma MacNeill added.

"Well, where is he then?" Mammy asked.

"Auch, he's probably busy writing his newspaper," Marseil replied. "What'she got to come back for anyway?"

Me, I thought. He promised he'd come back to me to teach me how to be a journalist.

"Well, why doesn't he write to us then?" Mammy asked. She folded her arms and I was suddenly cross with her disbelief.

"He did write to us though, Mammy, didn't he?" I said. "Mr O'Brady wrote and said that Lady MacDonald would help us and now Her Ladyship is here."

Mammy looked at the three of us, Marseil, Old Ma MacNeill and me, just like she had done outside the byre that day. The neighbours began to leave, but she stood there, shaking her head.

"I don't like it," she said. "Something's not right. I cannot believe the Laird has changed his mind."

I picked up a pebble and skimmed it across the waves. I hoped Mr O'Brady would write again, and that, even better, that he would return. I wanted to tell him that he was right about Peter, that he was not a monster, only a lad without a Mammy or a Da. There had been some talk of sending Peter away to the poorhouse in Lochmaddy, but Mammy said no, we would take care of him for now. How I wished Mr O'Brady was here on the beach beside me. I saw him so clearly in my mind, his tall, long-leggedness, the smell of his pipe tobacco, his easy laugh. I remembered his warm hand clasping mine. I had been keeping my journal just like he told me to and I wanted to show him. I thought of someone else I could show and I ran home to fetch it.

When I got to the school room it was empty and I took a rag and began to wipe the desks from dust. It was smaller than I remembered and when I sat at a chair my knees knocked on the underside of the table.

"You are bright and early." There was Her Ladyship standing in the doorway with a basket on her arm. She was dressed, I was disappointed to see, not in fine green velvet, but in a plain grey dress and sturdy men's boots. She looked very ordinary today. "Here," she said, reaching into the basket and handing me

Mammy's best dress. "Will you give this back to your mother for me and say thank you."

Your mother, I mouthed, turning her lovely pronunciation over in my mouth. I watched as she untied her bonnet at how her short dark hair gleamed in the light. She looked about her.

"Do you think the other children will come?" she asked.

"Oh yes, Ma'am, they will. I told everyone."

I watched her set her paper, pen and ink out on the desk. I remembered then what I had brought to show her and I shyly held out my sheaf of papers.

"What is this?"

"It's my journal. Mr O'Brady told me to write down everything that happened here whilst he was away. He's going to teach me to be a journalist. It's in English. Would you like to read it, Ma'am?"

She pulled a funny face at the mention of Mr O'Brady's name, but she took the papers and put them in her basket. Then she took out a book.

"Is that The Holy Bible, Ma'am?" I asked.

"The Bible?" She looked at the book on the table. "Why no, I didn't think to bring a bible. Is that what you normally study?"

"Yes, Ma'am. That's what the Society taught, you see, Christian Knowledge." I wondered whether I should recite something for her, seeing as it had once pleased Miss MacAllister to hear me do so.

"Hmm, Christian knowledge." She frowned and glanced at the book. "This is a book of poetry that I have borrowed from Reverend MacLean by Mr William Wordsworth. I have sent for more books though, a book of stories, and an Atlas."

"An Atlas, Ma'am," I asked eagerly, "of Europe?"

"Of the whole world, I should think," she smiled.

"The whole world, ma'am?" I asked, my mind boggling. "Would it fit in one book?"

She laughed and it was the most beautiful sound, like a clear burn tinkling over pebbles.

The other children began to arrive. Their parents too and even neighbours who did not have any children. They peeped through the doorway to get a glimpse of our new teacher for themselves, bowing and bobbing one after another. Mammy was not among them.

Then we settled at our desks and Cormac chose a seat beside me. Her Ladyship looked at us for a moment and I thought how we must look to her, like dirty little tatties, all different sizes, sitting in our rows. Cormac's sister Marie had a rattling cough down at the front and somebody else sneezed.

"Well," Her Ladyship said, clasping her hands together. "Let's start by writing down your names so that I can see who is here." She sat at her desk and dipping her pen in the ink, she looked at me.

"Morag, I know your first name, but what is your family name?"

I stood up. "MacDhomhnaill, Ma'am."

She paused and looked down at her paper. "Hmm. May I write it as MacDonald, as it's easier to spell?"

Around the class she went, asking everyone their names, and it took such a long time as she tried to spell them out in English. Fionnlagh became Finlay; Beathag, Betty. When she came to Seonaidh she was stumped.

"Say it again boy," she instructed, closing her eyes and tilting her head as though listening to music. "Hmm, yes, Johnnie I think." And his name was added finally in ink to her list. Once the register was complete, the lesson was nearly over and the class had become a restless sea of children. Her Ladyship did not have the Gaelic like Miss MacAllister to settle them with a sharp word. Instead, her lovely white hands fluttered like two butterflies, then she stood up and read to us from the book of poetry by Mr Wordsworth, her voice rising over the increasing rustle, shuffle and tapping of the children before her.

"Lo! where the Moon along the sky/Sails with her happy destiny,"

As she read, I listened to her lovely voice. Her face shone with every word, almost as though she were reading it for her own pleasure. I glanced at Cormac beside me.

He had pulled my slate in front of him and was licking his finger and rubbing circles upon it. He bumped his knee on the underside of the desk. "What do we need this for?" he whispered in a hot grumble. I shushed him and turned back to the class.

When the lesson was finished, I stayed behind and straightened the chairs.

"Well," Her Ladyship said. She put her hands on her hips and looked at me. "How do you think that went?"

"Went, Ma'am?"

"Yes, was the lesson a success, do you think?"

I looked at my hands. "It was a lovely poem, Ma'am," I said. "Perhaps next time we could do some arithmetic."

"Yes, I think we could do some of that."

"Could we count to one million, Ma'am?

She laughed. Then she tied her bonnet and swung her basket on her arm and I walked with her out of the schoolroom and back towards the colonel's house. She had a long, fast stride, and I did a little jog to keep up. Her Ladyship wasn't like Mr O'Brady, whose easy company encouraged the asking of questions. Instead, she strode along, her face closed, as though all her knowledge was hidden away inside her like a secret book.

"Look, there is a marsh orchid," I said, pointing to a tiny purple flower in the grass. "Mr O'Brady told me that they are usually found in Africa, Ma'am. In Africa, Mr O'Brady said, there are animals with big ears and ones with very long necks called..." I stopped, trying to remember.

She raised an eyebrow at me. "Giraffe." She smiled as she strode along. "Tell me, how do you know Mr O'Brady, Morag?"

I wondered about telling her of the mermaid's treasure, of how he had been sent, but instead I simply said, "He came to the village to help us, to stop us from going to America."

She stopped and looked at me in a puzzled way.

"Do you not want to go to America?"

"No. I don't want to go on a ship with the weevils, or sleep on a dock, nobody wants to go."

"Well, you don't have to go then, do you?"

I looked down at my worn shoe. I could now see my toenail peeping through looking at me like an eye. I shook my head.

"His Lairdship is making us go. My Da says it's to make way for the sheep and for shooting. We have to go, the colonel said, or we'll be removed by the constabulary."

"Removed by the constabulary?"

I looked up at her again and smiled.

"It's alright now, Ma'am, because Mr O'Brady said he was certain that you would help us. And Hilda said that the Laird sent you here. Sent you to show that he's changed his mind."

Her Ladyship put her hand to her mouth and I hoped she wasn't going to be sick again, she had gone a funny colour. She looked away at the sea to where the tide was very nearly in.

I had a question that nagged like a sore tooth.

"Mr O'Brady, Ma'am," I asked, my voice faltering, "is he in gaol?"

She looked down at me.

She put her hand on her forehead. "I don't know."

"But was he arrested, ma'am?"

She looked down at me again. "He was arrested, yes, for throwing a rock through the castle window, but he didn't do it of course."

My heart began hammering fast. "But if he was arrested, then he will be in gaol in Inverness castle."

She frowned. "Inverness? No, you're mistaken, why would he be taken all the way up there?"

I remembered Da's words. "My Da said he was taken to the Justice in Inverness because the justice is a friend of the colonel's. They are going to transport him."

I felt the tears pricking in my eyes and Her Ladyship touched my shoulder. "I will go home and write to Inverness immediately," she said. She gave my shoulder a small squeeze and she strode off up the road.

Chapter Twenty-eight

Sollas

"Hilda?" I opened the bedroom door and called into the hallway, listening for the girl's step on the creaky stair, but there was no reply.

I went back to the desk and looked out of the window that overlooked the drive, but there was no sign of Hilda there either. I had come straight home from the schoolroom, unease ticking inside me like a fast clock and I had read Morag's journal from start to finish. Each page was written in tiny careful spider writing so that no paper was wasted. I saw it in black and white, the truth of Godfrey's improvements, his map, slashed with lines and a circle around the word Sollas. He meant to clear everyone out, by whatever means necessary. And Mr O'Brady had been trying to help them. He had stood in Godfrey's way with his petitions and his newspaper articles and now he had been arrested. The Irishman has been stopped, he had said. I had written a letter to the sheriff in Inverness insisting on Mr O'Brady's innocence and it must be posted straight away.

I went into the hallway and called down the stairs for Hilda again, but there was no reply. I could feel that a door was open somewhere, for a warm salty breeze was blowing up through the house. I went down the creaking staircase and towards the kitchen at the back of the house. There was no sign of the girl there, though a kettle on the range was beginning to steam, and someone had begun to chop an onion on the rough wooden table. The back door stood open and a rectangle of sunshine fell onto the old tiled floor. I listened. There was a noise like the mewl of a cat. There it was again, as though it was in distress. I went to the open door and looked out. Four steep stone steps led down to a yard, across which I could see stables and a large stone water trough full to the brim from rainwater. But the yard was empty. There it was again though, that small cry, and I looked to my right to where the peat was stacked. On the other side of the stack was Mr MacInnes, one hand caught roughly in Hilda's hair, so that her head was tipped back against the wall her neck twisting away from him, his other hand inside the front of her dress.

"Hilda!" I said from the top of the step.

MacInnes dropped the girl and looked at me. I saw the beads of sweat standing on his red temple. He was panting. "We were just having a little sport, Y'Ladyship." He grinned. "Weren't we, Hilda?" Then he said something to her harshly in Gaelic.

Hilda was shaking violently and she began to cry, but she did not move. From inside the kitchen the kettle was beginning to slowly boil.

"Hilda, come here, come inside." I held out my hand to the girl, but she did not move, so I came down the steps towards them.

"She likes it, don't you, Hilda?" MacInnes said and he stood in front of the girl. I could smell his fetid breath.

"Get out of my way, Mr MacInnes." I could feel my body trembling, but I reached past him and pulled Hilda towards me.

As I turned and mounted the steps, pulling Hilda behind me, Mr MacInnes sprang forwards and grabbed roughly at Hilda's arm, so that she stumbled a little, giving a cry as she was pulled between us both. I stood on the top step and yanked Hilda hard, pulling her into the kitchen, and then blocked the doorway as Mr MacInnes came up after us.

"You won't lay another finger on Hilda," I said, shaking. "If you do, you will lose your job and I will have you removed from this island."

He stood on the step below leering up at me. "You have no idea, your Ladyship, do you? It's not me who's gonna be removed, it's you."

The kettle began to scream and I looked at him in confusion. Seeing he had gained an advantage, he made to step into the kitchen, but I leaned forward and with all my might, I pushed him backwards, so that he fell, hard, down the steps into the yard. He landed with his full weight on his arm. He gave a howl of pain and clutched his arm, cursing in Gaelic. I slammed the door shut and locked it with the key, then I ran through the house and drew the heavy bolts across the main front door too.

I went back to the kitchen. It was filled with steam from the boiling kettle and I lifted it off the heat. Hilda lay crumpled on the floor and was crying. She looked up at me and her face was dark with hate.

"What did you do that for?" she cried. "Why did you do that?"

I crouched beside the girl and touched her arm.

"Get off me," she screamed. "Don't touch me."

I stood up and wiped my brow. My hand was shaking.

"Hilda, I was trying to help you-"

"Well, you haven't." She wiped her eyes on her sleeve and looked up. "My uncle's going to lose his job now, he's going to be put out. He's got nowhere to go." Snot was hanging from her nose.

I knelt on the stone floor beside her.

"Hilda, I am going to speak to my husband, whatever it was that MacInnes threatened-"

"It wasn't MacInnes that threatened it. It was His Lordship himself."

I reeled back, felt the blood rush from my face, felt a swoop of dizziness pass over me.

"What did he threaten?"

The girl looked at my, my shoulders still heaving from left-over sobs, her voice coming out in hiccups. "He said, if I didn't do exactly what was asked of me, my uncle would be put out of the castle and off the estate."

"Well, surely he didn't mean that."

"He did, he did," Hilda said fiercely, and then her voice was a whisper. "Because the first night he came here, MacInnes was here too, and MacInnes, he grabbed me on the stairs, and he tried to push his- his, and His Lordship, he was on the landing above us and he saw it, and the next day, he said I was to think of my uncle and do whatever was asked of me. And then he turned and smiled at MacInnes."

I pressed my hand to my mouth, feeling how cold my fingers had become. The girl was staring at the floor, shivering now, despite how the room had grown stuffy from the trapped heat of the range. I stood up and lifted Hilda to her feet, taking her upstairs. The girl pointed towards a door, but opening it, I saw that there was only a pallet on the floor, with the thinnest of blankets, so I turned and took her to my own room instead. She was shivering so violently that I heaped the bedclothes on her and then climbed onto the bed too. I held the girl, stroking her hair, until her breathing quietened. I thought of what Hilda had said about the way my husband had threatened her, at what the girl must have endured because of it. I thought of the leering face of McInnes, his rank breath. What had he said to me, that I was going to be removed? He was insane and a drunk, I told myself, but there was a small beat of uncertainty.

I watched the sun move off the front of the house, and swing round to the side, and the room became colder. I got out of bed and went to the window. There was no one out there, and the road was empty too, but how long until MacInnes returned, or the colonel or Godfrey? I felt my heart harden like metal cooling to think of what Godfrey had permitted.

I was desperately thirsty. I left Hilda sleeping and went down to the kitchen. There was a pitcher on the table that was half-filled with water and the kettle had boiled dry. I looked out of the window and saw that there was a water pump out in the yard beside the big stone trough. I stood in front of the locked door, should I open it. Suddenly, it rattled hard. I jumped back, as it rattled again.

"Halo? Hilda? Hilda?" It was the cook. I went to the door in relief, my hand on the key to turn it, but then I heard the voice of MacInnes, saying something quietly in Gaelic, and the door rattled again. I snatched up the pitcher from the side and ran back into the hall, closing the kitchen door behind me. I checked the front door, but the bolts were still tightly drawn across. I went into the front room. MacInnes face suddenly leered up at the window, his arm at an un-natural angle, dangling from his side. I snatched the curtains shut, and he began to pound on the front door, cursing in Gaelic. Setting the pitcher on the floor I went and dragged the drop leaf table through the hall, and then one of the wingback chairs, and used them to barricade the kitchen door. I stood back, panting, then drank a gulp of water straight from the pitcher. The voice of the cook came through the front door now, calling, and I sat on the bottom step of the staircase, watching and listening until the cook's voice went quiet and the knocking stopped. Then I went back up to the bedroom.

197

Hilda was still asleep, her arm flung out, her cheeks stained with tears. There was a trace of resemblance to Duncan in the curve of her forehead and chin. I put the pitcher on the desk beside my letter to Inverness. Unsent and useless. What would become of Mr O'Brady now? I lay down next to Hilda.

When I awoke the room was dark and stuffy, but there was a faint pool of light from an oil lamp on the table. I sat up, looking about me, but Hilda had gone. I listened and heard the creaking of the boards, and as the door opened, I half-rose from the bed, in fear. It was Hilda, carrying a tray and another lamp in her other hand that cast dark circles beneath her eyes and left a smoky trail behind it. I fell back upon the pillow.

"I thought for a minute that you were MacInnes," I said.

Hilda put down the tray on the desk.

"You didn't unlock the door, did you?" I said, sitting up again suddenly.

"No Ma'am, and I put the table and chair back too. The range has gone out, so we'll have to make do with this. She passed me a small plate with hard oat biscuits covered in soft white cheese.

I got up and peered out through the crack in the curtain. It was so dark all I could see was my own pale reflection peering back at me. I turned to the girl. "Hilda, what do you remember of my husband?"

She sat down on the bed. "I didn't know Master Godfrey very well, being down in London as he was for most of the time. My uncle used to say he was a strange wee lad."

"Strange how?"

"He used to have these outbursts even at the age of five or six. No one could calm him, not even his mother, he'd go stiff with rage and lie on the floor."

Prone to outbursts, I thought. That's what he'd said about his brother. It was though he had simply swapped his own childhood with his brother's, the games, the adventures, everything had been swapped. "Did he get on with Alexander, as a child, I mean?"

"I don't know, Ma'am. Like I said, he was sent down to London when he was young."

"Leaving his youngest brother behind."

Hilda shook her head. "No, Godfrey is the youngest, Ma'am. He's younger by five years."

"No, that's not right, Hilda. If Godfrey inherited the estate then surely he's the oldest."

Hilda looked down at the bed and fiddled with the edge of the coverlet. When she spoke again, her words came out in a rush. "He didn't inherit the estate, he stole it, stole it from Alasdair."

I looked at Hilda in confusion, so she went on:

"The estate was supposed to go to Alasdair as he's the firstborn son, the heir. His Lairdship and Her Ladyship were very young when they met, he was just an officer in the army and she a lass of seventeen. The families disapproved and so they went away to Ireland where he had a posting and they lived there as common-law husband and wife. It's the custom in Ireland and Scotland and that is where Alasdair was born. A few years later when His Lairdship inherited the estate they were told Alasdair's birth wasn't recognised in England. He was counted as born out of wedlock."

I remembered Godfrey's words: *Alex is a thorough bastard.* I hadn't understood their meaning.

"His parents did everything to get Alasdair's birth right recognised, they even went before a Justice in Annan and they swore an oath, it was recorded in the back of her Ladyship's bible. The justice said that would be more than enough to settle the matter and Alasdair was raised as the future clan chief and taught how to manage the estate." Hilda looked up at me, her face a dark frown. "But Godfrey stole it from him."

I thought of the day I had met Godfrey. "It's all mine now," he had said, holding up his signet ring. There had been glee in his voice.

"But how did he steal it?"

"Last October, the old Laird died unexpectedly. It was a shock to everyone and Her Ladyship took it very hard. A letter was written instructing Godfrey to come up from London, but it was nearly a month later before he arrived. We heard a carriage coming up the drive, at speed, and we all went out to greet it. Her Ladyship, grey with grief, was leaning on Alasdair's arm. The carriage door opened and Godfrey stepped out with Colonel

Crawford at his side. He looked at us standing on the steps and all he said was, "I have some news. Father's title is now to pass to me." He'd come to serve notice on his brother. He had had a legal writ drawn up that his brother had one week to clear the castle and be off the estate."

"But how? After his parents had taken the oath that Alexander was the rightful heir?"

"Godfrey had been before an English court and he had it overruled. That's what he'd been doing down in London for a month. There was no record of the oath at Annan, you see, for his mother's bible had been lost some years back and the justice who had signed the oath was long dead. Her Ladyship pleaded with Godfrey, begged him not to put his brother out, but he would not listen. The shock of it all broke Her Ladyship's heart and she died that night. Then Alasdair quit the castle and he went away without a penny."

After what you have done?! Alexander had been dispossessed by his own brother.

I went quickly over to the carpet bag that lay beneath the window to show Hilda what I had found, but there was a sudden hammering at the front door. Without thinking I drew back the curtain and looked out. It was MacInnes and he stood below, with a flaming torch in one hand, his other arm in a sort of sling. He lifted the torch towards the window.

"Good evening, Y'Ladyship," he called. His voice was slurred and the torch made a circle as he swayed. "I thought you'd like to know, I've had word from the mainland. The colonel and His Lordship will be here tomorrow." He swayed a little more, spat on the ground, muttering something in Gaelic. Then he staggered away and took up guard at the entrance to the house.

Chapter Twenty-nine

Sollas

I walked up the road in the sunshine towards the schoolroom, eager to ask Her Ladyship if the letter to Inverness had been sent. All the way up the road I imagined it being carried away on a steamer across the sea, where it would be tucked inside a leather satchel and bumped all the way up the main door of the castle and given to the sheriff. And the sheriff would read it and, without having even a mouthful of breakfast, would go straight down to the gaol and demand the key. Then Mr O'Brady would get up off his thin wooden bed, and he would stretch out his long legs and yawn, and the sheriff would open the gaol door and brush off Mr O'Brady's suit for him, pass him his hat and his pipe, and say how awfully sorry he was for the misunderstanding. And then, I thought, my heart doing a little skip, Mr O'Brady would come back to Sollas, to me.

But when I reached the schoolroom and opened the door, there was no one there. The chairs were just as I left them, and there was no sign of Her Ladyship at all. I went out of the schoolroom and stood looking up the road towards the colonel's house, shading my eyes in the sun.

"What are you looking for?" It was Cormac. The other children who were following up the road behind him.

"I'm looking for Her Ladyship, but she's not here yet." I turned back towards the empty road.

We sat on the machair beside the schoolroom to wait for her. It was a hot, still day. Some children made daisy-chains, others wrestled in the grass, but after a while, they began to drift home until only Cormac and I remained. He picked stalks of grass and peeled them with his nail, and flicked seed heads into a shower in his lap.

I kept watching the road. Perhaps she was waiting for her books to arrive, her Atlas of the world.

When the sun had swung round the side of the church, Cormac stood up.

"Come on," he said.

"Where are you going?"

"Let's walk up to the colonel's house and see if she is there."

We stood up and my legs were stiff from sitting for so long, my eyes strained from looking. As we went up the road I saw that although the sky was still blue, clouds were bubbling up far out on the horizon; white mountains tinged with grey.

"Maybe she's sick," Cormac said as we walked past the reverend's house.

I thought of how she had been sick in our croft. "She was well yesterday."

"Do you think he will come back?"

"Who?"

"Mr O'Brady."

"Of course, he promised me he would."

He kicked a stone in front of him. "You're sweet on him, aren't you?"

"Don't be daft." I glanced at him, my cheeks growing hot, but he didn't look up. He was studying the ground in front of him.

"I've always liked you, Morag," he said, kicking his stone again so it bounced along in front of us. "But you're, well, you're a lot different to me." He gave me a tiny glance. "You're clever."

"You're clever too," I said quickly.

He shrugged. "Maybe, but you like letters, you like knowing things, you're like him."

I stopped in the road and looked at him.

"What I mean," he said, looking at his feet, "is that if he doesn't come back, well you know, I'm…"

But he didn't finish, because two riders were coming in a fast canter from the direction of the colonel's house, kicking up a cloud of dust in front of them, and as the dust cleared, I saw that it was Mr McInnes and the colonel. "You there," called the colonel sharply to us in English, "You children!"

We shrank back into the grass, two field mice awaiting the swoop of the hawk. Colonel Crawford drew up his horse so close to us I could see right up its shell pink nostrils, they looked as

202

soft as velvet. I looked up at the colonel, his face was set like stone.

"Do they speak English, well, do they?" he demanded of Mr McInnes who drew level on his own smaller brown horse. I saw that he was riding one handed, the other arm was strapped across his body.

Mr MacInnes looked down at me. His face had a sickly glaze and his eyes were glassy and rimmed with red as though he had not slept in a while. "She does - that one there."

"We have come to serve notice that Sollas has now been repossessed by the estate and is to be cleared immediately," he said. "MacInnes, give them the notice."

Mr MacInnes fumbled in the inside of his pocket and pulled out a rolled parchment, stamped with an unbroken red seal.

"This is from the Justice of the Peace in Inverness," the colonel said. "It is a legal document." He pointed to me with his riding crop. "You can be the one to deliver it, I think. MacInnes, give it to her."

MacInnes leaned down from his horse, and I saw him wince as he moved his injured arm. Dumbly I took the parchment, feeling the thick, patterned wax beneath my thumb. We were like cattle being driven down the road in front of the two men, the hot breath of the horses on our necks. Cormac's face was blazing and I could see his lip was trembling, like mine, but he did not catch my eye. I looked straight ahead, we were at rise in the road and from here I could see the reverend's stone house and the stone church, and there was the school room opposite, and a little further on were the rigs. I could see people bending and digging, I heard someone laugh. Smoke was rising in straight columns from the crofts beyond, I caught its toasted, peat smell, and washing flapped on a line in a sudden breeze. Down on the beach, two women were stretching out a fishing net between them to dry.

In the road outside the church, Peter was crouching, clinking his pebbles together. He looked up when he saw us and stood up, in that half-hunched position of his, his head bobbing on his neck.

"Peter," I called. "Run, run and find Mammy."

He gave a groan, flapping his arms against his sides, moaning and shouting, but he did not move. I saw the people in the rigs stop work and stand up, shading their eyes to see.

"Go on, Peter," I said, "run."

He wailed, but he did not move, and the women on the beach looked up too.

From behind us, I heard MacInnes snigger. "Is this your village watchman, a stupid daftie with a soft head?"

Cormac turned then and stopped. He snatched at the bridle of MacInnes' horse, yanking it hard. "He's not stupid, he's got more brains than you, MacInnes, you stinking worm."

"You little..." and he swiped at Cormac with his boot.

"MacInnes. We are on official business here, control yourself." Crawford barked.

"Walk on," he said, whether to his horse or to us, it was hard to tell. Peter first, flapping his arms and pulling at his clothes, and Cormac and I next with the two horses and their riders behind us. We were like a funeral procession, I thought, bearing the parchment in my hand, winding our way towards the village along the hot road. Having seen us, people were now coming in from the rigs.

There was Mrs MacRae and Cormac's Ma too. When she saw us, she began to cry out, "Cormac! Cormac!" and ran through the crops to reach us.

"Keep walking," the colonel instructed, flicking his riding crop against his boot, and even though Cormac's Ma had drawn level with us and was pulling at Cormac's arm, he didn't stop. Villagers had gathered outside the crofts too, twenty or so, then more, spilling out into the road, or up from the beach and in from the machair. I saw Mammy then, up on the peat bank, and she was running, running down the hill towards us with a peat iron in her hands. Peter lumbered away towards her.

"Stop here," the colonel said. He looked about him as people pushed closer in a circle. His horse was nervy of the crowd and tossed its head and struck the road with its hooves. I looked for Da, but I couldn't see him.

Mammy, though came pushing through, red faced, her forehead damp, and stood between the people and the factor, her peat iron by her side. "What is your business here?" she

204

demanded of MacInnes, "Why is my daughter with you?" She looked at me. "Morag? What is this?"

I lifted the parchment roll with a quavering hand.

"Give it to me," Colonel Crawford said, snatching it up from me. "Now, you will translate this."

He broke the red seal and unrolled it. Then he spoke in that frost-sharp voice of his.

"Notice is hereby given that you must all quit your dwellings forthwith. Every man, woman and child must vacate their croft and take all chattels immediately. Those that do not agree to go willingly to Langais will be removed by force, by the authority of the Inverness Constabulary."

My voice followed his, breaking like waves over large rocks. He lowered the parchment. Somebody coughed, but no one spoke.

"This notice has been signed by the Justice of the Peace in Inverness and is a legal document," he said. "Those that do not go peacefully will be removed and placed on the ship which will depart from Lochmaddy in two days' time."

All the eyes of the village were on me now and how I wished they were not. There was a ripple of shock as I translated what the colonel had said.

"We haven't had enough time," someone called out.

The colonel looked about him and MacInnes translated for him.

"You've had warning since March," the colonel replied. "Many of you agreed back then that you would go, you knew that this day was coming."

"What about our crops?" someone else said. "We can't leave those."

"Any financial loss will be fairly off-set against the rents you owe," the colonel said.

"But how will we feed ourselves?"

"Rations of meal will be provided."

There was a wave of despondency through the crowd and some began to turn away.

"But what about Her Ladyship? She was sent to help us," Cormac's Ma called.

"Her Ladyship?" the colonel asked, when he understood the question. He glanced at MacInnes, then gave a sort of dry laugh and shook his head. "No, no. Her Ladyship wasn't sent here to help you. She is feeble-minded, she has been taken away."

There was a gasp in the crowd and I saw Mammy shake her head.

I looked up at the colonel.

"And what about Mr O'Brady?"

He looked down at me in surprise, then his face darkened. "Mr O'Brady is in gaol at Inverness castle, awaiting sentencing. He will be transported to the colonies."

Mammy dropped her peat iron with such a clang that it bounced in the road and made Crawford's horse startle and dance. He thrashed it with his riding crop. Mammy stepped forward and put her hand on my shaking shoulder. She stared up at the colonel, her eyes flashing darkly.

"*Losgadh do chridhe ort!*" she cursed him. "The burning of your heart to you."

But the colonel only nodded to MacInnes and kicked his horse so that people had to jump aside as he trotted away. There was a moment when nobody moved or spoke, Mammy with her arms around me, and in that tiny instant I imagined that we were caught forever, like insects in a piece of amber, just as Mr O'Brady had described. But as the colonel and MacInnes left, the crowd stirred. People went into their homes, some cried out, or called on the Lord, others hurried to find their husbands and wives and children.

As the crowd dispersed, I saw Da, standing in the road, covered in stone dust from head to toe, white as a ghost.

We went into our croft and coming in from the bright sunlight it was utterly dark to our eyes for a moment, as though it were already empty. Da put his hand on Mammy's shoulder.

"It's time, Ceit," he said. His voice was hoarse as though full of stone dust. "Just as we agreed, we'll sell the pearl and we'll start again somewhere else."

My heart started hammering in my chest, my voice froze in my throat.

Mammy nodded and went slowly then to her wedding chest and knelt beside it. She pulled out Da's best suit and rummaged in the top pocket.

"Where is it?" she muttered. "It can't be gone." She began taking things out of her chest, the suit, her best dress, the Bible, shaking everything twice. My heart beat fast to watch her, but I could not speak. Mammy sat back on her heels, pulling off her kerchief, so that her hair tumbled free, she looked at Da.

"The pearl, Artair. It's gone." She looked at him with a stricken face.

Da came and knelt beside her, turning out all the pockets of his suit, turning The Bible upside down and giving all the pages a mighty shake. "Could Peter have taken it?" he asked. "Could the lad have taken it?"

"I took the pearl," I said, my voice finally breaking.

Mammy sat back and looked at me. "What?"

"I took it and I threw it into the sea."

Da stood up and stared at me.

"It was a mermaid's treasure so I took it and I threw it into the sea to ask the mermaid to help us."

He came over to me and for a moment I thought he was going to strike me. But he didn't, he just grabbed my arms and held them very tightly, looking at me in the face with his red-rimmed eyes.

"Why? Why? Why did you do that?"

I tilted my chin at him. "Mammy told me that the mermaid gave her that treasure for rescuing her. That's what she said, so I gave it back to the mermaid so that she would help us."

Da gave a groan then sank into his chair and put a white hand on his forehead. "This is what you get, Ceit," he said, "for telling her stories."

I looked at Mammy. My insides were crumbling, like a tower made of sand when the sea reaches it.

"You said that you saw a mermaid, you swore on cold iron you did."

Mammy stood up and her hands fumbled for the table and she sat down hard on the narrow bench, her hand to her face.

"You swore!"

Mammy looked up at me. Her face was so blank so that I hardly recognised her, then she blinked and frowned. "I did see a mermaid, Morag, and I will never forget it, but the story is not quite the way I told you." She swallowed hard. "Because the mermaid, that day, you see, the mermaid, it was- killed."

"What? No. You said you saved it, you turned to the crowd and told them, "No," and then you set it free."

She looked up at me and slowly shook her head. "No, I couldn't. I couldn't save it. The crowd was too quick, they were throwing stones, I couldn't save it."

I stared at her and she spoke in a flat voice. "A stone struck it on the head, and it vanished beneath the waves. Its body was washed up a few days later on the beach. The factor instructed it to be taken to the church and it was given a proper burial on Benbecula."

I stared at her. "But you told me you saved her."

She looked at the floor. "I wanted to, I tried to, but I couldn't. I wanted to tell you a happy story, with a happy ending." She put her hands in her face.

"Well who gave you the pearl?

She looked up. "It belonged to your Grandmammy. It was from France."

"And it was our only hope of escape," Da said. We've got nothing now, nothing. We're trapped." He stood up and turned to me. "When did you throw it away? Perhaps it can still be found."

"I didn't throw it away. I threw it into the sea. For help. And Mr O'Brady came, didn't he? To help us."

"And What's happened to him now? He's been locked up!" Da said. "He's going to be sent to the colonies for his efforts. What are we going to do, Ceit? There's no way we can send Morag to your sister's, they are stretched enough with all their mouths to feed, and now there's the lad, Peter, too."

Mammy looked up. "Where is he? Where is Peter?"

208

Chapter Thirty

North Uist

I was so thirsty that I could hardly swallow. The pitcher lay on its side on the desk, I had been to it so many times, running my finger, then my cracked lips around it, but there was not a single drop left. The sun blazed through the window and out on the moorland the pools of dark peat water glinted teasingly. I had lost track of time, even the sun did not seem to move, but only burned directly into the room that I was locked in.

We had been woken at dawn by the sound of splintering wood and battering, then heavy feet clattering on the stair. There was no time for anything, save to half-sit up, as Godfrey and the colonel had burst in to find Hilda and me clinging to each other in fright. The girl had been yanked away, out of the room. Godfrey had stood for a moment staring at me before turning on his heel, locking the door behind him.

So thirsty. I had spent some time calling to be let out, another portion of time banging with the flat of my hand against the wood, but this had hurt my throat and it had brought no one. Then I had stood staring out of the window and watched the colonel and MacInnes ride out, another two other men ride in, and then it was too hot to stand by the window anymore. I didn't sweat though, and if I had, I would have licked the salty beads straight off my skin. I lay on the bed staring up at the cracked ceiling. I thought of Morag's upturned face, full of hope, and my heart pinched. Had she waited for me today at the schoolroom? The letter to Inverness, unsent and useless, lay on the desk. I had not even been able to save Hilda. She had been dragged away.

So thirsty. I heard hooves on the drive and I went to the window to see. It was the colonel and MacInnes returning. "The constabulary will be here at first light," I heard the colonel say as he dismounted. "Make sure you get rid of the body."

I peered down onto the driveway, but MacInnes led the two horses away, awkwardly with one arm, and I heard Crawford come into the house.

"At first light," he had said. I saw the circle on the map around Sollas draw tighter.

Where was Godfrey? I had heard his voice once in the hallway and had gone to the door and called out to him. Why had he not come in? I wanted to confront him, about the hotel bill, the card chits, his brother. And to warn him, about Mr Brentwood. The sun moved round the side of the house and the room began to slowly cool. The door opened. It was Godfrey with a jug and glass in his hand. He came over to me by the window.

He set the glass down on the desk beside me. "You must be parched." He filled the glass in a great splash. It was the sweetest sound and it was all I could do not to snatch it out of his hand. He did not pass the glass to me straight away though, but picked it up and held it for a moment, as though admiring how the light played on the water, as though considering whether to give it to me at all. When he did, I gulped it down and poured another and another until the jug was nearly empty. Godfrey sat down upon the bed.

"Where have you been, Godfrey?" I asked, setting the glass on the desk and turning to him.

"Down to London," he said.

"About the estate, about the debts?"

He ran his hands through his hair. "What a mess," he groaned.

"Godfrey, I know about what happened last year about how you took the estate from your brother."

He looked up at me, the colour rising up his neck suddenly. "The estate was rightfully mine," he said quickly. "And the law agreed with me."

"But what about your parents and their wishes?"

"My parents!" he said it with such force that I stepped backwards. He narrowed his eyes at me. "Have you been listening to estate gossip?"

But my confidence grew. "It's hardly gossip. I know that those stories you told me, of your childhood, none of them happened to you, did they? They were your brother's stories."

He stared at me for a moment, then looked down at his hands. Ha! I thought, now I have got him on the back foot.

"The story of you swimming out to the Point, that wasn't you was it? It was your brother. And that ring, it was given to Alex that Hogmanay, instead of you."

His shoulders slumped and I felt sorry then, to have shamed him like that. I sat down next to him on the bed and reached for his hand, but he pulled his hand away and there was a look of hatred on his face.

"What do you know, of my childhood, Maria? Hmm? To be packed off to school when you were seven, where, where older boys would, well, they would..." His mouth worked, trembled a little, but nothing came out.

"It was for your health, Godfrey."

"Ha. My health. That's only what they said to people, but the plain fact is they just didn't want me. 'If he's too much of a handful,' I heard my father say to my mother, 'let's send him down to school.' Once a year my mother came to visit me, once a year! And then only to tell me tales about my wonderful brother. The riding, fishing and all the other adventures." He stood up abruptly, but kept his back turned. "I had nothing, and no one, and Alex had it all." He wheeled round. "And then when I was fifteen, I discovered that the estate was actually supposed to be mine, *mine*! It should have been Alex packed off to school, not me." His eyes were flashing with emotion now and I felt a flicker of fear at seeing the strength of it, as though something was being unleashed.

I could not help myself from asking him. "And how did you come to find out?"

"I was travelling up from London with an aunt to spend Hogmanay at the castle and she mentioned the business about the oath at Annan. About my parents getting a Justice to witness that Alex was their rightful heir. She thought I knew, you see."

When he spoke again the emotion rolled off him like a wave.

"I spoke to father as soon as I arrived. I asked him about why the estate wouldn't come to me. He said, unfortunately I wasn't clan chief material, that I would make a hash of it and he didn't want the place going to the dogs."

I watched him twisting the signet ring round and round on his finger. "Was this the same Hogmanay that Alex was given the ring?"

But he did not answer, only bowed his head and gripped his hands together until his fingers were white. I could imagine how galling it must have been to watch his brother receive the ring. For a second, I could see what pleasure there must have been in taking the estate from Alexander.

"I vowed then, that night, that the estate would be mine," he said. "I've waited all this time, only to be told there is nothing left. Well, I'm not losing it now, I will not lose it."

There was that strange high note in his voice and I thought back to what Duncan had said, of how Godfrey had become crazed when Alex got the ring, so crazed that he had run through the castle with the burning branches and had nearly set it alight. How no one could stop his outbursts.

I stood up to go to the door, but he stood up too and quickly pulled me towards him, squeezing my arm hard. "You are going to help me though, aren't you, Maria?" he said softly.

"Godfrey, please you're hurting my arm."

"I am at fault," he said, shaking his head. "With all this business with the estate, I have neglected you. How I wish I had been more attentive or I would have seen it."

"Seen what?" I asked trying to pull away.

"The return of your illness of course."

"What on earth do you mean?"

"I found that journal. The one you left in your room at the castle. What you wrote about marital relations is quite explicit."

I remembered my intoxicated entry about his nightly visits and I felt my cheeks grow hot. "That was private," I protested.

"Added to the feminist literature that you stole from the library and hid under your bed. And then you engaged in an intimate picnic with an Irishman you barely knew. It was documented in a newspaper, I might add."

"It wasn't like that."

"Really? MacAllen said he found you in a state of undress with your stockings thrown in with the picnic things."

He put his hand on my cheek, but it was not a tender gesture. I felt the pressure of his hand. His thumb began to dig under my jaw, his long fingers press very close to my eye socket. I made myself stand very still, I hardly breathed.

"And then only yesterday, you attacked a servant, broke his arm, then barricaded yourself in the house. When the rescue party came, they found you half-dressed and in bed with another woman."

"Godfrey, listen to me, please."

"No, you listen to me." He brought his face close to mine. "This is not normal behaviour and it is a husband's sad duty when his wife is of feeble mind to take the necessary steps to protect her."

He released me and I stumbled backwards.

"I'm not feeble-minded!"

"Your actions have shown otherwise, I'm afraid. You are clearly not of sound mind, Maria. Your aunt warned me, the doctor warned me, but I did not listen. I thought I could care for you, but now I see it is for your own safety and the safety of others that you are committed to somewhere that can care for you in the most appropriate way."

I understood his meaning then and panic rose in me. "What is this?" I cried. "What is this scheme?" And when he refused to answer, I pushed his chest with both hands so that he staggered backwards in surprise.

His retaliation was swift. He grabbed a handful of my hair and yanked it so hard, that my neck jerked and I cried out at the violence of it. He dragged me back to the bed by my hair and pushed me down. I did not dare to look up at him for fear of exciting his rage any further. I could feel his body trembling as he stood over me.

"Godfrey," I pleaded. "Think of my inheritance, of the money."

He laughed. "Ah yes. Your inheritance. I read about it in your Grandfather's obituary. It was Crawford who said I should go after it, that it could be the answer to my financial woes. He didn't think I could pull it off."

"But you need an heir to get the money."

He looked down at me with something like disgust. "Actually, it turns out that I don't. That's what I was in London for." He pulled out a paper from his jacket. "Do you know what this is, Maria?" He shoved it in my face and I only caught the name Doctor Fortnum and a signature. "It turns out that if a wife is deemed to be mentally unsound, her husband must immediately take possession of all monies belonging to her. It is a hard decision of course. But with no alternative, it is one that I have made."

With a mere stroke of pen upon paper I was to be locked away. Panic gripped me. I could not go back there, I would not. "Please, Godfrey, if you mean to get rid of me at least let me go back to my aunt. You can have the money. Please." I despised the pathetic tone in my voice, the crawling creature I had become.

"Your aunt?" he scoffed. "She doesn't want you. She was in on it in the first place. Do you know what she said to me that day you first came to lunch? "If you show Maria the library, she will definitely agree to marry you."

I stared at Godfrey in disbelief. My aunt had pretended to be asleep?

Out in the hallway I heard heavy footsteps and I sat up ready to try a last-ditch bargain.

"Godfrey, I know about your gambling debts. Look, I can sell my jewellery, my wedding ring, my clothes. I know you need money very urgently, I know about Mr Brentwood."

He looked surprised.

"I met his lacky in the velvet coat. The one you gave your watch to, the one who has been following us since London. The one who smashed the castle window."

His eyes glittered and a strange smile played on his face. "Ah, Mr Atkins. He did not break the window. I had a groundsman do it in order to arrest O'Brady. He was becoming troublesome."

"Listen to me. Mr Atkins is coming for you, Godfrey."

Godfrey gave a cold, high laugh. "No, Maria. He's not. Mr Atkins has come for you."

And with that he opened the door and the man in the velvet coat stepped in.

Chapter Thirty-one

The full moon was slowly rising over Eaval hill like an eye, pale and luminous. The midday nights were nearly here when the night would be no longer black, but would stay as a dark blue twilight and a thin streak of light would be always on the horizon. Those days were still a little way off though so I waited until darkness fell and then I set out.

My shoes hurt me so much now that I went barefoot. Quietly past the church and the school room. The moon watched me as I left the village. Wisps of cloud blew across it and its light came and went as though it were winking. It illuminated the road, then cast it into blackness, lit the white wing of an owl then caused it to vanish in the dark. Down below the machair I heard the surf breaking on the shore. The salt-breeze brushed my arms and legs.

As I reached the rise in the road, I turned to take a last look at Sollas. Darkness had folded the village into its cloak and I could hardly see it. All afternoon we had called and searched for Peter, half the village joining in, but he was nowhere to be found. Mammy said he would have been scared by the colonel's coming and had probably gone to up to the moors. I half expected him to rise out of the grass beside me, clinking his pebbles and making his soft sounds. How I wished for his presence when once I had so feared it. I set my face to the road again and continued walking, on towards the colonel's house. My heart started beating faster in my chest, but I had fixed what I was going to do in my mind. I could see now, in the distance, the dark outline of the colonel's house set up on its hillock against the night sky. Then, I heard the soft snicker of a horse and saw just ahead of me in the machair to my left there were two figures, one on horseback and the other searching for something in the long grass.

"It's not here," the one in the machair said.

"It can't be gone," the other on the horse said. "I left it here." It was the voice of Mr MacInnes, rough as sacking. I saw the outline of him get off his horse, unevenly, cursing in pain, then he went through the machair, kicking through the grass roughly.

"Maybe it wasn't dead," the other said.

"It was dead alright, I rode right over it and back again," came MacInnes" reply. He gave the grass a final kick, then turned back to his horse. "Come on, we'll have a look further down the road."

They led the horse down to the road towards me and my heart jumped in fright. I threw myself into the heather moor at the side of the road. I lay on my stomach and hoped the shallow ditch and the cloud-cast moon would hide me. I pressed my face into the scratchy heather, felt the peat earth in my nostrils and listened as the boots and hooves got closer.

"Crawford will hang you if I don't find it," the other said.

"Shut up," MacInnes replied. He was so close now that I could hear his raspy breath rattling in his chest, could smell the liquor coming off him.

"What was that?" he asked.

I did not even breathe, but my heart was thumping so hard in my chest that I was sure they could hear it. Now my breath was bursting in me, as though I had taken a gulp of smoke, I could feel it scratching in my throat wanting to burst out in a cough.

"Over here," MacInnes said and I knew that I was done for.

I heard his boots, closer still, when just beyond me, a grouse burst up out of the heather with a cry of alarm. The moon suddenly appeared and caught the white of its feathers.

"Just a grouse," the other said. "Come on, we'd better keep on looking."

My breath burst out of me as I heard them walk on down the road. I waited until their steps had faded and then I scrambled to my feet and ran. I stuck to the dark moorland, my feet tripping over rough ground, all the way to the colonel's gate. I stood looking up at the house and it stared back at me from its many windows. Every glassy eye was dark, save one on the ground floor that glowed dimly. My purpose beat through me and yet, in truth, I was scared. I had not said goodbye to Mammy or Da, or Cormac or anyone else, and now the chill that I would never see them again crept over me. But then I thought of Mr O'Brady, sitting in his cold gaol cell for something that he did not do when he had only come to help us and I felt bold. The words I would say formed clearly in my mind. I went up the drive and peeped through the lit window. An oil lamp burned on a table and by its light I saw three men asleep in fine-looking chairs. On a small table between them was a bottle of whisky, near empty. One of the men was the colonel, his sandy hair falling across his eyes. The second was a thin, pale fellow in a smart suit with his long legs stretched out in front of him. His head, on top of his long white neck, was propped up one fist. The third man wore a velvet coat, but although he was smartly dressed, his face looked rough and I could hear his snores through the glass.

I went up to the front door and lifted my hand to knock, but as I did so I heard a tiny tap. I looked around. There it was again, a tiny glass tap. Looking up I saw the pale face of Her Ladyship looking down at me from a window.

"Your L-," I began to say in surprise, but she put a finger to her lips with such force that the words vanished in my mouth.

She was pointing to the front door and showing to be very quiet so I turned the big brass handle and found that the door was open. I had only ever seen the outside of the Inn at Lochmaddy and this house was bigger than that. Looking up I could hardly see the ceiling and in front of me was a huge great set of wooden steps leading off into roof. I listened, I could hear the rumbling snores of the colonel to my left and there was the faint glow of the lamp beneath the door. Again, there was a little tap, a wooden one this time, coming from the darkness above the steps. Carefully, I climbed up them, clinging on to the rail as I went higher and higher. Half-way up was the head of a stag which nearly made me fall backwards with fright. I stopped, I could hardly see where I had started, or the floor above, and my head swam a little, my palm sweaty on the wooden rail, doubting that I could go any further. Another little tap, this time more urgent, and I pressed on reaching the top and catching my breath as though I had climbed a hill. I stood at the top, marvelling how there seemed to be another whole house up here, with doors and floors and ceilings too, just as Mr O'Brady had told me there was in London. A tap, tap, tap came from a door further along and I followed it in the dark, feeling my way along the cold wall.

Reaching it I gave a little tap back and Her Ladyship's voice came through in a whisper. "Unlock the door."

I felt then for the handle, felt something metal sticking out and I shook it hard.

"No, you must turn it," she said. I heard a click, and the door opened. Her pale face appeared and she pulled me into the room and closed it behind her.

The moon shone brightly through the window and for a moment I drew back, afraid. Her Ladyship's short hair was wild, sticking up in all directions, her face was sallow and her lips looked swollen and were trembling. I remembered about the colonel saying that she was feeble-minded and I was certain in that moment that it was true.

She gripped me with shaking hands and I smelled her awful, rank breath and I drew back in fear. "Morag," she said in a dry whisper. "What are you doing here?"

My purpose came back to me then and my voice came out in a tremble. "I am here to tell the colonel that I smashed the window at the castle."

"What?" Her eyes widened. "But why would you say that?"

"Because Mr O'Brady is in gaol and is to be sent to the colonies for something he didn't do."

"But you didn't do it either."

"It's my fault," I said, the sick truth of it clawing in my stomach. "I threw Mammy's pearl in the sea and now there is a ship waiting in Lochmaddy and we will be sent to America, so I might as well go to gaol."

Her Ladyship looked as though she might cry, but no tears came out of her eyes. She put her hand to her mouth. "Where is the colonel and my husband?"

"They are asleep downstairs with another gentleman too."

"And MacInnes?"

"He is looking for something on the machair."

She nodded and then turned quickly to the desk by the window. "Here," she said. "Take this. It is the letter I wrote to the sheriff in Inverness explaining that Mr O'Brady is innocent. Take it and send it. It will have better luck than your idea." The letter glowed white in the moonlight and she pushed me to the door.

"Go," she said, quickly pushing me out, "and be quick about it, Crawford's men will be here at first light."

Back down the stairs I crept, as fast as I could, though going downwards made me dizzy and twice I thought I would fall. In the hallway I listened. The colonel's snores had stopped. I froze by the door, waiting for his hand upon my shoulder, but then they started up again and, quick as a mouse, I tucked the letter in my apron pocket and darted out the door and away through the gate, not even looking back to see if her Ladyship was watching.

Half-way along the road home, I heard the voices of MacInnes and the other man coming towards me, and I cursed myself for not being smart enough to think that I would meet them on the road again. I dived into the nearest long grass, and lay flat, but they had given up searching it seemed, and the clouds had drawn in too, so there was hardly any light to see by.

"How many men has Crawford assembled for the eviction party?" the other man was saying.

"Two dozen constables and a few specials he hand-picked himself who really know their business and will get the job done," I heard MacInnes reply.

"Well let's get home and see if we can get a couple of hours sleep." The other man's voice trailed away into the darkness. I waited until the clip of the horse and their boots on the stones could no longer be heard.

I stood up cautiously and looked around. The moon was more thickly covered by clouds now and it struggled to peep out and see. I looked down to the beach, where the tide was half-in, and saw that something was lying there, down on the sand.

I peered in the darkness. Was it a clump of kelp or a seal? The moon burst forth and I drew back in horror. It was a large, pale body. I jumped down onto the sand and ran over to where it lay and I saw it was the body of Peter. He was curled on his side, as though he was asleep, but as soon as knelt and I touched him I felt how cold he was. I pulled him roughly onto his back and gave a cry, for his face was bloody and swollen and looked trampled as though by horses' hooves, and across his chest, was a dark, oozing puddle. A sob started in my throat and became a wail, I didn't care who heard me now. I threw back my head and gave a dreadful moan, for Peter, for Mr O'Brady, for Sollas. The moon drew the cloud over its face and refused to look. I looked down at him, how his big fists were curled, one around his three pebbles, and the other, the other, his fingers were already stiffening.

A shout came from up on the machair behind me, and I didn't even turn to look. Let them come, I thought. Then I heard the voice of a woman. "Down here!" she cried. I turned and saw flaming torches making towards me. Mammy was running across the sand. "Morag, Morag!" she cried, stumbling and falling on her knees and clutching at me. "Where have you been? Where? Oh, my love, my, oh, no."

She fell upon Peter then, keening. Others had reached us too. Marseil MacRae fell on her knees and stroked his pale hair, Da and Mr Morrison held torches over Peter's mangled body. I stood up, the wind had got up over the sea and I could smell rain. "It was MacInnes," I said to them all, "who killed Peter. And the eviction party is coming at first light."

Peter's body was carried off the beach and laid out in the schoolroom. Those that were still in their beds were summoned and Mr Morrison stood before the village, some still rubbing sleep from their eyes. Through the high windows of the schoolroom, I could see that black was already changing to indigo of dawn outside and the rain was beginning to catch on the glass.

"We understand that it will be today that the colonel and his men mean to evict us," Mr Morrison said, "with the support of the Lochmaddy constabulary and a regiment of soldiers."

A wave of sorrow and distress broke over the room. People clutched each other and cried out.

"We must have faith," Mr Morrison tried to lift his voice over the din, but even his booming sermon voice was washed away in the tide of sorrow and consternation.

Some at the front who had heard him cried out, "What's the point?" Someone else shouted, "What do we have left here?" and there were echoes of, "We're done for" and, "It's over."

Mammy stood at the front of the crowd, as still as a rock, watching the scene before her. Quick as a flash she climbed up on to Miss MacAllister's desk and stamped her foot hard, twice. There was immediate silence as the people turned to look at her.

220

"What's the point? I hear you asking, what do we have?" She cried out to the room. "Yes, we have nothing, and yet, when a poor, motherless boy came into our community, a boy who was the very least of us, we cared for him. Mrs MacNeill, you shared your crowdie with him. Marseil, you gave him clothes. Yes, we are nothing on our own, but together, together, we are something."

She stood tall and wild, my Mammy in her old work dress, staring fiercely down at us, and she looked at Da, who nodded.

"We have not endured famine, hardship, disease, and deprivation together to now be ejected like this. Are we not sons and daughters of Colla, of Conn of the Hundred Battles? Do we not have his blood in our veins? Do we not belong to this land more than any Englishman? We shall not be scraped lightly away like moss from a stone. No, we shall cling to it, bleed for it, rather than be removed, but we must all agree, to stand together, for if one agrees to go, we shall all be forced to follow."

The crowd before her said nothing, but every last person had their gaze fixed on my Mammy. From the back of the room, a reedy voice began to sing and turning round I saw it was Old Ma MacNeill.

A Chlanna Cuinn cuimhnichibh / Cruas an àm na h"iorghaile," Ye children of Conn/ remember hardihood in the time of battle"

It was a *brosnachadh,*a call to arms, an incitement to battle, and one by one, people added their voices to the ancient song.

* * *

Mammy pulled me up the hill towards the black flag. Her hand was wet and cold and squeezing mine too tightly. Our feet squelched and slipped in the peat bog, and the sodden heather and grass soaked through our shoes to our feet. My heart hammered in my chest like the waves at Cod Point, but Mammy wouldn't stop, and when I tripped and stumbled over a rock she dragged me on. *"Thugainn, Morag!"* she said in a voice that was so sharp, I swallowed my tears and stumbled on behind her. Mammy's pockets were bulging full of stones that clinked and bounced as she ran. The sack in her left hand bumped against her

221

leg. Her hem was stained and splattered dark with mud and wetness was rising like the tide up the back of her dress. The wind whipped the rain into our faces as we ran. I felt like I was swimming. I had a mouthful of water and everything was blurry. I am the rain and the rain is me.

We reached the flagpole, made from the boat's mast that had washed up on Sollas beach. It leaned in the wind as though it were still aboard the ship racing over the waves. Mammy dropped my hand, and the sack, and clung to the pole trying to catch her breath. Her breathing sounded like Mr. MacIver's jagged saw and her hair was plastered flat against her head so that her face was skull-like with two dark circles under her eyes. She had no bonnet. Her black bonnet was being used as the signal. It hung, sodden and miserable, like a dead thing, flapping half way up the pole. She yanked it down on the line of rope and pulled out the damask shawl from the sack. The fine blue shawl was quickly spattered with dark spots from the rain like blood.

Mammy suddenly froze and stared down at the Lochmaddy road below us. The rain was blowing across the bog in great rolling drifts so that the road appeared and vanished, appeared and vanished in the mist. Mammy gave a single terrifying shriek that ripped a hole in the mist and for a heartbeat the rain paused, cowering. In that moment I saw what she had seen. They were coming. Raise the flag, yes raise it up, for they were coming. Coming for us.

Chapter Thirty-two

"Your cash cow has escaped, Lord MacDonald. Mr Brentwood will be most unhappy." This was Mr Atkins.

"Find her and you'll get double what I promised you for delivering her to that hospital in Lambeth. And Mr Brentwood too," said Godfrey.

Torchlight reflected on the water. I crouched lower and held my breath. Footsteps and then another voice, the colonel's, said, "We need to make a move. If the constables and soldiers do not do this today, they will need paying for tomorrow as well, and they will need their board and lodgings too."

The frustrated escape of air from Godfrey's lips, then his boot kicked the stable door hard.

"Very well, Mr Atkins and I will continue the search. You and your men go on to Sollas."

"Have you seen my pistol? It was hanging on the door with my jacket."

I hugged the sack to my chest and did not breathe.

"For God sakes Crawford, take one of mine."

Footsteps departing, the torch too. Were they all gone? I peered around the stone trough and saw that the yard was empty. A lamp lit up the kitchen window, but I had to take a chance. I picked up my sack and quickly drew back the bolt of the stable door. The smell of mildewed straw and dung filled the night air.

"Hilda, come on, quickly now, come on."

Beside a pile of old tools in the corner, a dark bundle of clothes shifted. I saw it stand. The girl came trembling towards me, her eye half-swollen from where Atkins had struck her while looking for me. I went into the stable and held out my hand. "Quickly, come on."

"So, there you are." I wheeled around, it was Godfrey and he was blocking the doorway. I stepped backwards as he came into the stable towards me. My hand fumbled behind me for one of the tools leaning against the stable wall. It was a shovel and I swung it round and brought it crashing against the side of

Godfrey's head with all my strength. He fell straight down, onto the stable floor, and I did not know if I had killed him, only that we must run.

Out to the machair we ran, the sack thumping against my leg, to where the horse used for pulling the trap was tethered on a stake for the night. It snickered to see us and I took it by its head collar and held it still, whilst Hilda freed it from its stake. "Quick now, quick," I said to Hilda, shoving her up on the horse. I looked about, but saw there was no escape, for the machair only led down to the sea and the tide was nearly in. We would have to go around the front of the house and down the driveway. I reached into the sack. A half-remembered childhood tune began to play in my head.

Around the side of the house we crept, me leading the horse by the headcollar, Hilda half- slumped upon it. The horse's hooves seemed to catch every stone and make it sing out, 'look! They're here, they're here!' I held my breath, waiting for a shout. But when we got to the front of the house, the driveway was empty except for the heavy scuff of boot prints and hoofmarks that the constabulary had left behind in the gravel. Down the driveway I hurried, so that the horse broke into a trot to keep up with me. We only had to get to the road and then we would be free. At least it was cloudy so there was no moonlight. Only now and then the moon appeared, as though to watch our progress. The wind stirred the crops that lined the driveway and they waved us on, go, go, they rustled, keep going.

But at the entrance to the driveway, our luck failed. A broad-shouldered outline I knew so well blocked the way and I saw the curved glint of his knife. I drew the horse to a halt twelve feet away.

"You'll let us pass," I called.

"A valuable asset like you," he scoffed. "I don't think so. I've been waiting to cash you in for weeks."

"You will let me pass, Mr Atkins," I called. The song in my head was getting louder now. I stepped away from the horse to show him what I had pulled from the sack. The colonel's flintlock pistol. It had hung with his jacket on the backdoor as I had crept outside to the yard.

Mr Atkins laughed, an ugly sound.

"And you'd know how to use a pistol like that, would you?"

"My Grandfather taught me many things, Mr Atkins."

"Go on, then shoot it."

"I'll count to five. I'm warning you; you'd better move."

But he only stood there with the moonlight catching on his knife.

I aimed the gun. My hand was shaking badly, and I steadied it with the other. Then I pulled the trigger. Nothing. There was no spark and the charge did not light. Mr Atkins laughed again. I skimmed through the song that Grandpapa had devised: Load the powder in the gun /Wrap the ball up in its patch / Prime the flash pan/ pull the trigger, BANG. What was the missing line?

Mr Atkins came towards us, eight feet away now. There was nowhere to run. Six feet away, now four. So close that I could smell his fetid overcoat. It came to me: prime the flash pan *and cock the gun.*

I pulled the trigger. Bang.

Out on the road, I dropped the pistol and shakily mounted the horse behind Hilda then I kicked it on, hard. It broke into a quick trot and then a canter. I did not look back, but only put my arms around Hilda's waist, the square cornered shape of the sack's contents tucked between us, my fingers twined in the horse's rough mane. The rain began to fall, the glorious rain. I felt its cool relief on my chapped lips, sucked at the drops from my sleeve. But the wind was whipping in from the sea and the rain began to fall harder and harder. Soon it was no longer a relief, but a relentless icy curtain that chilled me to the core. The first grey dawn light was breaking. What did this day hold for Morag and the people of Sollas? I remembered the constables' rough boot prints in the gravel drive. This thing must be done today, the colonel had said. Oh Morag, Morag. Her small pinched face had loomed up out of the dark outside the colonel's house. She had been willing to sacrifice herself for Mr O'Brady. And what of him? Mr O'Brady? Would my letter ever reach Inverness? I did not know and I never would. My inaction was like an ink spot that could never be removed, that would stain me forever. No, there would be no peace. I tucked my face into Hilda's back for protection, was it wet from the rain or my tears? The girl was slumped like a sack of potatoes in front of me. On we went along the rutted road, the horse was tired and had slowed to a walk no matter how I kicked it on. Let them come, I thought, come and take me away. But no-one came. Hilda let out a cry. Looking up, I saw the wet slate roofs of Lochmaddy, and beyond that, waiting in the harbour, the masts of the tall ship bound for America.

The Battle for Sollas

They entered Sollas just after dawn, a dozen soldiers and other gentlemen on horses with two dozen of the constabulary marching on foot behind. Mr MacInnes rode up front beside Colonel Crawford, and through the rain, I thought I saw Mr Shaw, the Lochmaddy sheriff, at the rear. The rain was heaving down and the constables had their collars turned up and their hats pulled down low as they stopped outside the first crofts. Mammy, Da, Mr Morrison and Mr MacIver stood blocking the road at the head of a crowd of people, Cormac and I beside them.

Mammy had told the villagers in the schoolroom that a group of people becomes stronger when it stands together, and she was right. Now standing as a crowd, the people of Sollas had become something greater than their individual selves, made up of a hundred specks of dust, together we had become a large shadow beast, the Cu Sith itself that moved as one, spoke as one, and thought as one.

I reached up and held tightly to Mammy's hand and caught Cormac's eye -his terrified face was a match for my own. The eviction party had stopped a distance away, but we watched as Colonel Crawford kicked his horse forward in a brisk trot. I saw the flash of his shiny leather boot, and the horse's chest get closer and closer as he prepared to barge us. His horse drew up short though, tossing its head, snorting and dancing with fear at the shadow beast which blocked the road.

"We are here on legal business," Colonel Crawford said. "You have all been served notice and given time to quit since March. We are here to clear this village and you must disperse immediately so that the party can go about its business."

The crowd gave a low, muttering growl and stayed hunched in the road.

"We will not go," Mammy shouted. "Losgadh do chridhe ort!" She cursed him again, "the burning of your heart to you."

Crawford wheeled his horse about and consulted Shaw who had ridden to the front of the eviction party. I watched Shaw shake his head and point up to the stone church and then he rode away.

The colonel cast an angry look at us; his horse was lathered now in nervous sweat, pacing the road, its hooves striking the puddles in great splashes and he rode it up and down the line, past the constables, who shifted from foot to foot in the rutted road.

Mr Shaw came back, with Reverend Maclean hurrying along behind, skipping over puddles as best he could, his cassock flapping as he jumped. Mr Shaw brought him to the front of the party and the reverend stood before us. Rain dripped off his hat onto his cassock and his mouth opened and closed as he tried to think of what to say. He wrung his hands and looked up at the sky, but rain fell in his eyes and he looked hurriedly down, he was not used to delivering his sermon outdoors.

He lifted his hands. "People, I know and see your distress. But I urge you to go quietly and obediently in a way that is pleasing to God"

The crowd murmured.

"I urge you, go back to your homes, prepare yourselves, make peace with your situation, go in peace."

"Go back to your Church, you English puppet," someone shouted.

That was it.

Crawford, at the back of the line now, spun his horse around and with a violent kick, sent it leaping forwards, bucking. The other horses in the party responded, dancing and skittering forwards and sideways too. The charge was on, ten or twelve horses cantering towards us, the constables charging behind, with their batons raised. The crowd in the road scattered and dissolved, becoming individual specks again, and Mammy pulled me sharply against the wall of the nearest croft, as the horses went careering down the road, stones and mud flying from their hooves. All I could think of was Peter, and how he must have met his terrifying end. As the eviction party poured into the village, our crowd, which had melted, now re-formed and followed in noisy pursuit.

It was Old Ma MacNeill's croft that they came to first, opposite ours, banging on the door. Crawford was off his horse now with MacInnes at his side.

"Will you go to Langais?" demanded the colonel, MacInnes translating, but Mrs MacNeill shook her head.

"Out to that marsh?" she said. "And where exactly would I live ? I can't build a croft now can I?"

"Well, you shall board the ship to America then," the colonel said.

"An old lady like me, all the way to America? I will not go." She shook her head and folded her arms in the doorway.

Crawford nodded to MacInnes and a constable, and they shoved the old lady aside and pushed past her into the croft. A minute later, her chair was thrown out, its legs splitting in the mud, her mattress dragged beside it, bedsheets and clothes tossed out in the rain, her spinning wheel followed, smashing onto the road. A great wail rose out of Mrs MacNeil and it spurred the watching crowd, and we surged forwards, surrounding the party, pressing the horses and constables from all sides.

"Shame on you," Mr MacIver shouted. "Shame on you, MacInnes."

"This is a wicked and evil act," Mr Morrison cried. "In God's name have you no conscience at all?"

The colonel turned sharply to two constables beside him. "These men are ringleaders. Arrest them for inciting rioting and civil disorder, immediately."

Two constables came forward and seized them, and Cormac began pummelling his fists into the back of the policeman.

"And arrest this boy," Crawford said.

"No – Cormac," I screamed, grabbing hold of his arm as he was taken away. "No!" My grip on him was slipping, as he was sucked through the dense crowd like a man falling into quick-bog. He turned and looked at me one final time, then disappeared.

All around me, the people of Sollas howled in response and began a frenzied attack. A volley of stones was rained onto the eviction party and they responded, constables pounding their truncheons down wherever they could. I caught sight of Da, duckling beneath the swing of a truncheon, Mammy, running along the road. I looked everywhere for Cormac, but the crowd was too thick to get through and I was carried backwards, like down a river in spate. All along the road the crowd was savaging the edges of eviction party as it tried to go about its business, protected on either side by a line of police. Missiles and rocks were lobbed and thrown by the crowd, answered by the crunch of truncheons and the kick of boots. And yet still, as the party made its way from croft to croft, it left a trail of destruction in its wake. Each family tried to protect their croft, but they were told to quit, and when they did not agree, they were pushed aside, the furniture thrown out. At the MacRae's croft, I saw the thatch torn off with iron bars, Marseil and Seamus left under their bare rafters as the rain poured down on everything they owned.

Two lines of police formed and charged at us and Mammy shouted at everyone to disperse, sending people in every direction, running up alley ways, into the barley rigs, towards the stream. I caught up with her there, as she leaned on her knees to catch her breath beside Cormac's Ma.

"They've got Cormac," I cried. "They've arrested him and taken him away."

"Lord have mercy," Cormac's Ma cried out.

Mammy stood up then, her wild hair flying around her shoulders, but her face like flint, and she put a hand on my shoulder. "We will find him." Then she bent swiftly to refill her pockets with rocks and stones. "We'll go this way," she said to Cormac's Ma, pointing from the stream towards the crofts, "and surprise them."

We made our careful way up behind the crofts and Mammy motioned me to crouch behind a stack of peat. I hunkered down behind it, pressing my face into its rich earthy smell, tears leaking out for Peter who had hidden just like this only a few months before. Between the crofts, I could see that the eviction party had reached Aileen's door opposite us. Mammy put her finger to her lips and she and Marseil inched forward. I saw Aileen's pale face appear in the crack of the doorway and then MacInnes pull the door open widely and dragged her out with his one good arm. She had both twins in her arms; the larger one began to cry desperately, the other was pale and listless as the rain began to soak it. Mammy and Marseil crept closer, staying against the croft wall.

"Where is your husband?" Crawford demanded.

Aileen shook her head, "I have no husband, he is passed away."

Crawford shook his head in frustration, but I saw that his face was grimacing in a sort of pain. "MacInnes – clear the house," he said, but his breath was short and uneven.

MacInnes leaped forward grinning at Aileen as she stood up to her ankles in mud, his face close to hers, then I saw him put his filthy hand upon her breast. Two constables stepped forward to enter the croft, and at that moment Mammy gave a shriek and she and Marseil leapt out from their hiding place, pelting Crawford, MacInnes and the two constables with a torrential rain of stones. The men shielded their faces with their arms, all except MacInnes who could not protect himself seeing as his one good arm was upon Aileen. A stone hit him hard on his soft temple and he fell like a sack of wet sand to the ground. Mammy and Cormac's Ma ducked back behind a croft and disappeared. Mr Shaw the sheriff was coming up the road now, and Crawford looked up from examining MacInnes, his face was a strange, livid colour.

"This situation is intolerable. The damned women are savages. They've attacked my man," Crawford said, pointing to where MacInnes lay. "Someone will hang for this. And evict this woman too." He pointed at Aileen.

Mr Shaw stood looking down at the body of MacInnes in the road, and up at the trembling Aileen, clutching her soaking, wailing children to her. He shook his head, then looked at the colonel gravely.

"It looks to me that this man simply fell," Shaw said, "and bumped his head. Look, he's got a damaged arm, he probably slipped in all this mud."

"You must be joking," Crawford snorted, but his hand went to his chest, and he was wheezing. "You will do as I say," he said in a strange voice.

Shaw looked at him. "I will not, Sir. You will find that I am the agent of the Law here and I refuse to evict this woman. The Inspector of the Poor will need to be summoned to care for a great many of these families here if they are evicted today, and you will have to answer for that."

But Crawford did not reply, his mouth was opening and closing like a fish needing air and he was clutching his chest.

Now the battle was over, the stricken Colonel was carried off to the physician in Lochmaddy, and the body of MacInnes was slung in the cart beside him. The constables and soldiers had been ordered to fall back, and the rain had stopped, though the mud stood knee-high now in places. All about us, people were gathering up their belongings that had been trampled and broken, tending the injured who had been beaten, hit and stamped on, but there was no sign of Cormac anywhere. In the distance, up by the church, I saw Shaw talking to Reverend Maclean, and I ran, my bare feet slipping and sliding towards him.

"Sheriff," I called, "where is my friend? Where is Cormac?"

He turned away from the reverend and looked at me in surprise. "Morag?"

I wiped the mud that was caking my face as best I could. "They've taken him, sir, taken him away."

He nodded and his face was a small, set line in his beard. "The arrested men will be taken to Inverness."

"No, no, no." Tears were making the dried mud on my cheeks flow freely again. I thought of Cormac, down in the cells with Mr O'Brady, bound for the colonies.

He looked at me, then said, quietly, "Follow me."

Up to the stone church we went and Mr Shaw pulled out the key and opened the solid oak door. Mr Morrison's face appeared and the faces of three other men, and Cormac, his face mud-streaked as mine, and pale.

"Ah, thank goodness, Shaw," Mr Morrison said, making to step out. But Shaw shook his head. "Only the boy, I'm afraid." And he took Cormac by the shoulder and pulled him out.

The other men began to jostle at the door. "I'm sorry, sirs," Shaw said, "but you have been arrested by the Inverness constabulary and you must face the charges brought against you."

The men began to protest, but Mr Morrison turned to them. "We will have faith, and hope that this case is dismissed." He said to them, then he turned and nodded to Shaw as he re-locked the door. "Thank you for the boy," he called.

Cormac's Ma was coming running up the road, screaming his name.

Faith and hope. I suddenly remembered the letter and I fumbled in my apron pocket, and pulled out Her Ladyship's letter, crumpled and slightly damp and held it up to show him.

"What's this?" the sheriff asked frowning at the dirty, limp envelope in my hand.

"It's a letter for Inverness, from Her Ladyship."

"Her Ladyship?" He looked at me in surprise and took it, examining the loopy handwriting on the outside. "Her Ladyship is very unwell, she is being taken away."

"I know that, sir, but she wrote it to help a very good friend of mine, Mr O'Brady, who is in gaol there."

"Mr O'Brady?" He startled to hear the name. "I took him to the sheriff in Broadford three weeks ago, though it was clear he had done no wrong. He was going to be released the next morning."

"But he wasn't, sir. He was taken to Inverness before a Justice who was a friend of the colonel's. For transportation."

Mr Shaw shook his head gravely. "A Justice of the Peace has no authority to hand down such a sentence." He looked at my letter in his hand. "I will ride to Inverness immediately and give this to the sheriff principal myself." Mr Shaw looked at me and put his hand on my shoulder. "You must prepare yourself for bad news though, Morag, the transport ship left three days ago."

I looked up at the heavy clouds splitting with rain again, and the world receded like a huge wave pulling back from the shore, sucking everything with it. I fell down into the mud. A sound was coming out of me, a terrible sound, like the dragging of a bow across a fiddle, and the wave crashed back, and everything vanished.

* * *

I lay in my bed in the corner, unable to speak or move, my arms and legs were like wet kelp, I could only lie there watching and waiting. Cormac's Ma said call the physician, but Mammy said no, there was no need for a doctor, it was only a sort of grief and I would get better on my own, though I did not feel like I would ever get better. I watched the light reach the table, move across it, and then snuff out for four days in a row. Peter was buried. I lay in my bed and heard the village singing as he was taken past our door and placed in the headland next to my brother. All around me, people came and went, came and went, bringing news like driftwood on the tide. Mr Crawford was still unwell, and it had been agreed that nothing more would be done about the evictions this year, though each man had to give some cattle as a bond that they would go next spring. Da went to see some land out on Benbecula.

One the fifth day, I dreamt that the mermaid came for me. I was standing on the shore when she appeared, but her hair was not fair like Mammy had said, but long and dark. She beckoned to me so I waded out to her and she took my hand and pulled me into the sea. We swam out to where the water was deep and dark and then she pulled me down underwater, but she held my hand in hers to stop me from drowning. Her dark hair floated around her pale face and she was trying to say something to me, her lovely mouth forming an O, but I could not hear her. I opened my eyes. There was a tingling in my left cheek. The light was only just at the edge of the table, but there were footsteps in the road outside, and then the door swung open, and he was there.

Mr O'Brady.

A New Beginning

Dear Sir,

Forgive me for the strangeness of this letter and for the package that accompanies it. It is a long tale to explain how I come to have this in my possession and no doubt you will puzzle over the postage mark and marvel how it has travelled so far over the ocean to reach you.

Perhaps you heard of the wrecking of the SS Eliza off the coast of Newfoundland last year when one hundred and twenty-one souls were lost? My mistress and I were both on board having sailed from Lochmaddy, North Uist.

Having boarded the ship under somewhat particular circumstances we were forced to take a berth in steerage which was three decks below. Being late in the season for an Atlantic crossing, our passage was rough and all passengers were confined to their bunks for the last week of the journey. My mistress was most agitated about this and she refused to leave the foot of the stairs. Conditions in steerage were abysmal and with many families and children packed down below without proper facilities the situation quickly became unsanitary. The night before we were due to make land, the ship struck rocks and began to list. It was my mistress who saw it, being stationed at the foot of the stairs: the water was rushing in through the hull. She grabbed me from my bunk and shoving her sack into my hands she pushed me up the stairs. But she did not follow. Instead, I saw her wading through the water, back to a family with several children whom she helped to reach the stairway. The water was neck deep now and my last glimpse of her was as she dived beneath the water to reach more passengers. I never saw her again, but I know that many people owe their lives to her bravery and her strength. God have mercy upon her soul.

My mistress' wish was that this bible would be returned to its rightful owner and she guarded it with her life through the journey. I am fulfilling my duty to her by sending it to you. I know that you will do with it as you see fit. I only ask that you might remember my uncle, Hugh, and see that he is taken care of. As for me, nothing would induce me to ever cross the Atlantic again. My mistress' ambition had been to reach Hadley, Massachusetts which is where I find myself now. I have taken board in a small lodging house in return for helping with the chores in the mornings. In the afternoons I attend the Mount Holyoke Seminary for Women which is where I have learned my letters and now continue to study mathematics and science.

God bless you and keep you, Your Lairdship Alasdair.

Your faithful servant,

Hilda Duncan

Edinburgh 1865

"Will you tell us a story, Mammy?" the little girl asked, kneeling up on her bed.

"Auch," said her mother, standing up to close the window. "It might be too late for that."

"Please, please," said the little boy, bouncing on the bed.

The mother looked out at the Edinburgh rooftops, at a pigeon flying across the dusk sky. She had never quite got used to how small the sky was here, or how the rain smelt different, like metal. She pulled the casement closed.

"All right, but only until your father gets home. Then he and I have to finish writing our article for *The Courier*."

"Can it be about the Cu Sith?" the boy asked.

"Or a mermaid?" the little girl said.

She sat with the children on the bed, thinking of the story she wanted to tell them. It had no happy ending though. It ended with cattle forfeited and people drifting away, one family at a time. It ended with the death of her mother, aged forty-four. The kelping and then the Hunger had taken its toll on her chest. But it was a story that had to be told. It had to be remembered. She hugged her children sitting beside her.

"The story can be about the Cu Sith and a mermaid," their mother said. "But most of all, you need to know it is true story. The true story of a little girl who once made a wish by throwing a pearl into the sea."

The End

Author's Note

This book and all the characters within it are a work of fiction, but sadly the events it is based on are not. The Highland Clearances saw thousands of people being evicted from their homes across Scotland throughout the eighteenth and nineteenth centuries and they still have a legacy in the Outer Hebrides today. The Battle of Sollas in 1849 is remembered on North Uist through oral history and events and exhibitions run by Taigh Chearsabhagh Museum & Arts Centre as well as the Kildonan Museum on South Uist. I recommend you visit.

Although the characters of Godfrey and Alexander MacDonald are fictious, the dispossession of Alexander's title due to his illegitimacy is true. Their story is colourfully documented in a book entitled *A Romantic Chapter in Family History*, written by Alice Bosville MacDonald of the Isles and published in 1911. In it she notes that it was only the sudden and mysterious reappearance of the family bible many years later which enabled the title to be restored to Alexander's side of the family. You can still visit Armadale Castle on the Isle of Skye today although it was partially destroyed by a fire in 1855. The cause of the fire is unknown.

Acknowledgements

The idea for this novel first came to me as I cycled the length of the Outer Hebrides from Barra to Lewis on my own in August 2014. The weather was shocking, but the warm hospitality and kindness of the people I met on South and North Uist made a great impression on me. Thank you and I hope you will forgive me for any inaccuracies in this story or in the description of your wonderful landscape.

Thank you to all the people who read and critiqued the early drafts of this novel and to Livi Michael my tutor at Manchester Met University for her insights into writing historical fiction. A big thanks to everyone in Peak Scribblers who gave me feedback and encouragement when I needed it on a Tuesday night. Thank you to Eve Porinchak at Darling Axe for your edits and encouragement to actually get this book over the line. I couldn't have done it without your help or skill.

To my family - thank you for your tireless patience and forgiveness as I forgot lunchboxes and missed assemblies whilst working on the first draft. A special thank you goes to my sister Daisy who always cheered me on whilst telling me exactly what she thought. Your help has been invaluable. And I have to mention Joe who used his theatre skills to voice all the characters one wet afternoon – I have never laughed so much- you are so doing the audio book!

Finally, to my partner in crime and best friend, Oleg. Thank you. You know why.

Printed in Great Britain
by Amazon

16805267R00140